OPERATION COBALT

SUSAN HAYES

ABOUT THE BOOK

He's looking for a fight. She's looking for a hero.

Sergeant Dante Strak hasn't always fought for the right side. Now that he's part of Nova Force, he has a chance to make up for the mistakes of his past. After years of fighting, Dante believes he's ready for anything the universe can throw at him...until a sexy, stubborn doctor crashes into his life and changes everything.

Dr. Tyra Li is on Bellex 3 to help combat the arrival of cobalt, a new designer drug that turned half the population into addicts almost overnight. When a brazen attack turns her mission of mercy into a fight for survival, a split-second decision leads to unexpected consequences, and a chance at a future she never imagined.

Copyright © 2019 Susan Hayes

Operation Cobalt (Book #2 of Nova Force Series)

First print Publication: January 2019

Cover Design: Melody Simmons ~ ebookindiecovers.com

Editor: Dayna Hart

Published by: Black Scroll Publications

ISBN: 978-1-988446-25-7

For my Mum and Dad, for always believing in me. And for Karen. My best friend, my sounding board, and provider of laughs and support.

PROLOGUE

IN A GALAXY FILLED with different species, cultures, and governments, there is only one constant: trade.

In the aftermath of the Resource Wars, the surviving corporations grew strong enough to rival any government, shaping everything from colonization plans to intergalactic law.

To counter their influence and check their powers, the Interstellar Armed Forces created a new division – Nova Force. Their mission is to ensure the corporations play by the rules, by any means necessary.

Welcome to Nova Force. The last line of defense between the citizens of the galaxy and the corporations who believe that laws are flexible, and everything is for sale, for the right price.

CHAPTER ONE

"IT's the only thing that makes sense." Dr. Tyra Li could see her teammates weren't in agreement. They were all crowded into the space they'd designated the meeting room, because it was the largest one they had. It wasn't big enough, though. It was standing room only, all of them leaning against the grimy walls as they talked through their current challenge.

Barry Carver, the second-most senior doctor on the team, shook his grey head. "I'm sorry, but I don't see the correlation. The medic who made the initial report wasn't specific enough for anyone to make the leap you're making, Dr. Li. Just because two drugs cause violent outbursts and psychosis doesn't mean they're made from similar compounds."

"We need more than second-hand descriptions of the effects, we have to get our hands on an actual sample of this drug," Dr. Oran Castille chimed in from his corner. It was a common refrain from him, one they were all tired of hearing.

Tanis Vinos, the team's systems tech, shot an irritated look at Oran. "Why don't you trot down to the local pharma den and pick us up some, then? Oh, wait, we tried that. There's not a trace of the *fraxxing* stuff anywhere."

Frustration was making everyone short tempered. How could a street drug hit so hard and then disappear completely? "I know this has been a uniquely challenging assignment, but we'll get there in the end." Tyra looked around the room at the men and women who made up her team. They'd all joined Boundless to make a difference, to help people in crisis no matter the risk. Standing idly by wasn't in their nature.

Jessica scoffed. "There's no challenge here at all. Bellex 3 is hardly paradise, but the population is relatively healthy."

Riku hummed in quiet disagreement. "There may not be a drug problem, but these people still need us." He gestured out the dirt-encrusted window to the gray, dismal world beyond the glass. "We're the only qualified medical personnel in this entire district! Bellex Corporation should be ashamed of themselves. These are people, not animals. But they're treated like livestock, or worse. Makes me glad cloning has been outlawed. Can you imagine what the corporations would do if they could manufacture their workers the way they did the cyborgs?"

"They'd love to create another slave workforce with no rights at all," Tanis said. "Though that's damned close to what's going on here. Have you seen the tattoos? Cute little triangle symbol on their necks? They might as well be the barcodes they slapped on the poor cyborgs. Anyone with that tattoo has been chipped by Bellex so they can be scanned and tracked. It's horrible."

4

"We're not here to judge, Tanis," Barry said with a hint of reproval.

"Attitudes like that are how the corporations got away with abusing the cyborgs for so long. No one wanted to interfere. They were just vat-grown machines, so what was the harm? Only they weren't machines at all, and they suffered all sorts of atrocities because no one wanted to stick their neck out. The corporations have proven they can't be trusted with tech like that. Clones. Cybernetic implants. Nanotech. They've abused it all."

Barry stiffened. "We're here to help the people, not get involved in local issues. That's a key part of Boundless' mission statement. If we start interfering…"

Tyra cleared her throat. "I'm sure we're all aware of our mission statement, Dr. Carver, but I understand Tanis' concerns, as well. No one wants a repeat of what happened to the cyborgs. While we can't interfere, we can certainly document what we're seeing."

Both Tanis and Barry nodded in silent agreement.

"And while we are here, we can help these people as much as we can." She reminded them. "After all, while we're helping them, we're giving ourselves the best chance of finding some trace of cobalt. The blood samples we've taken from our patients have made it clear something is going on here. Most of our patients are sex trade workers, pharma peddlers, and street kids. The fact that none of them show any sign of the drug is one of the main reasons I believe it's not being used recreationally. That's the most vulnerable population. If they aren't using it, then it has to be the workers."

"I want to support you, Dr. Li, but once again, you're

using a lack of evidence as proof of your theories." Barry said.

Dr. Carver was steadfast and unflappable in a crisis, but he always needed a mountain of proof before he accepted any diagnosis or theory. It made him a valuable member of the team, but right now, she was frustrated no one else saw the patterns she did. It was as clear as *fraxxing* crystal to her. "If I'm right, then the only way to get proof is to test the factory workers."

"Our agreement with Bellex doesn't allow..." Barry started.

She cut him off with an angry slash of her hand. "I know. I know. But if I'm right, they might very well be in on this. You've seen the workers. The way they behave. Hyper- focused, frenetic, pushing themselves to the point of breakdown without slowing. That's not normal."

Everyone else remained silent.

"Alright, you're not buying my theory. Let's hear yours." She leaned against the wall and waited.

Jessica cleared her throat. "What if the original overdoses weren't from a drug *like* crimson. What if it was crimson, or at least a bad copy of it? Someone local tried to replicate it, but they got it wrong. The overdoses and deaths brought too much attention, so they closed shop and bailed. They'll probably try again with a new batch in a new district. We could stay here, help out the locals, and wait to see if the problem starts again elsewhere on the planet."

Several others nodded, and Tyra grudgingly accepted that they weren't going to see things her way. "Anyone else got a theory they'd like to put forward? Some angle we haven't thought of?"

No one spoke. She let the silence continue for a few minutes, then pushed off the wall she was leaning against and moved to the middle of the room "If that's everything, then let's call this meeting and get back to work. We'll revisit this discussion in a few days."

There wasn't much said as they filed out. Riku gave her a brief nod and a smile as he left, and Tanis bumped shoulders with her as she passed by. Once they were gone, Tyra sighed and looked out the window at the grim, colorless world outside.

There was something going on here, and she was going to prove it, one way or another. Until then, there was work to do.

TYRA RESTED her hand on top of Nico's, both as a comfort and to make sure the boy kept still until the tissue regenerator had completed its work. "You should have come to see me sooner. Your arm must have been hurting all day."

Nico nodded but didn't take his eyes off the rapidly healing wounds on his forearm. "It did. Lots 'n lots. But Livvy said I couldn't go until I brought in my share."

She bit back her opinion of Livvy, the adolescent girl who offered protection and dubious employment opportunities for the local band of street kids that called this neighborhood home. Not that most of them had homes. They were orphans and runaways, abandoned by their parents for reasons Tyra couldn't begin to fathom.

"How did you manage to scavenge that much with your arm all cut up? You must have worked very hard."

7

Nico looked up, his dirt-streaked face splitting into a gap-toothed grin. "I went down to the mag-train station and begged. People always give you more when you're bleeding. I even got more 'n I needed. I was going to go down to the market tomorrow and buy a hamburger. I never ate one that I bought myself." His eyes widened. "Or maybe I should pay you for fixing me? That's what real patients do, right?"

"You are my patient, but not all my patients pay me with money. Keep your coins and buy yourself a burger tomorrow." She smiled down at the boy. He might have been as old as twelve, but he was so thin and malnourished it was impossible to be sure.

"How do your other patients pay you?"

"Sometimes they bring me things they've made themselves, or they cook me a meal. Other times they help me get the things I need to help my patients." Tyra had spent the first years of her life in Xinshi, an Earth-based hive city on the coast of what had once been called China. Barter and trade were second nature to her, and she was happy to accept whatever form of payment her patients could afford – if they could afford anything at all.

Nico nodded. "I could do that. Bring you things. Help you help other people."

She had no doubt Nico could bring her plenty of things, all of them either broken, stolen, or both.

"What about working here, instead?" She gestured around the cramped room. What passed for the government on this corporate-controlled world hadn't wanted the Boundless team to set foot on the planet. It had taken an undue amount of outside pressure to force the governor's agreement. While he'd granted permission for

Boundless to come to Bellex 3, he had managed to express his displeasure in petty ways, like the building he had grudgingly allowed them to turn into a research and medical center. It was rundown and dirty, with entire rooms crammed full of trash, and wiring so old it could barely support their equipment. They'd managed to reclaim, organize, and sterilize the space they needed, but another pair of hands would be welcome.

Nico eyed her with a suspicion that made him look far older than his years. "Doing what?"

"Sweeping. Helping me and the other doctors organize this place. Maybe run a few errands? If you went to the market and bought us lunch every day, that would be a great help." It would also make sure that the boy got at least one meal a day he didn't have to scavenge from the automated organic waste bins. She was certain that was how Nico had gotten the cuts on his arm and hand. The clean slices had to have been made by a blade, and they were too uniform to have been made one at a time. He was lucky he hadn't lost his hand.

He considered her offer for a moment and then gave a slow nod. "I could do that. We're allowed to work for others, but only after we do our share. Otherwise, Livvy gets mad."

"Well, we wouldn't want to make her mad, would we?" Tyra checked his newly healed arm and was pleased with the results. There would be no permanent damage. While they were officially here to investigate the cobalt crisis, she saw no reason not to help the residents in other ways.

"Nope" Nico shook his head. "Livvy's real mean when she's mad. Not like you. You're nice, Doc Li."

"Thank you, Nico." She was about to put a layer of sealant over the freshly grown skin when someone shouted. Before she could do more than straighten, the shouts turned to fearful screams punctuated by the terrifying sound of blaster fire.

Nico sprang from the chair and raced toward the window. "C'mon, Doc Li!"

"We can't go that way, the window is stuck. I want you to hide in there, Nico. No matter what happens, don't come out, and don't make a sound!" She pointed to a dilapidated cupboard that spanned one wall of the room. There was just enough room for him to squeeze inside. She scanned the room, looking for anything she could use for a weapon and cursing her decision to leave her sidearm locked in her desk downstairs.

She turned back to the cupboard, expecting Nico to already be hiding inside. The doors were still hanging open, the space empty. Her patient was nowhere to be seen. Before she could figure out where the hell he'd gone, someone ran up the stairs. The footfalls were heavy, uneven, and coming her way. Tyra grabbed one of the cupboard doors, yanking it off its hinges and holding it over her head like a club as she positioned herself beside the door.

The door flew open and Oran staggered into view, one hand clasped to his shoulder as blood poured down his chest. She dropped her makeshift weapon and grabbed him instead. "What's going on?"

"Masked men. The burst in and just started shooting."

Fraxx. Where were they going to go?

She wrapped an arm around Oran's waist and leaned into him. "Come on. We need to find a place to hide."

Oran sagged against her with an agonized groan. "Where?" He was almost a foot taller than her and outweighed her by more than she wanted to think about, but she managed to help him across the room, away from the door.

"Doc Li. Here. Hurry!" Nico popped his head through the now open window, grinning like he was taking part in a new game and not a life-and-death moment. "I checked downstairs. They're looking for that guy right now, but they are almost finished clearing the bottom floor. They'll be comin' up the stairs any second."

"This is Dr. Castille, and he's hurt. Can you help me get him through the window?"

Nico nodded and stuck his hands through the window. "Hurry."

She grabbed her med-kit and tossed it at Nico before helping Oran to the window. To his credit, he managed to stay mostly quiet as they manhandled him through the frame and out onto the rusty remains of a fire escape. Nico used it like a playground jungle gym, climbing higher and exhorting them to do the same.

She ignored her own instincts, which were all screaming to get her feet back on solid ground, and followed Nico. He was a survivor, and if she wanted to be, too, she would have to follow his lead. Oran gritted his teeth and managed to make it up the ladder to the roof, but after that, he was almost spent. "My friend isn't going to be able to go much farther."

"He don't have to go far." Nico tossed the med-kit back to her. "Fix him. I'll get us out of here." The boy ran to the far side of the roof, rummaging through what looked like a bunch of haphazard junk. Tyra had no idea how that was going to help them get away, but Nico didn't want to die up here any more than she did, so there had to be a method to his madness.

"How are you holding up?" she asked Oran as she popped open her kit and grabbed a canister of redi-seal, a multipurpose foam that should seal his wound and work as a temporary bandage.

"Getting shot sucks."

"Yeah, I know. I got bad news for you, though." She tore open his shirt to expose the gaping hole in his shoulder, broke the seal on the canister, and tossed away the outer casing.

"What's that?"

"This is going to suck even more. Remember, no noise." She slid the sterilized section of the redi-seal into the open wound and pressed the plunger. The foam hissed as it expanded to fill the empty space, the heat of the chemical reaction sterilizing and cauterizing the injured area as it went.

Oran uttered a single, muted wail and then slumped over in a dead faint. She finished doing what she could for him and shoved everything back in her kit. He was stirring, but not fast enough. She made a fist with one hand and briskly rubbed her knuckles over his breastbone. "Come on, Oran, open your eyes. We need to go."

He groaned, but it took another sharp rub of her knuckles to get him to open his eyes. By then, his breath was coming easier, and a little of his color was back, signs that the anesthetic in the foam was taking effect. She was satisfied he'd be ready to run when the time came. If they had anywhere to run to. She looked back at Nico and was surprised to see he'd turned the pile of random junk into a workable bridge. It spanned the gap from their rooftop to the windowsill of a taller building next door. Nico was already partway across, and when he saw her looking at him, he grinned and gestured.

"We go this way."

"You're amazing, Nico. When it's safe, I'm taking you out for all the burgers you can eat."

The boy's brown eyes filled with awe. "Really?"

She nodded, slung her medkit over her shoulder, and pulled Oran to his feet. "You get us safe, I'll buy you an entire vat of cloned-beef burgers. Maybe even real beef if we can find some on this world."

"And I'll buy dessert," Oran chimed in weakly.

Nico was almost dancing a jig now. "Then you better hurry. Come on. It'll hold your weight, but we gots to go!"

Oran was moving a little better now that the pain had eased, and he managed to get himself across the makeshift bridge with minimal help, though it took both of them longer than she liked to get through the window. *I'm getting old.* If she survived this insanity, she really needed to work on her flexibility…and her cardio.

The moment her feet hit the floor Nico began hauling the bridge in behind him, erasing any sign of their escape. Tyra helped, and they had it almost inside when the air erupted with shouts and the ring of heavy boots on steel. Their mystery attackers were on their way up the fire escape.

They ducked out of sight and dropped their voices to hushed whispers. "Where to, now, Nico?"

"I'm taking you somewhere safe." Nico grabbed her by the hand. "Someplace secret."

Safe was all Tyra cared about right now. She needed to

get somewhere secure so she could treat Oran, find out if anyone else had gotten out, and then figure out who the *fraxx* had the balls to storm a volunteer medical center in broad daylight. If they'd been there for pharma, they wouldn't have gone looking for her and Oran. Whoever they were, they were there to do harm, and she had a sinking feeling that didn't bode well for the rest of her team.

All she had was a medkit, a wounded teammate, and a street urchin whose strongest motivation was his love of hamburgers. It would have to be enough.

DANTE SLAMMED his fist into the sparring bot with a satisfying smack. The owners of the club had issued invitations to Dante's entire team to use their training gym while the Nova Force's new base on Astek Station was under construction. The feel of the gym took Dante back to his life before he'd joined up, back when blood sports and hurting people for money were the only ways he knew to survive.

"You break it, you're buying me a new one, Strak!" Cynder, one of the cyborg owners of the club called out from across the gym.

"Don't listen to her. She's broken that poor thing more times than we can count. Lieksa always manages to put it back together again," Toro, the biggest cyborg Dante had ever seen, said before taking another swing at Cynder. The two of them were sparring in preparation for their next matches. Husband and wife pounded on each other with a ferocity that would have done real damage to a human.

"Don't worry 'bout your cute little bot. I'm pulling my punches. The IAF training gyms never had anything as robust as your toys, and I learned fast not to break them."

Jaeger, Cynder's other husband, looked up from the weight bench without bothering to lower the hundred pounds of weight loaded onto his bar, and stars knew how high the cyborg had the gravity dialed up in that area. Working out with cyborgs had been an eye-opening experience for Dante. For the first time in a long time, he wasn't the strongest one in the gym. Not even close.

"You want a real workout, Strak, you should go a few rounds with Cyn."

"Nope. I don't fight ladies. Not even ones that could kick my ass while hopping on one foot."

There were riffs of laughter from all around the training area. Cynder didn't laugh, though. She stepped away from Toro and looked straight at Dante, her expression solemn. "Personal rule?"

Dante tapped two fingers to his chest. "A promise I made to myself a long time ago."

Cyn dropped her head in a brief nod, pivoted, and moved back into range of her husband's blows. Some women took his stance as an affront, others as a challenge. He appreciated that Cynder hadn't. He didn't like to talk about the reasons behind that rule.

Thoughts of the past cooled his interest in working out anymore. He deactivated the sparring bot and headed for the showers. The water might be recycled, but it would be scorching hot, and that's all he really needed. The showers in the club's gym were built to accommodate their fighters, which meant that even his six-foot-nine frame fitted comfortably in the stalls. It was yet another reason he liked coming to the Nova Club. There was nothing here that made him feel out of place.

He'd traveled all over the galaxy, but this place was unique. It wasn't Astek Station itself– there was nothing comfortable about its cramped corridors, battered walls, and recycled atmosphere. It was the beings who had carved out a place for themselves in this collection of platforms and stations that floated out at the edge of known space. Humans, Torskis, Jeskyrans, Pherans, and cyborgs lived side by side, laughing, fighting, and loving each other.

It was a place where air was precious, and life was cheap. The Corp-Sec teams worked tirelessly to maintain some semblance of order, but it was a fight they'd never win. Astek catered to every vice imaginable, and there wasn't much that was illegal, so long as you had the scrip and the inclination to indulge. Not that he indulged in anything stronger than Ja'kreesh these days. The brewed stimulant was the Torski equivalent of coffee, and most humans couldn't handle the effect on their nervous systems. Being part Torski, it didn't bother him. There was a brew shop on the station that specialized in the stuff, and he'd become a regular customer.

He was still mulling over the quirks and qualities of their new base of operations when his comm-device erupted in a strident sequence of chirps and beeps. *Veth.* That was the priority message alert. He left the shower running and jogged over to where he'd left his belongings, rummaging through them until he found his comm.

He thumbed the control to audio only. "Strak here."

"This is Rossi. You've been tapped for a solo mission.

You've got ten minutes to get in uniform and report to the briefing room on the *Malora*."

"I'll be there." He didn't bother asking what the mission was. He'd find out when he got to the briefing. It wasn't common for Rossi to split up the team and even less common for Strak to be the one going in alone. For one thing, he was the *Malora's* pilot, and then there was the fact his appearance made him stand out. Whatever the assignment was, stealth wouldn't be part of it.

CHAPTER TWO

THIS IS the last time I make assumptions about a damned mission. Dante stomped out of his fifth bar of the day and narrowed his eyes against the afternoon sun. Bellex 3 might have been a beautiful planet once, but the corporate-owned world had long since been drained of resources and covered in factories and processing plants. This entire system was basically one massive shipyard, creating and assembling the components for everything from small shuttlecraft to military-class star destroyers. The planet's entire population worked for Bellex Corporation as freelancers, contractors, or indentured labor.

His transportation here had been part of his cover as a freelancer looking for short-term work. He'd caught a ride with one of the freighters that crisscrossed the cosmos, spending several days with Royan Watson, the pilot of the *Sun Sprite*. Royan's sister ran a cargo company out of the Drift and they'd been at the center of the rebellion that uncovered some of the corporations' darkest secrets. They were solid allies in the fight against the corporation, which made Royan's ship the ideal way to get onto Bellex unnoticed.

He and Royan used some of their transit time to rehearse a public argument that played out once they landed. It culminated in shouts, thinly veiled threats, and Dante getting 'fired.' Now, he was just another transient worker looking for a job until he could find a way off the planet. It was a common story, and it explained why he'd been the one tagged for this mission. The rest of his team were too military to ever pass for drifters, and two of them wouldn't be allowed in the system at all.

Bellex Corp was so protective of their industrial secrets the whole system was off-limits to anyone with cybernetic implants or anything that could conceivably be used to conduct corporate espionage. Aria and Eric would only be able to enter if Nova Force stepped in to override the restriction. It was an insane level of security considering he'd been in the heart of the system for several days and hadn't seen anything remotely classified. He hadn't found any sign of the volunteer medical team he'd been sent to locate, either. In fact, he couldn't find much to suggest they'd been here at all.

The address Boundless had on file turned out to be an abandoned building, and no one in the neighborhood would admit to knowing anything about the team, their mission, or the hastily painted over blaster marks and blood stains he'd found inside a building everyone swore had been empty for years. He'd found leftover medical supplies stashed in an abandoned room upstairs. In a neighborhood as poor as this one, the fact the supplies were still there, untouched, spoke volumes. The locals were too afraid to even enter the building, never mind talk.

By the end of his second day on the planet, Dante had grown frustrated enough he'd been tempted to ask what color the sky was, just to see if the inhabitants claimed they had never heard the word sky.

There was something off about the population here, too. He'd been to plenty of worlds like Bellex 3. Hell, he'd been raised in places not much different, but he had never seen beings behave the way they did here.

It wasn't everyone. There were still some people with resigned expressions and the slow, measured pace and stooped shoulders of someone who knew that there was no point in rushing through life because every day would be the same from now until they died. But everywhere he went, there were people striding through the streets with near frenetic energy and vacant eyes. For the first time in his life, Dante found himself moving out of people's way.

The black marketeers, bootleggers, and pharma dealers still plied their goods and made their money by offering fleeting escapes from reality, but there were fewer of them than there should have been. Bars, brothels, and pharma dens offered their wares along every block he walked, but none of them were doing a booming business. The harder the life, the more likely people were to escape the drudgery through their vice of choice. So, why weren't there more customers?

His briefing included the drug crisis that supposedly gripped this world, but he hadn't seen any of the usual signs of addiction or overdose. A former IAF medic who worked security at one of the factories had made the initial report and then disappeared, just like the Boundless team of doctors who had come to Bellex to help.

Boundless had been here less than two weeks before vanishing into thin *fraxxing* air. After four days of casually worded questions and countless visits to bars and backrooms looking for scuttlebutt, he was only certain of two things. Someone had erased all trace of the Boundless medical team's visit to Bellex 3, and whatever had happened to the doctors, it wasn't good.

He'd run into the same people once or twice, and it wouldn't take the locals long to notice that the hulking newcomer kept asking questions that had nothing to do with finding a job that would get him off the planet, or at least paying for the rundown room he kept so he had a place to sleep at night. The price was steep, too, considering the bed was too small, the walls were infested with lizards, and his fellow renters were a silent, shady crew who seemed to have an aversion to daylight and personal hygiene.

The *Malora* would be arriving in a matter of days with Commander Rossi and the rest of Team Three. The plan was for him to have scouted all of District Twelve and collected as much intel as he could before they got here to start the official investigation. If he didn't find a lead soon, the plan was officially *fraxxed*.

The streets were as quiet as they ever got in a place like this. The factories ran day and night, which meant the businesses did, too. It was another two hours until the next shift change, though, and the mid-afternoon sun had driven most of the off-duty workers inside. It was a good time to revisit the place the doctors had been using as a base. There wouldn't be many people on the streets to notice he was poking around the empty building again. Maybe this time he'd find some clue to tell him what had happened.

He scoffed at himself. "Yeah, sure. Maybe you'll find something you missed the last two times you were there. And maybe a flock of green fairies will descend from the sky and offer you cold beers and ice cream, too."

He was still grumbling to himself when an odd sound caught his attention. He jogged forward a few steps, trying to figure out what it was. A trash-choked alley opened onto the street, the narrow walls amplifying what he heard until it was unmistakable. Quick, light footsteps were coming his way, fast. He froze, considering his options. Did he follow his training and investigate, or stick to his cover and keep walking?

It only took him a nanosecond to make his decision. He turned and headed into the alley. If someone was running in this heat, they were either causing trouble or fleeing it. Either way, it was worth checking into. He only made it a few meters before the source of the noise appeared. She was short, with a matted ponytail of dark hair streaming behind her as she ran full-tilt toward him. Her head was down so he couldn't see her face, and she didn't see him at all.

"Hey!" He called out a warning as she closed the distance between them.

Her head snapped up, and he caught a glimpse of vivid green eyes wild with fear as she realized her path was blocked.

He expected her to slow down, but instead, she accelerated, coming straight for him with her teeth bared in a defiant snarl. She feinted left and then veered right trying to deke around him. He reached for her and she dodged, ducking under his hand only to lose her footing in the garbage that littered the alley. She went flying, smashing into the wall with enough force he winced in sympathy.

She was still trying to get back to her feet when he caught up to her. He reached down and grabbed hold of the backpack she wore, lifting her until her feet dangled half a meter off the ground. The little *peskin* was still fighting, thrashing in his grip and trying her best to land a blow as a string of curses in a variety of languages flew out of her mouth. He recognized Pheran, Galactic Standard, a few choice phrases in Torski, and some others he couldn't begin to guess.

She was far too well-educated to be a street rat, and her accent wasn't local, either. *Interesting*.

"I'm not with whoever is chasing you."

She raised her head to look up at him, still wary and defiant. "No? So you just make a habit of wandering into alleys and grabbing women at random? I'm in trouble, so if you're not going to help me, could you at least let me go so I can get out of here?"

He grinned as recognition dawned. She didn't look much like the polished and professional woman he'd seen in the holos provided at his briefing, but underneath the grime and exhaustion was the first real lead he'd found since setting foot on this *fraxxed* up planet. "I'm happy to help you, Dr. Li. In fact, you're the whole reason I'm here."

TYRA WASN'T sure she believed the walking mountain of

muscle who had her dangling in mid-air, but she was short on time and out of options. "Great! Who the *fraxx* are you? And more importantly, what are you going to do about the three guys trying to kill me?"

The big guy grunted. "Only three? They can't be trying that hard. My name's Dante. Sergeant Strak if you want to be formal. I'm Nova Force, and I'm here to find out what happened to you and your team."

Nova Force. Well, that explained the attitude. They were the elite of the Interstellar Armed Forces. "My team was wiped out by the same assholes hunting me right now. I'm the only one left." She didn't mention Oran. He was still alive, but if she didn't get back with the meds she'd retrieved from their old base, he wouldn't be for long. She'd tell her rescuer about him once he'd proven she could trust him…and if they survived the next few minutes.

He lowered her to the ground gently. "If I let go of you, are you going to bolt? I'm not really a fan of running."

"And I'm not a fan of dying. You protect me, I'll stick around. Just don't expect me to help."

He grinned, flashing a set of dimples that made her heart beat even faster. "I don't need your help, Shortcake. You just stay out of sight. This won't take long."

Shortcake? She opened her mouth to tell him what she thought of his nickname, but he pressed a finger to his lips and gave a sharp shake of his head.

She didn't hear anything for a second and was about to say so when she caught the distant sound of footsteps growing louder. *Fraxx*. He gestured for her to take cover behind a stack of abandoned crates. Whatever was inside was rancid, and a cloud of insects rose into the air as she slid into the gap, but it was the only place to hide.

She barely made it out of sight before the ones hunting her arrived. She still had no idea who they were or who had hired them, but whoever it was, they had to pay well. They hadn't stopped looking for her since the attack. The only reason she and Oran were still alive was Nico and his friends. They kept them hidden, fed, and as safe as they could manage. If it wasn't for Oran's injuries they'd still be safe, but he was dying, and she had risked going back to see if she could find the meds she needed to save him. They'd been on her seconds after she snuck inside.

The three men slowed as they spotted Dante standing in the middle of the alley. "You see a female run this way?" one of them asked.

"Yeah. And I gotta say, you three seem a little over-prepared for chasing down one itty-bitty female. She wasn't even armed that I could see."

The lead male pointed his blaster at Dante. "Which way?"

"What's it worth?" Dante drawled, ambling a few steps toward them.

Is he fraxxing *insane?* She wondered.

The others straightened up and raised their weapons. "It's worth your life. Tell us where she went, ya half-breed freak."

Dante uttered a heavy sigh and rolled his massive shoulders. "And here I thought we were getting along well. Then you had to start with the insults." He covered the last few feet of ground with unexpected speed and grabbed the leader by the shoulders, tossing him in the direction of the other two masked men. They landed in a tangled heap of limbs and weapons, and Dante charged in, fists swinging. The crates Tyra was using for concealment blocked her view after that. She briefly considered sneaking away while they were all distracted, but there was no way she'd make it down the rest of the alley without being spotted. Instead, she hunkered down and hoped that when the fight ended, she hadn't lost her only potential ally.

The fight sounded vicious. There were meaty thuds, grunts, and snarls, and then the wet, gut-twisting sound of bones snapping. There was an agonized wail, too high-pitched to be Dante's. The shriek ended suddenly, only to be replaced by the sound of blaster fire. A wild shot slammed into the crates protecting her, and the stink of scorched polymer hit her nose a few seconds later.

Adrenaline pumped into her system, and she had to fight through the urge to do *something*. Run. Fight. Move. Scream. Anything but sit there any longer.

More blaster fire, another pained scream and it was over. She pressed her hands against her thighs, trying to slow their shaking as silence returned to the alley.

"Dammit, I liked this shirt." There was no mistaking the deep rumble of Dante's voice.

Tyra breathed a sigh of relief and stood up. Dante stood in the middle of the alley, looking mournfully at a bloody gash on his forearm. He was the only one still on his feet.

The moment she reappeared, his head snapped up and he moved to block the view of the men behind him. "Stay there."

"I'm a doctor. Once you have them restrained, I can treat them, and you, too."

His dark eyes widened. "You'd treat the men who want

you dead? They might be the same ones who killed your team."

"I took an oath to preserve *all* life, not just the lives of the beings I like."

"Well, I'm sure they'd appreciate the sentiment -- if they still had lives left for you to preserve." He clamped a hand over his injured arm and walked toward her, still blocking her view. Apart from the blood on his sleeve and a swollen lip, he looked fine.

"They're dead? All of them? Didn't you need to interrogate them or something?" Part of her was relieved to know they weren't a threat anymore, but there was also guilt for feeling that way. She'd seen more than her share of violence growing up in Xinshi, one of Earth's original hive cities. She accepted that sometimes, violence was necessary, but she'd never been the cause before. Not until she'd come to Bellex 3.

Dante shrugged his broad shoulders with a nonchalance she found irritating. The man had just killed three other beings. Why wasn't he rattled, or at the very least, breathing hard? "I'm on undercover recon. No backup, no base of operations. Officially, my team isn't arriving for a few more days, so it's not like I can march into whatever passes for law enforcement around here and ask to borrow a jail cell to hold my newly captured prisoners."

"No backup? What kind of rescue is this?"

He curled his lip and she caught a flash of fang. "The kind who would appreciate a thank you instead of a lecture. I did just save your life."

"Right." She shook her head and tried to think clearly. It wasn't easy, but he did deserve a thank you. "I'm grateful you were here, and that you risked your life protecting mine. I shouldn't have come back here, but I needed meds…"

"You're hurt?" He was at her side in a second, his demeanor instantly changing to one of gentle concern.

It was the first calm moment since their meeting, and she took the time to get a real look at her rescuer, beyond his massive size and gruff demeanor. His hair was almost shaved at the sides and not much longer on top. It was a classic military cut, but nothing about him seemed military. He hadn't shaved in a few days, and his jaw was shadowed with a beard as jet black as his hair. She could see the top of some kind of tattoo along his neck and was struck with a sudden urge to pull back his collar and take a closer look. His nose had been broken more than once, and his features were too craggy and rough to be called handsome, but there was something appealing about him just the same.

Now that she was close to him, she could see that his eyes were a striking shade of midnight blue. And he had fangs. She should have seen it, but adrenaline and fear had fogged her perceptions. Her rescuer was part Torski.

"Shortcake, I asked you if you were hurt."

She blinked, and blushed as she realized he'd caught her staring. "I'm a little banged up and bruised, that's all. I've got so much adrenaline zinging through my system right now I can't even feel it. How's the arm? Do you want me to take a look at it?"

"Not here. I need to get you somewhere safe, first. Then you're welcome to play doctor with me." There was a wicked glint in his eyes as spoke.

Butterflies the size of asteroids took flight inside her

stomach at his words. What was it about this big, violent man that piqued her interest? *Probably the fact I haven't been laid in six months, and he just saved my life.*

She squared her shoulders and tried to muster a little dignity. "I know I should probably ask to see your ID or something, but I'm in over my head and I need to trust someone, so it doesn't matter if you're Nova Force or not. I need your help."

"I think we established that already," he drawled, tipping his head toward the pile of recently deceased attackers.

"Uh, yeah. But not just with them. I lied before. I'm not the only one who survived the first attack. Dr. Castille is still alive, but he needs the meds in my pack soon, or he's not going to make it. That's why I risked coming back."

"Interesting logic. You risked your life to save his. If you got caught, you'd both die." He shook his head. "How did you stay alive this long?"

"A street kid named Nico got us out and is helping us stay hidden. Oran, Dr. Castille, is with him."

Dante cracked his knuckles and looked around the alley. "Can you find your way to Oran and this kid from here? I hope so because we've got about three minutes before the next security drone sweep is due to overfly this sector. They're going to find those bodies, and once that happens, it's going to get very busy around here."

"I can find my way back." Nico had made sure of that. He'd described landmarks and street names to her repeatedly until they were both confident she'd be able to find her way.

"Good. Then get ready to haul ass. We'll be leaving in sixty seconds."

She cocked her head. "Why aren't we leaving right away? I told you, Oran needs the meds I'm carrying."

Dante was already walking away from her, back toward the bodies. "I need to ID your friends, first."

She watched as he stripped off their masks, helmets, and gloves with ruthless efficiency. He took quick scans of their faces and the palms of their hands with what looked like a basic comm-device, while she stood by, staring at the faces of the men who killed her team. None of them looked familiar.

Within a minute he was finished and coming her way. "Unless my ears deceive me, the *fraxxing* drones are early. We need to move. Now."

"This way." She pointed back the way she'd come and started walking.

Three steps later, she was swept off her feet and into Dante's arms. "Hey!"

"We're out of time, and I can run faster than you. Save your breath for giving me directions." He broke into a run, holding her close and doing his best to cushion her body against the worst of the jars and bumps.

She called out directions as he raced through the alleys and backstreets, and he followed her instructions without hesitation. It was oddly empowering to have this big, dangerous male obeying her every command. She was actually starting to enjoy herself a little despite the danger when he finally slowed his pace.

"We're not quite there, yet."

"I figured, but we're far enough away to start trying to blend in." He used his head to indicate several security cams overlooking the area. "The ones in the alley were all broken, but these ones aren't."

31

"Actually, most of them are inactive. The locals keep them that way. This sector isn't considered a security priority. No factories. No Bellex offices."

He dropped his head to give her an assessing look. "How do you know that?"

"Nico."

His lips twitched. "I can't wait to meet this kid."

"If we're trying to blend in, you should really put me down, now."

He pursed his lips and considered it, then shook his head. "Request denied. My job is to keep you alive until my team gets here. The closer you are to me, the easier my job is. Now, where do I go from here?"

"Straight for half a block, turn right at the alley marked with red graffiti, third door on the left. See? It's not that far, so you really need to put me down. I can walk the rest of the way."

"Nope." He set off again, ignoring the fact she was trying to wriggle free.

"This is ridiculous!" She swung her feet and managed to catch him in the side with her heel.

"It isn't, but it will be if you don't stop squirming." He tightened his grip and walked faster.

"Don't test me. In the last week, I've been shot at, chased across rooftops, and gone without food, sleep, or even a damned shower."

"Believe me, I'm aware you need a bath."

She cursed again, calling him every insult she could remember in every language she knew. They were at the door to the hideaway before she reached the end of her list, and the smug bastard carrying her was laughing at her for the last thirty paces.

"How long did you say it would be before your team got here?" She finally muttered, leaning out of his arms to knock on the door in the code Nico had taught her.

"Three or four days."

She groaned. Three days in Dante's company was going to be a test of her patience and sanity. Stars help her, it was going to be a test of her willpower, too. If she didn't kill him, she might just end up liking the arrogant son of a starbeast.

CHAPTER THREE

IN AN ACT that had become routine over the last two days, Dante walked the final visitor of the day to a small side door and let him out, then barred and barricaded the door behind him.

"You're the most paranoid man I've ever met," Tyra declared as she watched him secure the door. She insisted on walking with him as he escorted each of her drop-in patients to the exit, which gave them a few minutes of relative quiet before they returned to the noise and chaos of the upper levels. These stolen moments had allowed him to get to know Tyra a little at a time, and he'd started looking forward to each solitary encounter.

"Maybe. But you're not paranoid enough. People are actively trying to kill you right now, and you're carrying on like it's business as usual." He couldn't decide if Tyra was deliberately trying to make him crazy or if she simply wasn't aware of how dangerous this world was. He'd never met anyone so determined to take chances with their life for the sake of helping someone else. It was maddening and damned attractive, just like the rest of her.

"This is what I do. When I see suffering, I have to do something about it."

"Which is fine and noble and all that, until one of the ones you try to help turns on you. What do you think will happen to you, Oran, Nico, and the others if they find us? I'm good, Shortcake, but I can't save everyone."

Since they'd arrived at her bolthole two days ago, he'd watched in growing dismay as she had used almost all the medical supplies she had left treating street kids, criminals, and even a foul-tempered lizard one of the kids kept as a pet. She'd spent hours working on her fellow doctor, sacrificing sleep to watch over him as he slowly fought his way back from the brink of death. The medication she'd risked her life to retrieve had successfully countered the infection tearing through her teammate. Her dedication to her craft was impressive, but she seemed blind to the risk her patients presented and completely uncaring of the danger that one of them would sell her out for the price of a hot meal and a night's stay somewhere clean and warm.

Tyra didn't answer him, but the set of her shoulders tightened as she turned and headed toward the stairwell. He didn't like playing the heavy with her. She'd gotten under his skin in the short time they'd been thrown together. He found himself trying to find ways to make her smile whenever he could, despite the fact his job was to keep her safe, not make her happy.

Her choices frustrated him, her stubborn defiance made him crazy, and yet there was something about her that pulled him in and made him want to spend time with her. He just wished she could see that her need to help others was putting everyone at risk. These people were desperate, and that made them unpredictable, which was why he'd instructed Tyra not to mention who he worked for. As far as the others knew, he was a mercenary hired by Boundless to track down their missing doctors, nothing more.

The only one of the group he trusted not to sell them out was Nico. The kid adored Tyra, and it was obvious he would do anything for her. He shadowed her every move, only leaving her side when she sent him out to scavenge food or other necessities.

It had been amusing to watch Nico's initial reaction to him. He'd been sullen and distrustful at first, but once he accepted Dante wasn't a threat, he'd mellowed. He hadn't really thawed until Dante had pulled out some Bellex vouchers and offered to buy food for everyone. After that, the kid had accepted him into the group.

Dante felt an affinity for the boy. He'd spent time on the streets, too, though never in a place as rough as this one. It would be easy for Nico to let his circumstances twist him into an angry, bitter soul, but he hadn't. Not yet, anyway. The few times Dante heard laughter around the place, Nico was always part of the fun, and while he was distrustful and cautious, he hadn't closed himself off.

He followed Tyra into the main room, a big, open space the kids had filled with abandoned furniture and assorted junk. Some of the older ones had managed to patch the building back into the power grid. Dante had looked over their handiwork and made some improvements, showing the interested ones what he was doing, and why. He'd done the same when he discovered the lizard traps on the roof.

He'd given the want-to-be hunters a few tips on how to improve their snares and traps. The kids had to eat, and he wouldn't be around to buy them burgers for much longer.

Dante's stomach growled. A quick check of the time confirmed it was early evening. Time for him to check in with his team and organize food for this motley crew he'd fallen in with. "Hey, kid. You hungry?"

Nico's eyes lit up. "Burgers?"

Of course he wanted burgers. He never wanted anything else. "Yeah. You know the plan. Get enough for everyone, but only buy one or two from each vendor. And maybe get some fruit this time."

Nico wrinkled his nose. "Fruit?"

"Yeah. Fruit. Any kind. It's good for you. You want to get big and strong, you need to eat healthy stuff sometimes."

"It's mushy and gross," Nico declared.

"That's because you're eating it after it's old and rotten. See if you can find some fresh apples or something, okay?" Dante handed Nico enough money to cover the purchases. He'd be out of the local currency by tomorrow, and he couldn't risk hitting a dispenser to get more. Nico and his friends were watching Dante's room at the hotel, and while no one had come around yet, he wasn't taking chances. He planned to stay out of sight until Dax and the rest of Team Three arrived.

Once Nico was gone, Dante moved to a quiet stretch of hallway. He could still see into the room where Tyra and her patient were, though. He pulled his comm out and took a moment to activate the newly upgraded stealth settings, which now included encryption and signal masking. Once he was sure everything was working, he sent a ping letting the team know he was ready to report in.

A few seconds later, he got a reply and a familiar face appeared on the screen. "Buttercup! Good to see your ugly mug." Ensign Eric Erben, the youngest member of their team and the most gifted cyber-jockey Dante had ever met, was beaming at him from a seat in the cockpit of the *Malora*.

"Magi. Please tell me they didn't leave your irresponsible ass in charge of my ship."

Eric grinned. "Relax. Your baby is flying herself right now. I'm just monitoring communications and scanning the chatter to see if there's any mention of you or your two MIA doctors."

"Anything I need to know?"

"Yeah, it's too *fraxxing* quiet. Not a single mention of the dead bodies you left in the alley. Nothing about the doctors, either. Either Bellex 3 has the most incompetent security force in the galaxy, or someone with some serious muscle has suppressed the whole incident and anything related to it. Care to make a bet on which one? I'm giving ten-to-one odds right now."

Dante scoffed. "No bet. Security around here isn't that bad. They're stretched thin and focus their attention on protecting this place's secrets instead of keeping the peace, but I've got eyes on the ground, and they confirm the bodies have been removed."

"You have eyes on the ground? You running a spy ring down there, now?"

"Something of the sort. What's your ETA? We need to

get Dr. Castille into a real med-bay, and we could all use food, sleep, and a shower."

"We should be in orbit in sixteen hours, boots on the ground two hours after that. At least, everyone else will be. I'm staying on the *Malora*."

"Your implants?" Dante asked.

Eric's expression turned stormy. "Yeah. They've given Aria a waiver, but they're not keen on having me dirtside. Jokes on them. I'm just as dangerous from orbit."

"Trust me when I say you're not going to be missing much. This world is one big factory floor, and the population all work for Bellex one way or another."

"Charming. I'll stay up here and breathe all the nice, clean air and avoid the lizard burgers."

"Not funny, Magi."

The kid grinned. "Depends on which side of the screen you're sitting on. I'm having a nice synth steak with all the trimmings for dinner. What are you having?"

"Apples. I sent the kid out for apples."

Eric didn't stop laughing for a full minute, and by the time he was done Dante was already planning his revenge. He was also going to ask Rossi to quit sharing tidbits from his daily reports with the rest of the team. With his luck, they'd program the food dispensers to produce nothing but burgers for the next week he was onboard.

"Is the commander around? Much as I'm enjoying our little chat, I should officially check in."

"I'm here. Nice of you to remember who you're supposed to be reporting to, Sergeant." The screen split, and the face of his commanding officer appeared beside Eric's.

"Oops," Eric said before giving a jaunty wave and disconnecting.

"He really needs more to do, sir. Maybe get him to run a level six diagnostic on the engines once you make orbit?"

Rossi snorted. "Maybe. Magi's not my main concern right now, though. How are you and your charges doing?"

"We're fine, for now. Our unknowns are sweeping this sector more often, which worries me. Too many people know we're here. Eventually, one of them is going to talk."

Rossi narrowed his eyes. "I thought I told you to put an end to the makeshift med-center?"

"I tried, sir. But word spread and Tyra – Dr. Li – won't turn anyone away. She's as stubborn as a Nantari rhino and has no sense of self-preservation. Frankly, I'm amazed she's lasted as long as she has doing this gig." He'd skimmed her file. She'd joined the Boundless Program less than a week after graduating from a private and very expensive medical college. She was a crusader, probably compensating for the nice, comfortable life she'd had growing up by trying to help people who weren't born with the same advantages. Whatever her reasons, she took too many chances, and he'd spent most of the last two days trying to protect her from herself.

"Your mission is to make sure they both survive until we get there. Someone with some serious clout is making plenty of noise about getting those two doctors out of there in one piece, and I'm getting sit-rep requests every few hours from the brass. I do not want to have to relay bad news. Got that?"

"Yes, sir."

Rossi nodded. "Good. Do you have more intel on this supposed addiction crisis?"

41

"Some. You saw my report?" He'd talked to the doctor at length last night after she finally got Castille stable, and what she had shared with him was enlightening. He'd sent a preliminary report this morning.

"I did. What I want to know is what you think about her theory."

Dante didn't hesitate. "I think she's right. It's the only explanation for what I've seen since I got here."

"Please tell me that your belief in this theory hinges on more than the fact that the criminal element on this world isn't doing cobalt. I am not going to be able to sell that to the higher-ups without blood loss and a three-rank demotion."

"There's more. They won't talk to me, but a few of the pharma dealers spoke to my source and confirmed that they had a supply of cobalt for a while, but the supply just dried up."

"Your source is a street kid with a burger addiction. We're going to need hard evidence."

"I know. Once I get the doctors safely on the *Malora*, we'll find the proof we need to verify everything, but we're going to need to test the Bellex factory workers to do it. If cobalt is being consumed, they have to be ones using it. Dr. Li's theory makes too much sense for it to be anything else. You'll see what I mean when you get here. It's a damned nightmare."

"Getting permission to test Bellex's property isn't going to be easy. They're already trying to limit our access."

"We're Nova Force. They aren't allowed to do that."

Dax gave a stiff-shouldered shrug. "They're trying anyway."

"Believe me, sir, there are cobalt users here. Thousands

of them. I didn't see it, because by the time I got here the overdoses had stopped, and I didn't know what I was looking for. Now, I do."

Rossi scowled. "Where the *fraxx* did this shit come from and who is distributing it?"

"Good question. However the users are getting it, it isn't through the local pharma dealers. Not anymore. The ones on cobalt don't indulge in other vices as much. The bars, pleasure palaces, and pharma dens are all taking a hit." Now he knew what he was looking for, the signs were easy to spot. Cobalt didn't make the user high. It made them hyper-focused, energized, and prone to suggestion. They were so driven to accomplish whatever tasks they were assigned they became obsessive about it.

The ones that had nearly mowed him down on the sidewalks as they powered through their day weren't diligent workers, they were the addicts he'd come here to find. It was a plague of productivity. At least, that was Tyra's theory. If she was right, it was no wonder Bellex didn't want anyone investigating. Why would they want someone stopping the distribution of a drug that made their workforce work longer, harder, and without complaint?

Dax scrubbed a hand over his jaw. "If someone hadn't tipped us off in the early stages, we still wouldn't know about this. We haven't been able to track down Sgt. Markson, either. He made that report and then vanished into thin air."

"Lots of vanishing going on lately. I don't like it. First Markson, then they attacked the Boundless doctors and made them disappear. I bet there are others, too." Dante bounced his fist against his thigh in frustration. There wasn't much he could do right now. He had to protect his charges and stay out of sight. Once Tyra and Oran were safely on board the *Malora*, he could start working on the cobalt puzzle, but not until they were out of danger.

"I know that look. You're already planning what to do next. That's good. Just stay put until we're there to back you up. Too many members of this team have spent time in medical lately."

"I promise not to inhale any weaponized viruses until you arrive." Their last major mission had almost gone sideways when the perpetrator had tried to take out most of the team in a bio-attack.

"If you've got time to joke, then maybe I should get you to help Magi with that level six diagnostic when we get there."

"No, sir. I want to stay dirtside and find out who tried to kill Tyra and her entire team."

Rossi nodded. "I thought so. See you tomorrow. We'll alert you once we make orbit."

"Yes, sir. See you soon."

The communication ended, and Dante put his communicator away. When he looked up, the doctor was standing in the hallway. Her hair was tied back with a bit of string, and his fingers itched to undo it and let it fall around her face. Her hair was black with a few strands of grey sprinkled through it. Her brief said she was forty-two, though he wouldn't have known it by looking at her. The only parts of her that looked old were her eyes. He recognized the look. Most of his fellow soldiers had those same shadows in their eyes. The difference was, most soldiers he knew had learned to be cautious. They approached new situations and new

44

people with care. Tyra hadn't learned that lesson. She still trusted too easily and didn't guard herself at all. If he couldn't get her to protect herself, he'd just have to do it for her.

TYRA HADN'T LIKED BEING TOLD she was endangering the others, but she had to agree he had a point. Not that she'd admit that to him. He'd give her one of his cocky grins and call her 'Shortcake' again. She wasn't sure what annoyed her more, the damned nickname or the fact that every time he called her that, she got a little hot and bothered. There should be a rule that arrogant, pushy men were not allowed to be sexy.

Over that last few days she'd discovered there was more to Dante than his looming presence and complete conviction he was always right. He was kind and patient with the kids, given them tips on improving their home, and was spending a small fortune feeding them all. He was a constant, steady presence at her back, watching over her every move. It had annoyed her at first, but now she was growing to like it.

She found him in the hallway, speaking on a communicator. He finished his conversation, put away the device, then nodded in greeting.

"Everything okay?"

She felt like she'd been caught eavesdropping despite the fact she'd only caught the last few words of his conversation. "All good. That was your team, wasn't it? Are they coming soon?"

"Yeah. You and Dr. Castille will be safely on board our

ship this time tomorrow. You'll be out of this system and on your way home in no time."

"I'm not going anywhere."

The big man folded his arms across his chest and looked down at her with a dour look she'd come to know too well. He was in full bossy mode, which was as irritating as it was attractive.

"Your part in this is over. This is our investigation now," he declared.

He was right, again. This wasn't something Boundless would want to be involved in. They were a charitable organization who offered their medical services and expertise to those in need. They weren't a task force. She could leave tomorrow, rebuild her team and move onto the next place that needed her help. She could, but that didn't feel like the right choice. Not this time.

She drew herself up to her full height and mirrored his stance. "Do you have a doctor on your team? Someone who has firsthand experience with this drug and its effects?"

"No. But if we need one, we'll get one."

His dismissal stung. She marched over to him and poked a finger against the solid wall of his chest. "You've got one right here. I volunteer. In fact, I insist. I'm not going anywhere until this is resolved."

"You won't be safe here."

"As you've pointed out numerous times since we met, I'm not good with the concept of personal safety. Besides, I owe my team, and their families, the truth about what happened here." A pang of raw grief filled her chest, and her next words had to be forced past the lump in her throat. "My friends are dead, and I need to know why.

More than that, I want the ones who did this to be held accountable for their deaths, and I want to be part of that process." She hadn't even had time to grieve yet. No one knew where their bodies were. No one knew *anything*, and she wasn't leaving until that changed.

She expected an argument. Instead, Dante sighed and scrubbed a hand over his grizzled jaw, then gave her an understanding look. "I get it, but I'm not sure that's your call to make. Someone outside the IAF is very concerned about getting you and Dr. Castille out of harm's way. Someone with enough influence to make my bosses twitchy."

"I have no idea who that would be. Whoever they are, they don't have any say over what I do with my time. I came here to help these people. My job's not done yet."

"Uh huh. Well, like I said, someone's making waves." He shrugged. "But, if you can get that dealt with, maybe you should stick around."

She wanted to check the sky outside and see if it had suddenly changed color. Sergeant Stubborn actually agreed with her? "I thought you wanted me gone? Why the change of heart?"

"I never said I wanted you gone. I want you safe. The safest place I can think of for you right now is anywhere but here."

His expression softened, and for a moment she had the strangest desire to move in close and lean into him, borrowing a bit of his strength. He was arrogant, bossy, and as stubborn as a Braxian donkey. "The safest place I can think of is with you." The words were out of her mouth before she could stop herself.

She half expected him to laugh at her. Instead, he

reached out to cup her cheek in one massive hand. "You trust me to take care of you?"

She nodded, ignoring the way her heart was slamming against her ribs. "You saved my life once already. Of course I trust you."

"Thank you." He leaned down and brushed the lightest of kisses to her forehead. "If you trust me, then how about you stop arguing with me when it comes to your safety?"

She was too stunned by his kiss to do more than nod, despite the fact he was being bossy again. The man couldn't help himself.

"So, this is what it takes to get you to stop arguing with me?" he asked, his voice softer than she'd ever heard it.

"Apparently, but the effect is only temporary. I will try and listen to you more, though…when it comes to keeping everyone safe, that is," she retorted.

His lips twitched with the faintest hint of a smile. "Of course. Wouldn't want you to stop arguing with me completely, it would throw off our whole dynamic."

"We have a dynamic?"

"Maybe." He reached for her again, this time setting those big hands of his on her hips and pulling her in close. "We have *something*. Not sure what it is, yet."

She allowed herself a moment of indulgence and moved in so close she could feel his body heat warming her. He wrapped an arm around her waist, his hand spanning the space between her shoulder blades. She tipped her head back to find him looking down at her, his gaze full of fire.

"Yeah, this is definitely something," he murmured as he bent down to claim her mouth with a heated kiss.

Veth, yes, it was. She'd done her best to ignore the attraction brewing between them. She told her herself it had to be one-sided, that it wasn't a good idea, and even that she had imagined it existed at all. The moment he kissed her, all her carefully crafted denials went up in flames, and so did she.

He didn't stop with one kiss or even two. His hard body wrapped around hers, his mouth slanting across her lips as he turned them both and walked her backward until she was pressed up against the nearest wall. He towered over her, all power and strength. He could hurt her so easily, but as demanding as his kisses were, his touch was gentle, and she knew he'd stop if she uttered a word of protest. She didn't. It was insane, but she wanted this as much as he did.

Her hands were fisted in the fabric of his shirt and her head was spinning with desire when he straightened, abruptly breaking their kiss. He moved away so fast she didn't have time to let go of him, and he ended up pulling her with him for a few steps.

"What the hell?"

"We're about to have company, and it's coming in fast." He put himself between her and the door to the stairwell. "Go get your bag and be ready to bug out. Oran, too."

"Where can we go?" She had been too busy caring for Oran and the others to give much thought to an exit plan.

"No time for questions. Move your cute ass!"

It wasn't what he said that made her sprint for the treatment room, it was the look in Dante's eyes. He'd had the same expression when he'd told her to hide and walked out to meet the men coming to kill her. Something terrible was about to happen. Again.

Oran was awake when she flew into the room. "Get up. There's a problem, and we need to get out of here, fast."

Oran gave her a blank look. "What?"

"Shoes, Oran. Get your *fraxxing* shoes on right now!" She scampered around the room, gathering up her medical supplies and tossing them into her pack. There wasn't much left, and she was ready to go in less than a minute.

Nico arrived just as she was helping Oran to his feet. The boy was wide-eyed and panting, and one look at him confirmed for her that Dante hadn't been overreacting. "They're coming. You gotta come with me right now. Dante said so."

"Where? Who's coming?"

"The bad guys with the masks. I saw 'em on my way back. More than last time. Come on. Dante's waiting."

"How'd they find us? Where are we going?" Tyra asked as she moved in beside Oran to help him stay up. His wound was healing, but the infection had left him too weak to move fast.

Nico gave her a look of frustration he could have only learned from Dante. "I told you. We're going to Dante. Hurry! And I don't know how they found us. Maybe they followed one of the younger kids back from the market."

Or maybe Dante was right, and one of the people she'd insisted on helping had turned her in. *Veth.* Had she caused this?

CHAPTER FOUR

THIS WAS HIS FAULT. Dante felt the weight of his failure with every step. He'd let his interest in Tyra interfere with his judgment, and now everyone was in danger. He'd told the others about the pending raid. The kids had launched out of the room so fast they'd damn near created a shockwave. They'd flood the stairwells and swarm the exits, which was exactly what he needed them to do. They'd distract and delay the attackers, buying him a few minutes to get his charges to safety. If the universe was feeling kind, then the kids would all escape unharmed. He hoped for that, but his priority was saving Tyra and Oran.

He listened carefully at the stairwell before entering. There was plenty of noise, but it was all coming from the lower floors. Perfect. "Follow right behind me. No talking. No unnecessary noise. If they hear us, we're *fraxxed*. Clear?"

Tyra, Oran, and Nico all nodded. "Oran, you're with me. Nico, stick with Dr. Li. If it goes to shit, you get her out of here and don't look back. We'll meet at the rendezvous site we talked about, okay?"

"Yessir," the kid nodded intently and moved closer to Tyra.

He winked at Nico, turned, and headed into the stairwell, bringing Oran with him. He couldn't save them all, but Nico had risked his life to get Tyra and Oran to safety during the first attack. It wouldn't be right to leave him to fend for himself.

He only took a few steps before realizing Oran wasn't strong enough to make the descent in time. Without a word, Dante turned and pointed to the injured doctor, then tapped his own shoulder. Oran got the message and gave a shamefaced nod. Dante leaned down and hoisted the other man across his shoulders in a fireman's carry. It wasn't dignified, but he was there to protect Oran's life, not his ego.

They only descended a single floor before exiting the stairwell again. He led them a few meters down the hall and stopped beside what looked like a random pile of debris. He moved an upturned desk aside, and shifted a broken door out of the way. Behind it was another door, this one still intact and set into the wall.

"Woah," Nico breathed. "Secret door!"

"I found it when I was doing some recon my first day here," Dante answered, keeping his voice low. He shifted Oran's weight to a more comfortable position and muscled the door open. The motor that powered it had long since died, which was probably why it had been ignored and eventually forgotten. There weren't many beings on this planet strong enough to open it.

The room itself was small, with a few empty counters

and shelves holding a few dust-covered bits of tech that had become obsolete more than a decade ago, along with a few items he'd placed there in case they needed a bolthole.

"Inside." He gestured for Nico and Tyra to get out of sight. He carefully set Oran back on his feet and turned his attention to the door. It only took a few seconds to move the desk and other junk back into position. Before he slid the door closed, he grabbed a light cube out of his pocket and tossed it to Nico. "Activate that for me."

He slid the door back into place, reaching through to rearrange the junk one last time so the doorway was completely covered. Once they were all safe inside, he allowed himself a mental sigh of relief. They were as safe as he could make them. "We can talk now, but no loud noises. That includes sneezing, coughing, or knocking over any of the shit in here. That happens, we're in a galaxy of trouble."

Everyone looked up from their spots on the floor, their eyes full of questions. Unsurprisingly, it was Tyra that spoke first. "Why are we still in the building? I thought the idea was to get away from these guys?"

"Nico, how many men did you see?" Dante asked.

"Lots. A dozen, maybe more. I had to circle around to get past them. They were all around."

"That's why," Dante said. "I'm betting they've got men watching every door, and probably the roof, too."

"But you sent everyone else out there!" Her tone was hushed, but there was no missing the edge to her words.

"I did. This way, they have a chance to escape, and the chaos they'll cause should make it almost impossible for the ones coming after you to be certain you and Oran didn't slip away in the crowd. They'll search the building and post a watch, but we're relatively safe in here, so long as we don't tip them off."

"If they're watching, how are we getting out of here?"

He pointed upward. "Same plan as before. My team will come get us in one of our shuttles. All we have to do is stay quiet until I get the signal. These guys might want you two dead, but I'm pretty damned sure they're not going to blow up a clearly marked military shuttle to do it."

"We're staying here until tomorrow?" Oran asked. "Uh, how's that going to work? There's no running water or well, anything in here."

Dante pointed to a small door in the back wall. "There's a closet through there with a bucket and a handful of rags. I stashed some water in here the other day, and I've got enough food tabs and light cubes to see us through."

"You were prepared for this," Tyra stated.

"I always have contingencies. In my line of work, backup plans are a requirement if you don't want to wind up dead."

"You could have shared your plans." Tyra's expression was hard to read in the dim light, but he got the impression she was pissed at him.

She had every right to be mad. He'd put her at risk because he'd gotten distracted. That was on him. Not telling her about his backup plan was the only reason they were safe right now. "If I had told you, there'd be a chance we were overheard. Either that information would now be in the hands of the men trying to kill us, or there'd be more people in here. Either way, it wouldn't be safe anymore."

She looked around the small space and then back at

him. "We could have fit a few more in here. They're in danger right now, and it's my fault."

"These kids are in danger every second of every day they exist. That's not your fault, that's the grim reality of this place and every place like it."

"That's not an excuse. We should have done more. Taken some of them with us."

Her voice was heavy with guilt and regret. He folded his arms across his chest and stared at her. "Which ones would you save, then? Give me their names."

"What?"

"Give me the names of four people you want to save. Now."

"I – Nico – and uh…"

"Nico is already here. Name four others."

Seconds passed in silence as she struggled to make her decision. Her mouth opened several times, but she never uttered a name.

"Do you understand, now?" he asked, feeling like a monster for making his point this way. He'd rather have her back in his arms, soothing her fears and stealing more kisses, but that couldn't happen. He wouldn't let himself get distracted again.

She nodded slowly. "I couldn't make the choice. I make life and death decisions for my patients every day, but this is different."

"Medical triage is brutal, but there's a logic to it. There's no logic to the choice you were trying to make, and we couldn't take the time or the risk."

"You tried to tell me this before. When you said you couldn't save them all," Her voice cracked on the last word. She drew her legs up and wrapped her arms around them, pressing her face to her knees.

Fraxx, he hated seeing her like this, but it had to be this way. It was the only way to keep them all safe.

He walked to the back of the room, as far away from the door as he could get, and pulled out his comm. It was time to let his team know what was happening.

Rossi opened the link within seconds, his expression grim. He knew what it meant that Dante was calling outside of their assigned contact times. "Report, Sergeant."

"We've been compromised. Packages are secure and undamaged, sir."

"For how long?"

"Long enough, sir." He didn't bother with details. This had to be a short conversation, just in case someone had the tech to trace his signal.

"Rendezvous?"

"Unchanged."

Rossi nodded. "Remember your orders, Sergeant."

"Yes, Commander." He saluted just as the screen went blank.

"Sergeant? You ain't a merc?" Nico scowled at Dante as he put away his comm and returned to the group.

"I'm not." Dante didn't see the need to continue the ruse any longer. "I'm with Nova Force."

Nico and Oran gave him identical wide-eyed stares, but Nico spoke first. "I heard 'bout you guys. You make the corporations behave themselves, right? You're really Nova Force? Where's your uniform?"

"I'm undercover, kid. My uniform is back on my ship, which will be coming to pick us up tomorrow."

"Us?" Nico's dark eyes gleamed with hope.

"Yep. Us. You're a key witness, so you're coming, too. I thought you might want to try out the burgers on our ship the *Malora*."

"Wow. I'm gonna meet a real live commander and eat Nova Force burgers!"

"Yes, you are. Only you don't need to call him commander. You just call him Fido."

Oran chuckled softly. "I think I'll stick with commander, myself." He'd taken a seat on the floor with his back to the wall. "How's the ship set for ice cream? I promised Nico a whole lot of desserts, too."

"We've got ice cream, cookies, and I think there's even a recipe for chocolate cake programmed into the food dispenser."

Nico's eyes gleamed. "I'm definitely coming with you guys."

"Good choice," Oran muttered. "Soft beds. Real food. Hot showers. *Veth*, I cannot wait."

Tyra raised her head to look up at him, a ghost of a smile on her lips. "Sounds good to me, too." She lapsed into Torski. "Thank you for saving him."

"We're not safe yet," he reminded her in the same language. He'd taught himself Torski a little at a time growing up. He didn't have much connection to that part of his heritage, but at least the language skills proved occasionally useful.

"So that's it? We sit here until they come and get us?" Oran asked.

Dante activated another light cube and set it on a dusty tabletop. "That's the plan. It'll be boring, but I prefer boring to running hellbent for leather and trying not to die."

Everyone nodded in silent agreement. There were a few minutes of quiet, then Nico cursed and reached for the tattered bag he always carried.

"Almost forgot. I got food." He pulled several wrapped packages out of a plastic bag, and a few seconds later the small room was filled with the scent of greasy meat, warm bread, and something achingly familiar.

"Is that apple pie?" Tyra asked.

"I told you to get fruit, kid. Not apple pie. Actual apples." Dante tried to sound irritated, but the aroma of spiced apples and pastry had him grinning inside. After a lifetime of eating vat-cloned proteins, food tabs, and algae broth, good food had been one of the highlights of IAF basic training. Every day, the base's kitchen had made mountains of pie to go with the evening meal. He'd done hours of punishment duty peeling the apples for those pies, but it never dampened his love for the dessert.

"Fruit, fruit pies." Nico shrugged. "Same thing, right? The pies are fresh. They took 'em out of the oven while I watched." Nico set down the food on the floor between them, beaming.

Even Oran perked up at the scent. "Best smell in the world."

The scent. It was unmistakable, and it would give away their presence to anyone walking by. Dante looked around the empty shelves, trying to come up with a plan to at least partially seal the door.

"What do you need?" Tyra asked, already rising from the floor.

"Something to make sure our friends out there don't catch a whiff of our dinner and get a sudden hankering for apple pie. I need to seal this door."

58

She eyed the doorway and nodded. "I've got something that should work."

His brows raised, and she gave him a cocky grin that sent a jolt of lust straight to his cock. "You think you're the only one carrying around all sorts of useful items just in case things go sideways? I'm a doctor, remember? Improvisation is part of the job description." She left his side to retrieve her pack, rummaging in it until she came up with a canister he recognized.

"Is that redi-seal?" he asked, impressed by her thinking. She'd been through seven kinds of hell this week, and she was still at the top of her game.

"Yep." She returned to the door and handed the cannister to him. "I can't reach the top of the door, but you can. You know how to use it?"

"Yeah. I've used it to plug holes in a few of my friends over the years."

"I hate that stuff," Oran muttered.

"You shouldn't. It's going to save your life again," Tyra replied.

Dante snapped the cap off and maneuvered the tip into position. It would be a messy, imperfect seal, but it should be enough to keep them safe until it was time to leave.

DINNER WAS A QUIET AFFAIR, all of them lost in their own thoughts. Tyra kept thinking about the others. Had they made it out of the building? Had one of them given up her location? Questions kept buzzing around her head as she ate.

They shared the food Nico had acquired and agreed to

save the food tabs for the morning meal. By then, hunger would make the bland but nutritionally balanced paste more appetizing. As they'd eaten, they could hear the occasional booted footfalls outside the door, and each time it happened, they all went still and silent, barely breathing until the footsteps faded away again. By the time the meal was done, the fear and uncertainty had gotten to them all.

Oran claimed the corner farthest from the door and fell into a restless sleep. He was still weakened from his injury. Tyra suspected most of his issues weren't physical, though, but mental and emotional. He wasn't coping well with the stress of their situation. This was his first mission with Boundless, and she suspected it would be his last.

Nico stayed close to her for the next hour. He whispered almost non-stop about getting to go on a real spaceship, asking her and Dante countless questions about the *Malora*, Dante's teammates, and what flavors of ice cream were programmed into the food dispensers. Dante answered every one of the boy's questions in his low, rumbling voice, and she marveled at his patience. Dante could be blunt, violent, and frustratingly stubborn, but he had hidden depths and a kind heart, two traits she wouldn't have expected from someone who'd chosen the life of a soldier. She found him intriguing, and after the kiss they'd shared, she couldn't deny the attraction she felt for him.

As time passed, the questions came slower, and Nico's voice grew softer as he fought to keep his eyes open. She laid her hand on his head, stroking the boy's hair the same way her mother had done for her the nights she couldn't sleep. It wasn't long until Nico finally drifted off.

Unwilling to linger over the bittersweet memories of

her mother, Tyra carefully extracted herself from the sleeping boy and walked over to Dante so they could talk without disturbing the others. "I know I said it before, but I want to say it again. Thank you for saving him."

Dante was sitting with his back to the door, acting as a final barrier between the three civilians and any potential threat. He looked at Nico and then at her. "You don't need to thank me. I didn't do it for you."

"I'm thanking you because he isn't old enough to understand the choice you made, but I do." She sat down beside him and stretched her legs out beside his. Her feet barely reached his knees, and one of his thighs were as big around as both of hers put together.

"I don't think I did it for him, either. He's a good kid trapped in a bad life. It's not much of a kindness for me to take him to the *Malora* and show him what things could have been like if he'd been born somewhere else, or to someone else."

"Then why?"

"Because I was being selfish. I like him, and I didn't want to leave him behind."

She turned her upper body toward him and set a hand on his arm. She'd been itching to touch him again since their interrupted kiss. "That doesn't sound like selfishness to me. That sounds like kindness."

He grunted, his features folding into a stormy frown. "I doubt he'll think of it that way when we drop his ass back in this hellhole and leave. You and I will move on to the next mission, and he'll be back here, taunted by the memory of soft beds, good food, and a safe place to sleep."

"Maybe we won't have to do that." She was just musing aloud, but the idea struck a chord with her.

"He's not a pet, you can't keep him."

"Why not?" she retorted before she could think about what she was saying. "He's got no one to take care of him. Bellex won't even acknowledge his existence until his sixteenth birthday when he's legally able to work. Until then, he's a non-entity."

"And if he lives that long, they'll find him, scan the chip in his neck, and assign him a job to pay off his family's debts."

"Those chips are an abomination," she muttered, then frowned. "Wait, what debts?"

Dante's expression darkened as he pointed to the sleeping child. "That tattoo. The triangle with the three dots marks him as a debt carrier. Whoever his family was, they were indentured to Bellex. Unless someone cleared their ledgers after they died, the debts become Nico's responsibility once he's of age."

"But that's criminal!"

He shook his head. "Actually, it's legal, for now. That's why Nova Force exists. The corporations keep coming up with new loopholes and ways to twist existing laws, and we do our best to stop them."

"He's a child. How can they do that?"

Dante reached for her hand and slid it down to his wrist. Belatedly she remembered the cut on his arm. "Sorry. Is it still bothering you?"

"It's healing fine," he said dismissing his injury with a shrug. "As for how the corporations get away with crap like this, it's because they have the money and the means. Take this planet. The inhabitants here aren't citizens of any world or colony. Because of that, they have no rights or protections. They're staff, and this place is a classic example of how corporations treat their workers."

Tyra had spent time on colonies, stations, and planets across the galaxy, but she'd never been on a corporate-owned world before. She'd been too busy trying to fix the immediate problems she saw to really look at what was happening. She should have, though. She'd lost her parents to corporate greed when she was still a girl. She'd let herself be blinded to the truth. Or maybe she hadn't wanted to see it, because it would remind her too much of what she'd lost.

"What would happen if someone were to remove Nico's chip? And maybe got rid of the tattoo that indicates he had one."

Dante's frown deepened. "I don't know, but I'm sure Bellex wouldn't like it if you tried. As far as they're concerned, he's their property. They don't give up their assets easily."

"Believe me, I know all about that." She didn't want to remember how she'd learned that lesson, so she turned her attention elsewhere. "Will you let me check that cut? All you let me do was put some ointment and a dressing on it, and that was days ago. It might be infected."

"You can check the cut right after you tell me why you changed topics so fast."

She raised her gaze to find him staring down at her with interest. "I'd rather not talk about it."

"And I'd rather not have you poking at my owie. We don't always get what we want in life."

"Did you just call the three-inch gash on your arm an owie? Is that the official military term?"

"Nope. I'm sure there's an official four-syllable word

for it that involves two different acronyms and a whole lot of red tape."

"If that cut is infected, you're not going to be at your best tomorrow. It's been brought to my attention that you're my best chance of getting out of here in one piece. So, give me your arm, Sergeant. Now."

"You're adorable when you try to tell me what to do." He grinned at her, then rolled up his sleeve to reveal his heavily muscled forearm and portions of at least two tattoos. When he reached the dressing, his movements slowed, and she noticed he was taking care not to press down on the injury.

"I'm not adorable at the best of times, and this is far from the best of anything. I'm tired, unbrushed, unwashed, and generally disheveled."

"You're still adorable. That's my opinion, and it's not going to change. Trust me, bigger, tougher beings than you have tried to change my mind before. It never works."

"That would sound more intimidating if you weren't the same the man who is kicking up a fuss because he doesn't want me poking around his booboo."

Once he had his sleeve out of the way, she eased the dressing off to take a look. "This is why you didn't want me looking, isn't it?" She gestured to the wound, which was looking red and slightly inflamed.

He shrugged. "It's a minor infection. It's not like my arm is going to rot off before we're back on the *Malora*."

She rolled her eyes. "You're not the doctor here. I can name a half-dozen bacteria that could actually cause that to happen, and three of them exist on this planet. You should have told me." She got to her feet, retrieved her bag from the table where she'd left it, and brought it back with her, along with one of the light cubes.

He watched her in silence until she settled beside him again, then moved in close and laid his injured arm across her lap. It was the closest they'd been since he'd kissed her, and the memory of that moment made her pulse kick up a notch.

She retrieved a fresh dressing pack, some antibacterial wipes, and the last of her ointment from the pack and laid them out beside her. "Once we're safe, I want to take another look at you. The ship's med-bay will have healing accelerant and everything else I need to fix you up, right?"

Dante sat a little straighter. "My baby's got a fully equipped med-bay, complete with a brand-new diagnostic computer program and an auto-surgery pod."

"Your baby? I thought the *Malora* was an IAF ship." She kept talking as she cleaned the wound, pausing now and then to shine the light over the area.

"She is. But I'm her pilot. I miss being in the cockpit." Dante raised his hand and skimmed it through the air like a child imitating a ship in flight. "That was my dream when I was a kid. I was obsessed with anything that flew. Skimmers, military vessels, freighters—I had every type and model memorized."

"So you joined the IAF to become a pilot?" she asked as she worked. It was easier to do her job if her patient was distracted, but she was also curious.

He laughed, a deep booming sound that warmed her soul. "*Fraxx*, no. I was recruited for the infantry. My job was to shoot things until I ran out of ammo, then punch them until we won or I died, whichever came first. I didn't start flight training until after I was seconded to Nova Force."

"Interesting description of your career. Why did you choose it if it wasn't what you dreamed of doing?" She'd known she would be a doctor from an early age. The accident that killed her mother and crippled her father had determined her path, and she hadn't let anything get in the way.

"Lack of options, mostly. My dad wasn't much of a family man. He left for good before I could walk. My mom, she tried, but she was really only good at two things: singing on stage and falling in love with losers. I joined the IAF because a recruiter I knew pointed out that my careers as a cage fighter and part-time enforcer for the local criminal element were going to lead to a short, violent life, so why not sign up? I'd still live a short, violent life, but I'd be paid well and fed even better."

"You were a cage fighter? As in, bare-knuckle brawling, smash the other guy's face in, last one standing gets the prize?" There were fight clubs and organized matches in just about every place she'd ever visited. In a galaxy where almost everything was legal so long as the corporations got their share; pharma, fighting, gambling, and the sex trade were all highly profitable, and popular, pastimes. She was no saint, but there was something about watching beings deliberately hurt each other that twisted her stomach into knots.

"I was, yeah." He tapped a thick finger to the crooked bridge of his nose. "I'll have you know my face was busted by professionals."

"More than once, by the look of it." She gently stroked

her finger down the side of his nose. "I could reset that for you if you wanted me to."

He didn't move as she touched him, his gaze never leaving her face. "I like it this way. Reminds me of where I came from."

"I like it, too." She moved her hand away and dropped her gaze. She kept her head down and her eyes firmly locked on his injury until it was redressed and covered in the last of her sealant.

Across the room, Nico stirred and muttered something incoherent in his sleep.

"He's probably dreaming about burgers," Dante joked.

"No doubt. Or the desserts Oran promised him." She looked over at Nico, then back to Dante. "You're good with him. And with the other kids, too. Do you have any of your own?"

"*Veth*, no. No kids. My life is too crazy for anything like that. I couldn't even manage to keep my marriage intact."

"You were married?"

"For a brief time, yeah. My marriage imploded because I changed careers."

She could understand how that could happen. They were very different people, but their careers had similarities. They were both nomads, going where they were sent to do jobs that required long hours and total commitment. She glanced down at his arm as she made a quiet confession. "At least you gave it a shot. I never even got close."

"You were focused on helping others. Nothing wrong with that." He chuckled. "Besides, according to all my friends, you never know when the right person will come along. They keep telling me all I need to do is keep my eyes open."

"You, too, huh?"

"All the time." He shifted a little closer to her. "I've got a complaint, doc."

"What is it? Is the sealant stinging too much?" She looked up to find him watching her with a grin that put his dimples on full display.

"No, it's fine. I just realized that you got me to talk about myself this whole time, and the deal was you were supposed to be telling me how you know so much about corporations wanting to hold onto their assets."

"I don't remember agreeing to anything like that," she replied with a grin of her own.

"So, it's going to be like that, huh? I'm a trained investigator, Shortcake. I will find out what I want to know."

"You're welcome to try, but I doubt you'll get far. Especially if you're going to keep calling me that ridiculous nickname."

"What's wrong with Shortcake? It's sweet, delicious, and well…short. Just like you. If you don't like it, what about Tiny Tyra? Mini Medic?"

She glowered. "Not funny. I don't go around calling you Sergeant Stubborn or Muscle Mountain."

He snorted with laughter, muffling it behind his hand until he composed himself again. "Okay, point taken. Though honestly, I kind of like that last one."

"You would." She finished putting away her supplies and had to stifle a yawn as she turned off the light cube she'd brought, leaving the room far darker.

"Tired?" he asked.

"Yeah. But we need to stay awake in case something happens, right?"

"Only one of us needs to be awake at a time. Get some rest, short—Tyra. I'll wake you up in a few hours so I can grab some shuteye."

"Promise you'll wake me up to take a shift?"

He reached out and cupped her cheek in one massive hand. "If I need to sleep, I'll wake you." He leaned toward her and for a moment she thought he might kiss her again, but all he did was touch his lips to her hair before letting go of her again. "Get some rest."

She considered moving, but the truth was she didn't want to leave Dante's side. He was a comforting presence in this strange, threatening world she'd been thrown into. "Would you mind if I slept here, beside you? I don't want to disturb Oran or Nico."

It was the weakest excuse she'd ever used, but Dante didn't call her on it. "Not a problem." He lifted her backpack and set it down beside his thigh. "This will work as a pillow. You going to be warm enough?"

"I'll be fine." The building was warm during the day, but the nights were cold enough she'd miss the threadbare blanket Nico had given her to use as a bedroll.

"Now who's being stubborn?" He skinned off his shirt, revealing a heavily muscled chest covered in tattoos. Some of them were words in Galactic Standard, others looked like Torski symbols, and she could make out a bird of prey soaring across his ribcage.

"You're going to be cold if I take your shirt," she argued.

"I'm part Torski, which means I run hotter than

humans. I'll be fine. Take it." He patted the floor beside him in invitation.

She curled up next to him, her head on the makeshift pillow, and he draped the shirt over her like a blanket. It was still warm and smelled of him, a lingering scent of cloves and spices. "When it's my turn to take a watch, I'll give this back to you, so you can sleep in comfort."

"Sounds good."

She closed her eyes and tried to get comfortable. After a few minutes of tossing and turning, Dante laid his hand on her shoulder and used his thumb to stroke a pattern of soothing circles across her skin.

"Sleep now. I'll be right here. Nothing's going to happen to you while I'm here, Tyra. I promise."

She believed him. He might be stubborn and pushy, but he was also the reason they were all alive right now. It had been years since she'd trusted anyone to take care of her, but she trusted him. "One day, when this is all over, will you tell me about your tattoos? They're beautiful."

"Have a drink with me when we're back on the *Malora*, and I'll tell you all about them. Good night, Shortcake."

"Night, Muscles." The last thing she heard before falling asleep was the soft sound of his laughter.

CHAPTER FIVE

DANTE WAS on his way to the ship's small gym when he heard Tyra talking to someone farther up the corridor. In a move that was getting to be a habit, he turned on his heel and ducked into the first room that was open. It wasn't that he didn't want to see her. If anything, it was the opposite. Since their kiss, he hadn't been able to go five minutes without thinking of her, and that was a serious problem.

She hadn't slept well that night they'd spent in hiding. Each time she got restless, he'd put his hand on her shoulder or stroked her hair until she quieted again. He'd stayed awake all night, watching over her and the others while they slept. He was honored that she trusted him to protect her when she was at her most vulnerable. The problem was she was still vulnerable and would be until this mission was over. Until then, he couldn't allow himself to get distracted again. If he did, he risked losing her before he got a chance to know her better, and he wanted that more than he liked to admit. Every time he considered tracking her down and kissing her senseless again, he reminded himself why he was staying away. It was the only way to keep her safe.

It had been two days since they'd returned to the *Malora*, and the entire team was stuck onboard, waiting for clearance to proceed. Dax hadn't gotten permission to bring the shuttle in to pick up Dante and his charges. He'd ordered the mission anyway, and Bellex had retaliated by burying the team in red tape.

The only one enjoying the current state of affairs was Nico. He roamed the ship at will, but his favorite places to be were the mess and the ship's entertainment lounge. He spent a fair bit of time with Tyra, too, and he always seemed to know when Dante was in the cockpit of the *Malora*. He'd come by to chat with him for hours about anything and everything that passed through his young head.

"You hiding from the kid, the doctor, or both?" Dax asked from the shadows. Dante hadn't noticed him until his commander spoke and turned away from the viewing port to look his way.

Dante bristled. "I don't hide from anyone, sir."

"Then you're doing a remarkably good imitation of it right now. You've been ducking into rooms and lurking behind corners since you got back." Dax folded his arms over his chest and cocked his head to the side. "As a friend, that concerns me. As your commanding officer, it looks like an issue I need to resolve. So, what the *fraxx* is going on with you, Buttercup?"

"Off the record?"

Dax nodded. "Computer, lock the door to this room." He issued the command and pointed to the table and chairs that took up most of the available space. "Sit down and tell me what's going on."

"It's not a big deal. I'm just trying to put some distance between myself and Dr. Li right now."

"Personality conflict? I know you were having trouble getting her to listen to you down there. If that's the case, you two need to figure it out. She's volunteered to stick around and help us on this case, and we could really use her help."

Dante grimaced and rubbed the back of his neck. "Conflict? Uh, no. That's not the issue."

"Then what's the problem?"

"You remember the mission to Victor Base?"

Dax nodded. "It was only a few months ago, of course I remember. That's where we learned about the Gray Men and we all damned near died."

"And you reconnected with Trinity, which complicated things," Dante added.

"Yeah." Dax grinned. "She was worth almost dying for." It took a moment for him to get the point Dante was making. "Wait. You and the doctor got uh, complicated?"

"Nothing happened. I mean, I kissed her once, but then we got attacked. An attack that occurred because I let myself get distracted."

"I read your report. The most likely scenario is that one of the people she tried to help gave you all up for a reward. If you had really been distracted, you wouldn't have been prepared for that possibility. You had a plan, and it kept you all safe until we got to you. Mission accomplished."

"I should have insisted she stop treating people. Kept

her safely stashed away until pickup. Because I didn't do that, we got attacked," Dante said.

"Maybe." Dax rapped the tabletop with his knuckles. "But you know better than to let the bad days get to you. I know that's easier said than done, but it's important to keep perspective. You did good work down there. You saved three lives and brought us the one person who has seen cobalt and its effects. Without Dr. Li, we'd still be in the dark."

"Not that it does us much good to know what to look for when we can't get back on the planet." Dante thumped his fist on the still-shiny surface of the table in frustration.

"Actually, we can, but it means we're going to have Bellex visitors onboard. I received our clearance a few minutes ago. I was deciding who to send down when you came in."

"I volunteer." This was exactly what he wanted. Off this ship and back to work.

"I figured you would. As your friend, I think you should stay here. If you've got feelings for the doctor, then hiding from her isn't going to do either of you any good." Dax sighed. "But as your commander, I know you're more useful to the mission dirtside. Get packed, you leave in thirty minutes. That should get you off the ship before our guests arrive. If you're headed back to the planet, I don't want the Bellex reps seeing your face. You're staying off the books for the time being."

"That's fine by me. Who are you sending with me?"

"You'll go with Blink and Sabre. Trip is going to stay here and give your doctor a hand with the research side of things. Trinity and I will deal with the corporate types. One of them is just a representative, the other is a Bellex-backed doctor who wants to *help* us with the investigation."

Dante snorted. "Tyra's going to love that."

"Speaking of, are you going to tell her or the kid you're leaving? As your friend, I'm strongly recommending you do so."

"I uh, damn. I guess I should." It was a new idea for him. The only people who cared about his comings and goings were on this ship. He hadn't had anyone else to keep informed since Tish had walked out of his life. "Can you keep an eye on Nico for me?"

"You know it. He can hang with Magi. That might keep our resident whiz-kid distracted from the fact he's stuck onboard. Colonel Bahl is tearing through the red tape right now, and I think Bellex is finally starting to realize the magnitude of their error, stonewalling her and restricting our access to the planet."

Dante grinned. "The colonel is a dragon best left sleeping. She's one scary lady when riled."

"Indeed, she is. But if you ever call her a dragon in her hearing, I won't be able to save you. Go say your goodbyes and get your gear packed. I'll let the rest of the team know we're a go."

Dante snapped off a salute and headed out. The corridor was quiet when he stepped into it. He'd pack, then say some brief goodbyes heading out...if there was time.

TYRA WAS CONFUSED and a little hurt. Dante had been avoiding her since they'd arrived on board—an impressive feat considering he was a damned big man and the *Malora* was a relatively small ship. The last time she'd seen him for more than few minutes was on the shuttle ride to orbit. He'd escorted them into the shuttle bay and introduced her to the other members of his team. The next time she looked around, he'd vanished.

Later she discovered he'd gone straight to the med-bay to get his injured arm treated. Cris, the team's medic, let her know that Dante had gotten it cleaned up, received a shot of healing accelerant, and had Cris give him a clean bill of health.

Whenever there was a briefing, he was the last one to arrive and the first one to leave. She'd sent him a message asking how his arm was healing. He'd been slow to reply, and when he did, it was a brief note thanking her and stating he was back at full strength.

Clearly, he'd changed his mind about them. Not that there was a *them*, exactly. There was attraction, sure. The man was hotter than a supernova, and while she was over forty, she wasn't dead. He'd kissed her, so he must have felt something for her, too, but the moment the danger had faded, so had his interest.

At least he'd kept his promise and supported her desire to stay on and help find the source of the cobalt. She was convinced the drug was the reason almost all the Bellex employees had become near-mindless drones. Nico and the other kids had confirmed that the strange behavior started only two months ago.

The timeline fit, but there were still too many questions. Why had there been a rash of overdoses and drug-induced violence that affected the entire population? Where was the drug coming from? And how was it being dispensed now that the pharma dealers' supply had dried up? Bellex had to be involved in the vile mess, but she didn't have a clue how she was going to prove it.

"But I'm going to find a way," she muttered to herself as she headed down the ship's main corridor. She'd been summoned to a meeting with the members of the team. Hopefully, Commander Rossi had good news to share. The only one enjoying their enforced hiatus was Nico. The entire crew had adopted him as an unofficial mascot, and he was basking in their attention, especially Dante's. He was also eating his body weight in synthesized food every day, and she could already see the changes good nutrition and getting a decent night's sleep could make. At this rate, his friends on the surface wouldn't recognize him when he came back.

Veth, she hated the idea of sending him back to his old life. If there was a way to break him free of Bellex's grip, she'd find it. Even if that meant calling in every favor she was owed. A long time ago, someone had stepped in and helped her when no one else would. She would honor his memory by doing the same for Nico.

She reached the door of the briefing room and activated the chime to announce her presence. She'd quickly learned that most of the doors on this ship only opened for the crew. If she wanted access to anywhere outside the common areas, she had to get one of them to let her in. It was mildly annoying, but she understood. This was a fully armed IAF frigate as well as a mobile military base. They had protocols, and their own secrets to protect.

The door slid open, and Cris greeted her on the other side. The handsome blond lieutenant had a natural charm about him that was at odds with his precise and polished accent. "Hi. Welcome to yet another meeting. Despite appearances, we occasionally do actual work." He winked at her. "Just not at the moment."

She entered the room and looked around. Commander Rossi was seated already, and at his right was Lieutenant Trinity West. Ensign Erben, the one Dante called Magi, was working with a three-dimensional holographic interface projected over the table, but he was moving the data so quickly she couldn't make out what any of it was.

"Planning counts as work," she replied, earning her a smile from Commander Rossi.

"Yes, it does," he agreed and gestured for her to take a seat.

"It barely counts. I still can't believe I'm stuck up here for this mission. They let Blink go dirtside, but not me? Do they have any idea how dangerous that woman is?" the ensign muttered.

"No, and that's the point," Trinity said.

"Get over it, Magi. Not everyone gets to go on every mission. Plus, as you've pointed out several times already, there are no lizard burgers in our galley." Cris pointed out before sitting down across from her.

"The rest of the team has gone down to the planet?" Tyra had assumed the others were on their way.

Commander Rossi frowned. "Didn't Dante let you know?"

"I haven't seen him today. Did...did they take Nico with them?" Learning Dante had left without saying goodbye stung a little, but if he'd taken Nico..."

"Nico is still staying with us for now. Safer that way."

Dax frowned in obvious agitation, then added, "I thought Dante was going to tell you about this before he left."

"He didn't." He'd clearly moved on. It was time she did, too.

"You left Buttercup in charge of conveying information? He who doesn't like to utter more than a dozen words a day?" Eric shook his head in mock dismay.

"One more word out of you, Ensign, and you'll be starting that level six diagnostic Dante wants done on the engine," Rossi warned.

"Sorry, sir. Shutting up now, sir."

"Buttercup?" The way Dante's team bantered with each other had surprised her at first. Her few experiences with members of the IAF had given her the impression they were all about sharp salutes, polished boots, and protocol. Team Three were different. They traded insults, teased each other, and while they clearly respected their commander, they seemed almost allergic to protocol.

"That's Dante's nickname," Cris said in his elegantly accented voice. "Before you ask, he got tagged with that long before he came to Nova Force, and none of us know the story behind it."

"And believe me, I've tried to find out. I'm pretty sure he threatened to pulverize anyone who talks," Eric chimed in.

"I'm sorry you weren't informed about the team's departure, Dr. Li. Erben, when we're done here, I want you to outfit the doctor with one of the new communicators. Make sure you brief her on how to use the encrypted channels, too. That should make sure no one's left out of any other important updates."

"Yes, sir." Eric beamed at her. "Once I'm done kitting

you out, Dr. Li, you'll never want to go back to your old tech again. If you give me your comm now, I can switch everything over and have it back to you shortly."

"Thank you." She pulled out the basic communicator they'd given her when she arrived on the *Malora* and slid it across the table to Eric. It was good to be part of a team again, even if it evoked a sense of guilt. Her team was gone. Men and women she'd been responsible for had died. Joining a new team so soon after their loss felt like she was disrespecting their memories, but it was also the only way to get justice for them.

"Now we've got you caught up, I'd like to move on with the briefing. We've got about thirty minutes before our guests arrive. Before they set foot on this ship, I want everyone to know the plan."

"Guests?" Eric asked.

"Bellex is sending two representatives. They're to be read in on the investigation and will be staying on until we close this case."

"Aw, they're sending spies. How sweet. You want me to prep the standard welcome package for them?" Eric was grinning with almost maniacal glee as he asked the question.

"You know it," Dax replied.

"Do I want to know what that means?" Trinity asked.

"It means we'll be watching the watchers. From keystrokes to communications, I'll be monitoring everything they say or do. I'll also be activating the *Malora's* counter-surveillance functions to protect our network and secure all crew-only areas with extra measures." Eric glanced over at Tyra. "We giving the doctor full access?"

Dax nodded, his gaze firmly fixed on Tyra. "You know we already vetted you so you could stay on and help us with the investigation. I'd like to give you full access, but before I do that, you'd have to agree to sign some non-disclosure agreements."

"More?" She had already filled a myriad of forms and agreements just to be allowed what limited access she had.

"More," Dax confirmed.

"So much more," Trinity added with a laugh. "My previous assignment was all highly classified, and it still took me a staggering amount of paperwork to be allowed to join this merry band of lunatics."

"We're glad you did, though, Trin, and not just because the boss-man is a lot less grumpy now you're in his life," Eric said.

Trinity blushed. "Thanks."

It hadn't taken long for Tyra to figure out the commander and lieutenant were a couple. It was yet another surprising discovery about the way the team functioned. Most places she'd worked, including Boundless, discouraged workplace romances. Apparently the IAF, or at least Nova Force, felt differently.

Dax cleared his throat. "Dr. Li, you didn't give me your answer, yet."

"Oh, right. Yes. My answer is yes. Whatever it takes to find out what happened here and bring those responsible to justice. I lost teammates down there, and I owe them answers."

Everyone nodded in silent understanding.

"Dante told me how you felt. I'm glad you're staying on to help us." Dax stood and walked around to her side and offered her his hand. "Welcome to the team."

She rose, took his hand and shook it, feeling a surge of satisfaction. "Thank you, Commander."

Dax grinned. "It's going to be nice to have someone around here who actually uses my title."

"I'll behave when we have company, Fido, sir," Eric said.

Trinity rolled her eyes. "I'll believe that when I see it."

Dax returned to his seat. "Now that you're unofficially official, there are a few more things we need to cover before our guests arrive. There are two of them. One's a straight-up corporate rep, the other is a doctor." He looked at Tyra. "Dr. Debba Downs is on Bellex's payroll, and she's here to 'observe and assist' the team. She's going to want access to the med-bay, so you and Trip are going to have to keep an eye on her and make sure she's not interfering with samples or altering your data."

Cris groaned. "Who agreed to let her be part of this at all?"

"Colonel Bahl did, because it was the fastest way to get Bellex to agree to surface access. As it is, I was supposed to wait for them to meet the entire team before sending anyone down. I don't want them seeing Dante though. Everyone's files have been redacted and firewalled for this mission, and Bellex has been ordered to allow our team through without scans or security checks. They're not happy about it, but they eventually agreed."

"I bet the colonel told them what happened to the last corporation who refused to let Nova Force investigate," Eric said.

"What happened?" Tyra asked.

"We put them out of business," Dax said with deep satisfaction.

"And if Bellex had anything to do with the cobalt, the cover-up, or what happened to your team, we'll do the same thing to them," Trinity declared.

Both Cris and Eric cheered, but a stern look from Dax settled them quickly.

"Facts first. Right now, we don't have a lot of those. Our job is to keep the Bellex people away from anything important and be prepared to act fast once the team on the ground finds anything useful. Witnesses. Evidence. Actionable intel."

"A sample of cobalt would be nice, too," Cris said.

"That's on the top of the ground team's most wanted list," Dax said, then sighed. "Speaking of wish lists, the Bellex people have a few requests of their own."

"Let me guess. Full cooperation, total access to any and all data they deem pertinent to the investigation, private rooms, encrypted comms channels, and daily foot rubs," Eric quipped.

"You're close, but lucky for you, no foot rubs were requested. They are adamant that they receive a full debriefing from you and Dr. Castille, though, Dr. Li."

Bellex had insisted they needed to speak to her from the moment they'd learned she was alive and well. Nova Force had denied all attempts to have her returned to the surface or delivered to one of the dozens of stations and shipbuilding platforms in the system, citing the continuing threat to herself and her injured teammate. "They're welcome to ask me anything they want. Everything I remember is already on the record." Tyra frowned. "Apart from the names of the individuals who protected us down there. I'm not putting those children at risk, especially not with Nico here."

"Magi will keep an eye on Nico and make sure he knows who the newcomers are. He's a smart kid—once he's aware of their presence, my bet is he'll give them both a wide berth. As far as I'm concerned, he's a key witness under our jurisdiction until the investigation ends," Dax said.

"Thank you. I have no idea how to go about it, but if it's at all possible, I'd like to try to find a way to keep Nico from going back. He's got no one else, and I hate the idea of leaving him behind."

Everyone went quiet. "We can't save them all, Dr. Li. You know that," Cris said.

"I know. But Dante taught me that sometimes, we *can* save one."

Dax rapped on the tabletop. "Damn right we can. I make no promises, Dr. Li. But I'll see what I can do."

Hope bloomed in her chest, and Tyra found herself breathing easier. It wasn't hard to see why this team followed Dax Rossi with such devotion. He was the kind of leader who inspired everyone around him. "Thank you so much. I know it's a long shot, but I have to try."

"One more thing before we wrap up," Dax said. "Once Bellex has what they need from Dr. Castille, he's been cleared to leave the system and head home."

"He'll be happy to hear that. Doctors really don't make good patients. I suspect he won't be signing on for any more Boundless missions, either."

Trinity sat a little straighter in her chair. "Why not?"

"This kind of work isn't for everyone. We get a lot of young, eager doctors looking to do some good while adding to their resume. They often do one or two missions and then decide it's not the right fit for them. The experience is valuable, but they have to endure long hours, poor working conditions, bad food, and in a worst-case scenario, something like what happened to us."

"This was his first mission with Boundless, right?" Trin asked.

"Correct. To be honest, I'm not sure why he even signed on. He graduated near the top of his class, had sufficient experience and commendations to be hired most places, and he didn't strike me as the humanitarian type. He was a last-minute addition, too. When one of my regular doctors had to step away to deal with a family matter, he ended up being the replacement."

Trinity glanced over at Dax. "More feathers to ruffle?" she asked.

"Do it."

"I'm sorry, do what?" Tyra asked.

Trinity gave her a reassuring smile. "I'm going to take a closer look at Castille before he leaves to make sure we're not missing anything. I'll need to talk to you too, just to get your impressions of him for my files."

"He almost died down there. Do you really think he could be part of all this?" She couldn't imagine it. Oran wasn't even a good poker player. How could he hide a secret that big?

"What I think isn't relevant. We just need to collect all the information we can and sort it out later," Trinity said.

Cris leaned in and added, "It's the same process as making a difficult diagnosis. You have to gather all the facts and look at them with as little bias as possible to make sure you're not overlooking anything. We can't come to the right conclusions if we don't have all the facts."

"I understand. I'm here to help in any way I can, just

tell me what you need to know," she said. Cris' explanation made sense, but it didn't ease her discomfort at knowing they were going to investigate Oran. Worse, she knew what was happening, and couldn't say anything. Dante's untalkative nature was starting to make sense, now. When your work was full of secrets and you didn't know who to trust, it was safer to say too little than too much. How did Dante and the others live this way?

CHAPTER SIX

THE TRIP back to District Twelve's spaceport was simple enough the shuttle's computer could have handled it alone, but Dante left it in manual mode. It had been too long since he'd piloted. Being back in the cockpit helped smooth the ragged edges off his mood and let him focus on the mission ahead. At least, that was what he was trying to focus on, but every few minutes he'd be back to thinking about Tyra. He knew the team would take care of both her and Nico, but protecting them had been his assignment, first. Leaving them behind had unsettled him in ways he hadn't expected.

He'd found Nico in the galley and explained that he needed to go dirtside for a bit. The boy hadn't been happy to learn Dante was leaving, though he hid it behind an unending litany of questions. In the end, Dante had given the kid a one-armed hug and left, feeling an unfamiliar sense of guilt as he ran the whole way to the shuttle to make up for lost time. There'd been no time to talk to Tyra. He'd have to send a note soon and apologize for that, but she'd understand. She was part of this investigation because she wanted answers more than anyone. She'd be happy to know things were finally in motion.

His comm alerted him to an incoming message from Magi. He transferred it to the main console, read it, and winced.

In briefing right now. Rossi thought you'd briefed the doc before leaving. She didn't even know you were gone. Not your best move, Buttercup. Suggest you fix it.

He drummed his fingers on the console as the surface of the planet grew larger in his displays. He'd screwed up.

"I'm an idiot," he muttered and reached for his comm. "Computer, take over piloting the shuttle."

"Yes, Sergeant Strak," the ship's computer replied.

He typed out a quick message, read it over, and deleted it. It took four attempts to come up with something he hoped didn't sound completely pathetic.

Shortcake,

Sorry I left without saying goodbye. I meant to, but time got away from me.

Take care of yourself and Nico and watch your back around the Bellex reps since I can't be there to watch it for you.

D.

PS I know I still owe you a drink and a chat about my tattoos...and anything else you want to know.

He sent it before he could change his mind. Once that was done, he pushed all thoughts of the dark-haired doctor aside and set his mind to the task at hand. If he wanted to have that drink with Tyra, he needed to find a sample of cobalt and enough evidence to bring down whoever was making and distributing it.

Lt. Aria Jessop popped her head into the cockpit a few

minutes before they breached the planet's atmosphere. "Ready to give up the stick?"

"Not really. I've missed this part of my job." He might not be ready, but to protect his cover he needed to be out of sight before they made contact with the spaceport, so he grudgingly rose from his chair.

Aria moved back, giving him enough room to clear the door and ease past her so she could take over as pilot. "I'll see you once our boots are dusty and we're in the clear. Sabre and I will make sure you have a nice, smooth ride."

"Appreciate it. This is not my favorite part of the plan."

Aria laughed. "Just do what I do. Take a nap."

"I did not just hear you say that, Blink," Lt. Commander Kurt Meyer barked from his seat. "No sleeping on duty."

"If I'm locked in a box, my only duty is to pretend to be cargo. I can do that awake or asleep, sir," Aria retorted with a grin.

Kurt just shook his head. "Are you going to be this full of sass for the whole damned mission?"

"Very likely, sir. It's been a while since I got to breathe anything but recycled air. I'm looking forward to spending time in a place with gravity, atmosphere, and natural light." Aria ducked into the cockpit whistling a chipper tune that had both men share a look of dawning horror. Aria Jessop was a woman of many skills - a first-rate interrogator, a brilliant investigator, and a fierce fighter. There was only one thing she had no talent for: music. She didn't let that stop her though. When she was in a good mood, she sang, hummed, and whistled constantly.

"It's going to be a very long mission," Dante said with a groan.

"Quit complaining. You'll be in a nice, soundproof box for the start of it. Right now, I'm tempted to trade places with you."

In order to protect his cover, Dante wasn't arriving as part of the team. He'd be arriving as cargo. No one was allowed to search a Nova Force officer or their equipment, so he'd be carried in on a hover-sled with the rest of the team's gear. It wasn't a fun way to travel, but it gave him the best chance of returning to Bellex with his cover intact. It meant he'd be operating on his own again, but this time, his team wouldn't be far away if things went sideways. Not that he expected that to happen.

Now that Tyra and Nico were safe in orbit, there wouldn't be any more distractions. It was time to get to work.

Tyra walked out of her meeting with the Bellex representatives feeling like she needed a long hot shower and a very large drink. They'd kept her in the small, uncomfortable room for hours, hounding her with the same questions asked a dozen different ways. Dr. Downs had started off being professional and courteous, but as time passed the doctor had become increasingly difficult, questioning everything from Tyra's recollections of events to her medical credentials. The Bellex corporate rep, Chad Everest, had played the role of 'good cop,' speaking kindly, offering to fetch her a drink, and generally making a show of being an ally in the room. It had been an almost laughable display. Downs was all business, from the severe cut of her clothes to the tight bun that held back her dark hair. while Everest was an easygoing blond with a ready smile and a slightly rumpled suit.

She only got a few steps before Eric appeared in the corridor in front of her. The entire team had changed into fresh uniforms before meeting the new arrivals, and the switch had transformed them into the sort of soldiers she was used to. Sharp salutes, brisk movements, clipped sentences, and perfect posture.

Eric was still in uniform, but his sympathetic smile told her he was his usual self. "You survived the grilling?"

"I did, but barely. I've already told them they can't speak to Oran until tomorrow. He needs another day of rest before dealing with them."

"I know you can't be in the room with him while he's being interviewed, but what about Lt. Caldwell? He's got both the medical credentials and investigative authority to make sure they behave themselves and don't push Dr. Castille too hard," Eric suggested.

"That's a great idea, thank you, Ensign. Do you think the lieutenant would agree to do it?"

"I think Trip would be happy to help, and you don't need to call me by my rank. You're officially on the team, now, so it's Magi unless there's a VIP in earshot." His dark eyes lit up with amusement. "We don't bother with protocol on this ship unless we absolutely have to."

"I noticed. I ran my team the same way." It hurt to refer to them in the past tense. Her friends were gone. There'd be no more late-night sessions or early morning banter over breakfast. Jessica had told her last bad joke, and Riku would never brew up another pot of green tea. *Veth*, she was going to miss them all so much. How was she going to go on without them?

"You okay?" Eric asked.

She shook her head the slightest bit. "I think it just hit me that I don't have a team anymore. I've been keeping myself so busy I haven't let myself really process the fact they're gone."

Eric's eyes darkened to almost black, and he gave a small nod of his own. "Yeah, I know how that goes. You put all those feelings in a box and think you've got it handled. You convince yourself everything's fine, and then boom—grief grenade—no more box." He flicked his fingers out to mimic an explosion.

"Exactly."

"We're going to find the ones responsible. That will help. So will the occasional application of ice cream and alcohol. I'm not a doctor, but after what you just went through, I'm prescribing at least one of those. Come on, we're going to the galley. If we're lucky, Nico left us a few scraps."

"I should really get back to the medical center and check on Oran."

"Trip's there with him." Eric pulled a sleek piece of tech out of his pocket. "Besides, I'm supposed to be giving you a quick lesson on how to work this little beauty."

"That's my new communicator?"

"It is, but it's so much more than that. It's got everything from encryption functions to an emergency locator beacon."

"I can see the need for encryption, maybe, but why would I need an emergency beacon? I'm not going anywhere. Dante and the rest of your team are the ones headed into danger."

"And now, I *really* need ice cream. I still can't believe

Bellex won't let me set foot on their precious planet. Mercs, pharma dealers, and criminals, sure, but a cyber-jockey is not to be trusted?"

Eric held out the comm and started walking backward. "Come on, Dr. Li. Ice cream and new toys. You know you want some of that."

She laughed and followed after him. "Okay. But only because I want to know how to work this new communicator. I'm not really much for ice cream."

"You're not? Well then, more for me and Nico. What's your poison, then? Cookies? Cupcakes?" His grin turned wicked. "Shortcake, maybe?"

Oh no. "How the *fraxx* do you know about that? I've tried telling him not to call me that, but he won't stop. Please tell me the others aren't going to start using it, too."

"Nope, I'm the only one who knows. I was transferring your data onto this device when a message came in from Dante. It was addressed to Shortcake. Is that really what he calls you?"

"Yes! Because I'm short and he thinks it's funny. Which it isn't. And I'm not that short." It was hard to resist the urge to demand Eric hand over her comm immediately

Eric looked down at her, brows raised. "You're not exactly tall, either."

"No one is tall compared to that walking mountain of muscles!"

The young ensign whooped with laughter. "Damn, I think you just gave Dante a new nickname. I cannot wait to tell the others."

"That's not the only thing I've been calling him," she muttered.

"No? Please, do tell."

This would be her revenge for calling her Shortcake. "Sergeant Stubborn."

This time, Eric didn't stop laughing for a full minute. "This keeps getting better," he said when he could finally speak again.

"It wasn't very nice of me, considering he saved my life and all, but that man is just so…so…"

"Yeah, I know." Magi set off again, and a short time later they were in the mess.

He didn't say much more until they were seated across from each other. The table was battered, dented, and worn, and the chairs were unpadded metal, but what the area lacked in comfort, it made up for with the quality of the food. The dispensers' menus were impressive, with items from different world and cultures, as well as a vast number of basic comfort foods.

Eric had ordered a massive bowl of chocolate ice cream half buried in hot fudge sauce, while she'd opted for a slice of apple pie that reminded her of Dante.

She figured she'd waited long enough. "Can I see the communicator while you eat?"

"Sure." He pushed it across the table to her. It didn't work too differently from the one she'd already been using, and she had it activated by the time she took her first forkful of pie.

Dante's message was at the top of the list, and she read it over between bites of dessert.

"Is he always like this?" She asked, waving her fork at the screen.

"I didn't read the message, but judging by the number of times I saw him dodge you since he got back, and the fact he didn't talk to you before he left, I'm going to guess

94

he's doing his stoic, 'no distractions, the mission is all' schtick."

"So, that wasn't my imagination? He's avoiding me?"

"Definitely. Which isn't normal for him. Dante's a good guy, but he's not very subtle."

She scoffed. "That might be the understatement of the year. He had no problem bossing me around before we got here. He was in my face, telling me what I needed to be doing and then glaring at me if I didn't do it fast enough."

"Did he do that thing where he thumps his fist against his thigh like he wants to hit something?" Eric asked.

"All the time."

"Yeah, he does that when he's worried. Keeping you safe was his prime directive, and from what I hear, you didn't make that easy." He held up a hand. "Not blaming you for that. You had a job to do, too. But Dante takes it personally when someone he's responsible for is at risk of getting hurt."

"I can't see that happening very often. He's like a mother hen on steroids."

Eric sighed and put down his spoon. "A few months ago, he was assigned to keep an eye on a certain cyber-jockey who was messing around with some dangerous software. It wasn't his fault, but things went sideways fast." He pushed up the sleeve of his uniform, revealing a mass of scar tissue on the dark skin of his arm. At the center of the scarring was a data port.

Intrigued, she reached for his arm, stopping short of touching him as she remembered he wasn't her patient. "What happened? Those look like electrical burns."

"They are." He turned his head and pushed back his tightly curled hair to show her more of the same scars around a second data port behind his ear. "Dante was there when this happened. He's the reason I lived, but I don't think he's forgiven himself for letting me get hurt. It doesn't matter that there was nothing he could have done to stop it. So, if he was tough on you, it's because he was trying to keep you safe."

"He did keep us safe, even Nico. And I was wrong to make it so difficult for him. I'm the reason they found us."

"Maybe. Or maybe they found you some other way. The people hunting you were well-equipped, focused, and determined. We got confirmed identities on the men Dante took down in that alley. They were mercs, the kind that do their job well and don't ask questions." Eric tugged his sleeve back into place and resumed eating. "I didn't tell you my story to make you feel bad. I just wanted you to know that Dante's got his reasons for being the way he is."

"That still doesn't explain why he was hiding from me and then sends me a message telling me he wants to have a drink when he gets back."

Eric chuckled. "I've known him a few years. In all that time, I have never heard him call a woman anything but her given name. I think you've gotten under our Buttercup's skin."

"He might have gotten under mine, too, but it's a little hard to do anything about it when he won't stay in the same room with me.

"He's got a one-track mind. Right now, he's all about the mission. Later…" Eric winked. "I bet when he gets back, he's got a different goal in mind."

Her cheeks heated and she dropped her gaze to her dessert. "We'll see."

"You know my name means wise man, right? Trust in the Magi, for he is wise and all knowing."

She looked up and was met with a cheeky grin. "I make it a point to never trust anyone who speaks about themselves in the third person."

"That's a terrible policy." He gestured to her communicator. "Tell him you'll meet him for that drink when he gets back. I bet he answers you before you finish your pie."

"Do they only hire pushy people for Nova Force, or do you learn the attitude after you get the job?" She set down her fork and typed out a short reply to Dante.

Hi,

Don't worry about me. I've got Trip and Magi watching out for me, and Nico, too. Finished my interrogation with Bellex. Unpleasant, but nothing unexpected. Stay safe, and I'll see you when you're back on board.

T. (and quit calling me Shortcake!)

She sent it and went back to her dessert. He'd sent his message hours ago, and despite Magi's assertions, she didn't expect to hear from Dante any time soon.

Less than five minutes later, her comm chimed. She ignored it long enough to take the last bite of her snack, but her pulse was racing by the time she glanced at the screen and confirmed the message was from Dante.

"Told you so," Eric said, picking up his empty dish and stepping away from the table.

"How'd you know it was from him?"

He chuckled and placed his metal dishes into the cleaning receptacle. "Your expression made it pretty obvious. It's kind of adorable. I'm headed out. Come see me later, and I'll show you how everything works on that device."

"I will." She waited until he was gone to read Dante's latest message.

Shortcake isn't going away. Get used to it.

Are you on an encrypted channel? I don't want Magi reading our messages.

D.

She laughed. Somehow, she didn't think something as minor as military encryption would stop Eric if he wanted to read something.

Magi just gave me one of your team's fancy communicators, but he left without telling me how to use the advanced functions. You'll just have to behave yourself until he shows me how to encrypt our chats.

T.

She was blushing when she sent the last message, and when the minutes stretched out without a reply, she wondered if she'd gone too far. She'd cleared her dishes and was heading for the door when the chime sounded again. She didn't look at the message until she was in the small but comfortable room she'd been assigned.

Let me know when it's safe for me to misbehave. I need to go. I've got a lead I need to follow up. I will talk to you again, soon. I promise.

D.

"And he's gone again." She sank down onto the edge of her bunk with a tired sigh. At least he wasn't hiding from her anymore. After the way this day was turning out, she'd consider that a definitive win.

A quick check of the time told her she had an hour or so before the team normally met for the evening meal. She had enough time to shower, change, and then check on Oran and Nico. After that, she was going back to work. There were still a few blood samples left to test. Maybe one of them contained traces of cobalt.

Missions like this were why she'd signed on with Boundless, and why she stayed year after year. When Axion's negligence killed her mother and poisoned her father, no one had come to help them. There were antidotes. Treatments that would have allowed her father and scores of other survivors to make a full recovery. Instead, they'd been abandoned while Axion hid behind walls of denial and tried to cover up the entire tragedy. She wouldn't let that happen to someone else.

Eventually, Axion had paid for their mistake. One day soon, Bellex would, too.

CHAPTER SEVEN

"I WAS GONNA clear out your room if you didn't show your face by the end of the day." The unkempt man behind the desk looked at Dante with mild suspicion. "You ain't been around for days."

"I had a hot streak at the tables and didn't want to jinx it by walking away," Dante shrugged as he pushed a stack of vouchers across the greasy, stained desktop. "That should cover what's owed, and another week in advance."

The clerk snatched the money with greedy fingers, counting it before he bothered to respond.

"Must have been some hot streak. You need me to keep your winnings for you? Got a safe in the back. Very secure."

"That's the last of it. Lady luck didn't stick around for long. Don't suppose you know where I could find a job?"

"Maybe. What you good at?"

"Fighting and drinking, mostly."

The clerk snorted. "Drinking won't pay the rent. Fighting...maybe. Lemme ask around." His bloodshot eyes narrowed. "Any job I get for you, I'll want a finder's fee. Only fair, you know."

"Only fair," Dante agreed. He had no intention of letting this waste of oxygen find him a job, but he had to keep up appearances.

The clerk nodded and started to turn away, but then he paused and turned back to face him. "Nearly forgot. You got a message. Some kid left it for you a couple of days ago." He wandered around the cramped office, rifling through the clutter and refuse for several minutes while Dante fought to hide his impatience.

If there was a message for him, it had to be from Livvy or one of her crew.

"Found it." The clerk pulled out a tattered piece of paper and handed it to him. It had been a while since he'd seen paper, and took it with care, half afraid it would fall apart before he could read the note scrawled on it in uneven block letters.

Go heer. Tawk to Jake. Go aftr dark.

Livvy

Beneath it was an address.

"You know where this place is?" he asked the clerk, covering everything but the address with a thick finger before showing it to the other man.

"That's Jake's place. Two blocks down, turn left, take another three-block walk. Big red sign."

"Thanks."

"If you value your eyesight, don't drink anything but the beer."

He sighed. Why did clandestine meetings never happen at places with good food and decent drinks? "I won't."

He shouldered his pack and headed upstairs to his spartan room. He needed to notify his teammates about the lead, prepare for this meeting, and see what Magi could dig up on the address and the owner.

His comm chimed before he reached the door to his room. He checked, assuming it was Kurt or Aria asking for a status update. The name on the screen made him smile. Tyra had answered him. When he hadn't heard from her in the last few hours, he'd assumed she wasn't going to respond. After ditching her for the last few days, he wouldn't have blamed her. He had never been so happy to be wrong.

It didn't escape his notice that she was using the nicknames for his teammates. He was happy she was bonding with them, but Trip and Magi were both good-looking guys. Cris was still pretending he didn't have a thing for Aria, and Eric had a weakness for older women. Dante belatedly realized that volunteering for this mission meant he'd left Tyra alone with two of the galaxy's most eligible bachelors. He slammed his fist into his thigh. *Fraxx.*

He checked the room as they exchanged messages. What little he'd left here hadn't been touched, and according to the motion-activated surveillance system he'd left running, nothing bigger than a lizard had been in the room since he'd left.

He was laying out what he'd need for tonight's meeting when Tyra's last message came through. There was no missing her flirtatious tone, and he damn near cheered as he read what she'd sent. If she was ready for him to misbehave a little, then he'd be happy to oblige. A few flirty messages wouldn't qualify as a distraction, and when he got back…

He checked the time and swore. So much for not getting distracted. He still hadn't checked in with the others, and the sun would be setting soon. He fired off one more message to Tyra and got back to work. Magi could send him the information while he made the walk to the address Livvy had sent him.

By the time he reached the bar, he knew the layout of the place, the names of the staff, and he had enough information about Jake to know Livvy had pointed him in the right direction. The bar was nothing more than a front for Jake's more profitable businesses: black marketeering and information peddling.

"Magi couldn't have found out about this guy before? It would have been nice to have this information the last time I was here." He growled under his breath, certain that Aria and Kurt would hear him. He'd set his comm to broadcast on one of the encrypted channels, ensuring there'd be a full audio record of everything that went down once he entered the bar.

"Despite his claims, Magi is not all-knowing," Kurt said, his voice conveyed by a micro-transmitter embedded in Dante's left ear.

"And you're not invincible. Tell me again why you're doing this meet solo?" Aria added, her tone disapproving.

"Because you and Sabre couldn't pass for disreputable types if your lives depended on it. The way you walk, talk, and move is straight up military, and there isn't an IAF outpost for light years."

"I'm not sure if that's an insult or a compliment," Kurt replied.

"You're less than five minutes away. If shit goes sideways, you'll know the same time I do, and I'm pretty sure I can keep myself alive for five minutes without your help."

"You're just saying that because you took down three armed men with your bare hands the last time you were here," Aria said.

"And this time, I got to bring a blaster." The ride inside the cargo crate hadn't been pleasant, but it had allowed him to bypass security and bring along a few of his favorite weapons.

He approached the address Livvy had given him. "Going in, now."

"Good luck," both his teammates said, then lapsed into silence.

The place looked like it might collapse at any moment. It was in the oldest part of the district, and time had not been kind to the neighborhood. The road was pitted with potholes. There were no sidewalks, only well-worn paths in the cracked and dusty ground, and the buildings had been blasted by the wind and weather for so many years there wasn't a scrap of paint left on them. The only color on the whole street was the flickering red glow of the sign suspended over the front door of Jake's like a welcome sign hung on the gates of Hell.

Things didn't improve once he stepped inside. The interior was dimly lit and reeked of stale booze, unwashed bodies, and other scents he didn't even try to identify. The floor beneath his boots was sticky and uneven, and by the time he reached the bar, he was already looking forward to getting back to his room and having a long sonic shower.

"What can I get for you?" The man at the counter

asked in a voice that held no warmth or welcome. Even if he hadn't already seen a holo, Dante would have been able to guess this was the man he'd come to see.

"Information." Dante leaned against the counter, which creaked under his weight.

"I only talk to customers. What'll you have?"

"Got any Torskian ale?" It would be a minor miracle if they had any in stock, but the alcohol content would be strong enough to kill any bacteria it came in contact with, so it was worth a try.

The man looked at him for a moment and then nodded. "Got a bottle in the back. Won it off a guy a while back. You want it, I'll get it, but it'll cost you."

"That's fine." Dante reached into his pocket and made a show of removing a generous number of corporate vouchers. "Keep the change."

Jake took the money, nodded, and walked away. "Be right back."

Dante stayed where he was, casually glancing around to get a read on the other inhabitants of the bar. He'd counted four on his way in, and from where he now stood, he could see a fifth, seated at the very back of the room. None of them looked threatening. He'd garnered mild interest upon entering, but everyone had returned to their muted conversations within a few seconds. There was no reason for him to feel uneasy, but his instincts told him something was off.

He hummed a few bars of a song his mother had always loved to let his teammates know he was still alright.

"All good?" Kurt asked.

Dante hummed again, adding an affirmative note to the beginning of the tune.

He was starting to wonder where Jake had gone when the big, burly man lumbered back into view. He held a pint glass in one meaty paw, and he was eyeing the glass with something like apprehension.

"This stuff pours slower than shit," he said as he set it down on the counter in front of Dante.

"The slower the pour, the better the brew. At least, that's what I've been told."

"I'll take your word on that. I tried it once and couldn't taste anything for three days." Jake held out his hand. "Now that you're a customer, name's Jake. What can I help you learn today?"

Dante took the offered hand and shook it. "Dante." He'd kept his first name the same for this mission. It made things simpler. "A friend suggested I talk to you about finding a source for a pharma called cobalt."

Jake's ginger brows raised. "Does this look like a pharma den to you? I deal in booze and information, that's it."

"And that's what I'm here for. Information. I'm trying to track this shit down, but nobody seems to know where to find it. I've got friends who would love to be able to offer pharma with that kind of kick." He took a sip of his ale and was surprised at the quality. The place might be a rathole, but somehow, they'd gotten their hands on some premium liquor.

"Your friend sent you on a wild comet chase. There's no cobalt. Not anymore."

"You're telling me you don't know anyone who has even

a single dose? That's all I need. If I can get that to my friends, they can figure out how to replicate it. The finder's fee would get me the hell off this rock." He kept sipping the drink while he talked. His Torski constitution could handle a little booze.

Jake lowered his voice. "I heard Bellex banned the stuff when it started killing their workers. Seized the whole supply. They'll tolerate damned near anything, but only if it doesn't affect their production schedules."

"There's got to be some left over, somewhere. I'm willing to pay. If it's a fair-sized sample, I'll even pay in scrip." Scrip was hard currency, far more valuable than the vouchers corporations paid their workers. A voucher had to be redeemed at a corporate-controlled business, and most of them were specific to the company that issued them. Yet another level of control the corporations maintained over their workforce.

Jake shook his head. "I can make some inquiries, but I can't make any promises."

"I appreciate the help." Dante raised his glass in thanks before taking another, longer, drink. If there was any cobalt left in the district, he had no doubt Jake would find it. Hard currency was a powerful motivator.

The barman nodded to the drink. "How's the ale? Never had someone in here who actually knew what it was supposed to taste like."

"It's good. Whoever you won this off of had expensive taste." Dante tried to set the glass down, but the counter seemed to tip away from him. He ended up slamming the drink down.

"Glad you're enjoying it. I wasn't sure how I was going to slip you enough of the drug they gave me without you noticing the taste. Good thing you didn't order the beer."

Fraxx. He tried to reach for his weapon, but all he managed to do was thump himself in the chest with his arm. His legs felt like rubber, and the room was starting to spin. Black dots danced in his vision, blotting out Jake's jeering face. Furious, Dante lashed out at what he hoped was the barman's head. His fist smacked flesh, and Jake grunted in pain.

Dante kept swinging wildly, connecting with about half his punches. He knew he was going down soon, but every second he fought back, his team was closing the distance. If he could just stay on his feet until they got there…

The next time he swung, his right leg gave out, and he dropped to his knees with a bone-jarring crash that drove his teeth together. Something hard and heavy slammed him from behind, and then there was nothing but a rising tide of pain as blows rained down on him from every direction. As the dark waters of unconsciousness washed over him, he held onto the hope that Kurt and Aria would get to him in time, even if it meant listening to Aria say 'I told you so,' for the next six months.

TYRA WAS IN HER QUARTERS, playing cards with Nico when her door chime sounded. "No peeking," she told him before setting down her cards and crossing the small space to the door. "Who is it?" She asked, raising her voice so it carried through the metal door.

"It's Commander Rossi."

She pressed a button on the keypad and the door slid open. Dax stood in the corridor with Cris at his side.

Neither of them was smiling. "Commander. Is everything alright?"

He gave a sharp shake of his head. "I apologize for the intrusion, but something's come up. May we come in?"

"Of course." She stepped back, clearing space for the two men. Her quarters weren't spacious. There was a single bunk, a small table with two hard-backed chairs, and not much else. Dax spotted Nico at the table and turned to Cris. "Can you take Nico out for a few minutes?"

"Sure." Cris gestured to Nico. "Come on, you little card shark. You promised me I'd get a chance to win my money back. I want a rematch."

Nico grinned and scooped up the cards, along with the remains of his winnings – a stack of cookies. "Double or nothing?"

"You're playing for money? He's a little boy!" she exclaimed, overdramatizing the moment for Nico's benefit.

"We're playing for vouchers, and this kid counts cards better than some professional gamblers I know." Cris tousled Nico's hair and led the boy out of the room.

Once the door closed, she dropped the act and turned to face Dax. "What's wrong?"

"I need you to go to the med-bay and start prepping for a trauma case. Trip will join you shortly and act as your assistant. I'd like Dr. Castille moved to a room across the hall, but only if you think he's ready to leave the med-bay."

Her training took over. "I need information, starting with an ETA on my patient and who it is. Can you tell me what happened? What's their condition? And why aren't they being taken to a med center on Bellex?"

Dax's expression darkened. "It's Dante. He was following a lead and walked into a trap. He's been taken."

Her heart twisted in her chest, but she locked down her reaction and tried to stay focused. "I'm going to need specifics on his current status."

"He was drugged and went down fighting. His backup didn't get to him in time, and his attackers managed to move him before they arrived. We're tracking him. His current status is unknown until we can retrieve him. When that happens, I need you to be ready. We can't take him to a local med center because we don't know who we can trust down there."

"And there's a good chance they won't know how to adapt treatment to his Torski heritage, either. You're correct, he needs to be brought here. I'm going to need access to his medical records. There's a tissue cloning system on board, right? I'll go to the med-bay and start synthesizing blood type-matched to Dante. Do we know anything about what he was drugged with?"

"By the time you get to medical I'll see to it you have everything you need. His files, whatever information the field team has on what happened, you'll have it all."

He gave her a grim smile. "We *will* get him back, Tyra."

She managed a tight-lipped smile in return. "I know you will, and once you do I'll do whatever it takes to keep him alive. He saved my life twice, it's time I balanced the scales."

"I'm glad you're here to take care of him." Dax paused, then added. "He's having trouble admitting it, but Dante's glad you're here, too."

She snorted. "We'll see how he feels about me after I've had him at my mercy for a couple of days in the med-bay.

Sergeant Stubborn is about to find out what it's like to be the one getting ordered around."

Dax's eyes twinkled with momentary amusement. "Sergeant Stubborn, huh?"

"I think it suits him better than Buttercup."

"So do I. While you've got him hostage in medical, you might want to ask him how he got that name."

"I will." She pointed to the door. "I should get going. The second they have him, I want to be patched through to their comms. I'll walk them through treatment and they can give me a full report on his condition."

"You got it."

They left her quarters and split off. She set a brisk pace as she headed for the mag-lift that would take her to the medical bay. Despite Dax's confident words, there was no way to know if his team would get to Dante in time, or what shape he'd be in when they did find him. All she could do was prepare and hope that Dante was strong enough, and stubborn enough, to come back to her.

CHAPTER EIGHT

"DANTE. Hopefully, you're awake and hearing this. We're coming to get you. Hang in there." Aria's voice was a tinny whisper in his ear. He'd heard her message repeated several times now, but he had no way to respond. His jacket was gone, and so was his holster and weapon. His comm was in his jacket pocket. No doubt they'd destroyed it as soon as they found it. Fortunately, that wasn't the only trackable tech he was carrying. The earpiece was tagged, too.

He was secured to a chair by what felt like cables, and more of the same stuff bound his arms and legs. Whoever had done it had taken care not to give him any slack to work with. He was trussed up so tight he couldn't even take a deep breath. Not that he was going to be doing any deep breathing for a while, not until his busted ribs healed. He'd taken inventory of his injuries once he'd woken up, and the list was longer than he liked. His face was battered, one eye was swollen closed, and the coppery tang of blood on his tongue told him he either had a split lip, some loose teeth, or both. He couldn't see his hands, but judging from the pain and the fact he couldn't move the right one much, he'd guess it was badly broken. He was a bruised, bloodied mess, but his ego had taken the worst beating. He'd *fraxxed* up. Badly. Livvy had betrayed him, which meant he'd misjudged the girl - something he didn't do often. Now, instead of working on the mission, his teammates were putting themselves at risk to rescue him.

A door opened somewhere behind him, and two sets of footfalls announced he was no longer alone. "Why are we waiting for him to wake up? Why not just shoot him full of that shit and call it a day?"

That didn't sound promising.

Dante forced himself to keep his head down, relax, and slump against the restraints despite the pain. For now, it would be best if they thought he was still asleep.

"Because he was dosed with enough sedative to drop a Nantari rhino, and even so, it took five men to take him down. Remember what happened to the overdose victims?" The second speaker sounded older, and his unaccented words indicated that whoever he was, he wasn't local.

"They blew up like a supernova and started tearing into anyone or anything around 'em."

"I'd like to avoid having that happen again. Since I have no idea what would happen if I give him the neuro-enhancer before the sedative leaves his system, we're going to wait a little while longer."

Neuro-enhancer? That sounded like corporate-speak for cobalt. If they had some here, then maybe getting his ass kicked would be worth it, after all.

"Got it. Can we at least do the rest of the procedure while we're waiting?" the first man asked.

"Your impatience is going to be your downfall. Rushing leads to mistakes, and mistakes are messy. The people I answer to do not like mess."

"I keep telling you, we didn't mess up the Boundless assault. How was we supposed to know the street rats would help them doctors?"

"If you'd taken more time to watch and plan, you would have discovered the connection."

There was a rattle as several items were set out on what sounded like a metal tray, then the lights in the room brightened. A moment later, a pair of well-worn boots appeared in Dante's limited field of view. "If we hurry, we can do this while he's still out."

"And again, you rush headlong through life so quickly you missed the signs. Our guest is already awake."

There was movement behind him, a rustle of fabric, a soft footfall, and then a searing pain on the side of his neck. He snapped his head back, hoping to connect with something breakable like his assailant's nose, but he hit nothing but air.

"Trying to get a few more licks in before the end?" The one with the cultured voice stepped around to show himself for the first time. Well, most of himself. His face was obscured by a privacy screen that distorted his features. Black market tech—rare and expensive.

Everything else Dante could see of his captor spoke to one thing—money. His all black clothing was understated but tailored to fit him perfectly, and his shoes were polished to a gleaming shine. His hair was blond and cut in a military style, but nothing else about him suggested he was a soldier.

The man's neat and tidy appearance was a vivid contrast to the room they were in. It was grimy and worn, with a dirt floor, and a few opened crates with strange markings that might have been an alien language or an unfamiliar corporate logo.

"Who the *fraxx* are you and what did you do to me?" Dante snarled. All he had to do was buy enough time for his team to reach him.

The man gave an eloquent shrug of his shoulders. "I suppose manners would be too much to expect given the circumstances."

Dante bared his fangs. "Ya think?"

"You back off, or I'll pull those fangs of yours out of your head and wear 'em as a necklace." The second male finally appeared. He was on the short side, with a florid complexion and cold, hard eyes. Apparently, the hired help was expendable, because he had no mask to hide his identity.

"Enough. We're not here to indulge your violent side. Dante here is a prime specimen, and I intend to keep him that way...for now. I need more test subjects, and I am looking forward to seeing how his mixed heritage affects the process."

"He don't need his teeth to be test subject," the other man grumbled.

Mr. Money tapped a finger on a slender band of polished silver on his left wrist. "And I don't need you interfering in *my* work. You've spilled enough blood already. More than you were authorized to."

Red Cheeks blanched and lapsed into silence.

Dante listened to their conversation with interest. They were being careless, letting details slip that made him believe they already considered him a nullified threat. But if that was the case, then why was one of them hiding his face?

"What did you do to my neck?" Dante asked when the silence stretched out too long.

"A minor procedure. I inserted a chip. You are now corporate property."

"The hell I am. I'm a free citizen. You can't go around tagging people and claiming they're indentured servants, that's illegal!"

Money smiled and made a rolling gesture with one hand. "Legality is a lovely, bendable concept. Especially in a place like this."

"Places like this shouldn't be allowed to exist."

"Dante. ETA sixty seconds." Aria's clipped words were music to his ears.

"A mercenary with a moral code? How interesting. I imagine that makes for some long, sleepless nights as you try to justify your decisions. I have good news for you, though. In a few minutes, you're not going to have any more inner conflicts. You'll be at peace. No moral quandaries or questions about your place in the cosmos. You will know your role and embrace it." He walked to a rickety table and picked up an injector.

Adrenaline hit Dante's system like a jolt of electricity. There was no way in hell he was going to let them inject him with cobalt. "I thought you said you wanted to be sure the sedative was out of my system, first."

"Given the conversation we just had, I'd say that's already happened. You are coherent, alert, and had a normal response to pain stimuli. It's time to proceed. The sooner this is done, the sooner I can leave this dismal place."

"Want me to hold him?" Red Cheeks asked with a grating, cheery tone.

"Please."

Dante gritted his teeth and flung himself sideways in his restraints. The chair rocked, and at least one of the legs uttered a creak of protest at the abuse. One of the few details he'd been able to observe while he was faking unconsciousness was the fact his chair was made of a lightweight polymer. If he applied enough force, it would break. He'd done it before by accident. Now, he needed to do it on purpose.

He did it again, and this time the chair toppled, sending him crashing to the floor. His ribs screamed in agony, and his hand felt like it had been dipped in burning rocket fuel, but he ignored the pain and kept fighting against his restraints.

"Dammit! I told you to hold him!" Mr. Money barked.

"I'm trying." Red's voice sounded from somewhere near his feet, and Dante kicked out with both feet in that direction. He connected and managed to twist his head around in time to see Red stagger backward into Mr. Money. The injector flew one way, the men went another, and Dante knew he'd bought himself a few more seconds.

A red light began strobing and Mr. Money cursed. "Someone's tripped the proximity alarm. Stay here and deal with him. And remember, no permanent injuries!"

Dante managed to grin despite his pain. His team was here.

Red seemed to sense the balance had shifted. The

arrogant sneer was gone, and he kept eyeing the door Mr. Money had just walked through.

"You got friends?" he asked, flicking his gaze between Dante and the doorway.

"I do." He managed to kick free of the bindings holding his legs and rose to his knees. His arms were still bound behind him, but at least he was mobile again.

"Then that asshole ain't coming back for either one of us."

"Not likely. If you give yourself up, they'll hand you over to the authorities."

For a moment, Red looked like he was considering it but then shook his head, one hand rising to rub the side of his neck. "That's not an option for me."

"Then I suggest you run." There was no place on the planet Red could hide now that Dante had seen his face. Encouraging him to leave meant there'd be one less threat to his teammates.

"That's not an option for me, either." Red drew something from behind his back.

That's my blaster. Dante lunged to his feet and charged straight at Red. Head down, legs pumping. No way in hell he'd let one of his friends get shot with his damned weapon.

He was still two steps away when Red pulled the trigger. The blast hit him in the shoulder, searing away his shirt and frying his skin as it tore through his body. He had enough momentum to keep going despite the pain, crashing into Red as his legs gave out.

The last thought he had was of Tyra. She was reaching for him, but he didn't have the strength to lift his arms.

She called his name as she faded away, and he fell into darkness.

TYRA PACED THE MEDICAL BAY, waiting for news. She already knew it wouldn't be good. She had the same heavy, sick feeling she got sometimes when a patient was about to crash on her. She'd learned not to question those feelings. Something had gone wrong, and Dante was going to need her. "Do we have enough blood on hand?" she asked Cris.

"We should be okay."

"Synthesize another batch."

Cris' fingers flew over one of the consoles. "Done. Do I want to ask why?"

"Gut feeling."

"Should I call Dr. Downs? I'm just a medic. If things didn't go well down there, she's more qualified to help."

"She's also a Bellex employee, which means she can't be trusted. It's got to be us. Besides, you're not just a medic. You've got more practical experience and better skills than some doctors I know."

Cris grinned. "Thanks."

Tyra started pacing again. She had to keep her emotions locked down, but it wasn't easy. She was worried. More than she should be, considering there wasn't anything between her and Dante but an interrupted kiss and a few flirty messages. Later, she'd have to think about that, but first, she had to repair the damage the stubborn fool had done to himself.

The waiting ended a few minutes later. "This is Nova

Ground Team to the *Malora*. Retrieval mission successful, but we have wounded," Kurt's deep voice filled the room.

"This is medical. Who is injured and what's their status? I'm going to need details."

"It's Sergeant Strak, ma'am. He's unconscious and has been since we found him. He took a blaster bolt to the shoulder. It's...it's bad. I've applied wound sealant, but the bleeding won't stop. He's got multiple fractures to his right hand, and he's struggling to breathe. Med-scan indicates broken ribs, blood loss, and a punctured lung."

"Send me the report from the scanner. What's your ETA?"

"We're breaking every law and protocol to get to you as fast as possible. ETA, sixteen minutes."

Dax joined the conversation. "Make it fifteen or less. Ignore all protocols and redline the engines."

"Yes, sir," Aria replied.

"This is Caldwell. I'll meet you in the shuttle bay."

"Roger that. Revised ETA, nine minutes." Aria spoke again.

Cris grabbed the already-loaded gurney and made for the door. "You got this?"

She waved him on. "Go."

"Commander, the lieutenant is on his way to meet the shuttle," she said.

"I'll have West meet him there," Dax replied.

Dante's medical scans appeared on a wall monitor. What she saw gave her hope. He wasn't going to enjoy the next few days, but there wasn't anything here she couldn't fix. "Okay, Kurt. I've got the reports. Here's what I need you to do..."

CHAPTER NINE

TYRA STIFLED a yawn behind her hand and got to her feet. Not even coffee was staving off exhaustion anymore, but she was determined to stay awake until Dante woke up. He'd want to know his condition, and she was the best one to answer any questions. At least, that was her official reason. Unofficially, she knew she wouldn't sleep until she'd heard the familiar rumble of his voice. It wasn't the first time she had to treat someone she knew, but it hadn't made it any easier to see him lying on the operating table, bloody and still.

His medical file told the story of a man who had suffered more than his share of painful injuries. Some of them were related to his days as a fighter, most of them had been incurred after he joined the IAF. He'd been shot, battered, stabbed, and even blown up—more than once. Dax had given her access to more than just Dante's medical data, though. There were incident reports, statements, and even a list of commendations. She'd read through them while she waited for him to wake. In almost every case, he put himself in harm's way to protect someone else – the same way he'd told her to take cover before taking on her attackers single-handedly the first time they met. He might be overbearing and arrogant, but there was no denying how attractive his protective streak was... even if it might get him killed one day.

Today would not be that day, though. He was going to make a full recovery thanks to the care his teammates had given him in transit back to the ship. He was already stable by the time he arrived in the med-bay, and it had taken less than two hours to repair the worst of his injuries. What he needed now was time to heal, and she'd made some preparations to ensure that was exactly what he got - whether he wanted it or not.

She'd been monitoring his vitals from a workstation in the corner of the med-bay. He was resting comfortably, thanks to the pain-blockers coursing through his system. The anesthetic was already out of his system, and from what she was seeing he should be waking up soon. She rose from her chair and stretched, triggering a series of cracks and pops in her joints. "I'm getting too old for all-nighters," she muttered softly before walking the now-familiar route around the med-bay. She'd walked this path often in the last few hours. The movement helped keep her awake and allowed her to check in on both occupants of the room, Dante, and Nico.

Magi had brought the boy to see Dante once he was out of surgery, but all attempts to get him to go to bed had failed. Every time he was removed, Nico snuck out and returned to the med-bay, sitting outside the door in silent vigil. After the third escape, Tyra had suggested he stay with her. She'd tucked him into the bed right next to

Dante. The boy had settled down after that and fallen asleep about an hour ago.

He must have lost his parents suddenly, too. Now, he was afraid of losing Dante the same way. However this mission ended, she was more determined than ever to make sure Nico never returned to Bellex 3.

She stopped beside Nico's bed, drew the blanket up over his shoulders, and stroked his hair.

"Something wrong with the kid?" Dante's question came out as a cracked whisper, but it was still enough to startle her.

She turned to smile down at her patient, who was already looking better thanks to the heavy doses of healing accelerant she'd pumped into his system. "Nico's fine. He was worried and kept sneaking out of bed to check on you, so I let him sleep here."

"He was worried about me?" Dante looked over at Nico with surprise. "He's a good kid. I'm sorry I scared him."

"You scared us all."

He was quiet for a moment, then said, "I'm sorry about that, too. I've been screwing up a lot lately."

"Thanks to your friends, you're going to be around to make up for it. How are you feeling? You ready to drink a little water?"

"I probably feel better than I look, and yeah, I'd love some water. How are Blink and Sabre? Any injuries? Did they catch anyone headed out of the building?"

"Your teammates are fine. Not a scratch on either of them. I don't know much about what happened, but I do know they didn't bring back any prisoners." Tyra pressed a switch, and a robotic arm moved a glass of water to the side of his head, tipping it so the straw reached his mouth.

Dante took several sips before saying anything else. "No prisoners? Damn. They must have got away." He tried to sit up. "Why can't I move?"

"Because there's a restraining field set up around your bed. And before you ask, no, I'm not releasing you until I decide you're ready."

"Let me up, Shortcake. I have work to do."

For once, his nickname didn't annoy her. She was too happy to have him back to care what he called her. "Not happening, Muscles. The only thing you're going to do for the next twenty-four hours is lie still and let yourself heal. You had a lot of holes in your body for someone who promised to be safe."

The field was set up to allow him some movement, and it was enough for him to reach out and take her hand. "You told me to be safe, but I never told you I would be. Doing my job means taking risks."

"I'm starting to figure that out." She squeezed his hand, enjoying the chance to touch him this way. "So, I guess that means I'm going to have to get used to worrying about you."

His eyes lit up, and his fingers tightened around hers. "Yeah?"

"Yeah. But don't let it go to your head." One thing had become clear to her as she'd waited for the team to reach Dante – despite his decision to keep his distance, she cared about him. It wasn't logical, rational, or likely wise, but that didn't make it any less true.

He tried to rise again, growling in frustration as the field stopped him from rising more than a few inches.

"Turn this off, and I'll show you how happy I am to know you're going to keep being worried about me."

"Not a chance. You're staying put. You had a pneumothorax and it's going to take some time to heal."

"I had a what? Use smaller words, please. I'm the cannon fodder, remember?"

Her brow furrowed. "You're a lot more than that. And a pneumothorax is a punctured lung."

"I did? Must have done that when I broke the chair, or maybe when I charged the guy holding my blaster."

"You did what?" She stared at him in amazement. "Was that necessary?"

"Well, yeah. If he was going to shoot anyone with my own damned weapon, it was going to be me, not my teammates."

"You're insane."

"Maybe. But I also know that I couldn't live with myself if my mistake cost one of my friends their life."

As much as she wanted to, Tyra couldn't argue with his logic. "Speaking of your friends. I should let them know you're awake. They'll be happy to hear it, and I know the commander wants a brief summary of what happened to you tonight." She held up a warning finger. "A *brief* one, you hear me? The pain-blockers are keeping you comfortable, but you went through some serious trauma tonight. You need to rest."

"I hear you." He grinned, though she could already see he was starting to tire. "I like it when you try to boss me around."

"While you were gone, I got promoted to full team status. You know what that means?"

He shook his head, still grinning.

"I did some reading on IAF rules while I was waiting for you to wake up. It turns out that when it comes to the health of this team, I have complete autonomy. Not only do I outrank you, Sergeant, I outrank everyone on this ship."

Dante's eyes narrowed, his expression as mutinous as Nico's when someone tried to suggest he'd eaten enough burgers for one day. "I don't think Rossi is going to be on board with your interpretation of the rules."

She made an airy, dismissive wave with her hand. "Oh, I already discussed it with him. He's in agreement."

"*Fraxx.* I was gone one day, and you're already conspiring with my commander?"

"You were gone longer than that, Dante. We might have been on the same ship, but you left me alone long before you headed back to the surface."

"I know. That's one of the things I need to make up for once I'm out of this bed. I'm not good at multitasking. I try to focus on one thing at a time, and I thought the mission had to be my focus." He gave her a wry, but tired, smile. "Right before I blacked out, it occurred to me that I might have my priorities wrong."

"Next time you need a little clarity, how about skipping the part where you nearly lose your life?" She stroked her fingers over his cheek, being careful to avoid his injuries.

"Deal." He turned his head, pressing his cheek against her fingers. "Next time, I'll come to you first."

"You'd better. Patching up your owies is getting to be a habit." She let her hand linger for a few more seconds, but she could see Dante was starting to fade, and he still needed to talk to Dax before he could rest again. Eventually, she moved her hand from his face and eased her fingers out of his grip. "I should let the commander know you're awake."

"Yeah. I need to tell him what happened, and who we need to look out for." His eyes suddenly opened wide. "Hey, how's the analysis of the cobalt sample coming? You have it, right?"

"What sample?"

Dante tried to sit up again, but this time he remembered the restraints and stopped himself. "Dammit. I need to talk to Rossi, now. They were going to inject me with cobalt, but I knocked it out of the guy's hand. If it wasn't bagged as evidence, then it's still down there!"

She put a hand on his good shoulder. "I'm sure they brought anything they thought might be relevant. You relax and try not to get yourself too worked up. Your system doesn't need more stress."

"Dante?" a sleepy voice interrupted before she could say anything else. "Dante! You're awake."

Nico bounded out of bed and was at Dante's side in seconds. "You okay? Doc Li says you was shot."

"I was, but Dr. Li fixed me up. I'm going to be fine, kid."

Nico looked up at her as if seeking confirmation. "Really?"

She nodded. "Really, truly. He's going to be in the med-bay for a day or two, but that's all. He'll be back in the cockpit, ready to give you flying lessons, in no time."

"I get to fly the ship?" Nico's eyes lit up like stars.

"Maybe. But there's a rule that you have to get a solid eight hours of sleep a night to be a pilot." Dante raised his dark brows. "I heard you've been sneaking out of bed to check on me. You keep doing that, I can't let you sit in the pilot's seat."

Nico nodded hard. "I'll sleep now. Promise."

"That's good. Do you think you could stay with Dante for a few minutes while I contact the commander and tell him Dante's awake?" Tyra asked.

"I can do that. Did I really know 'bout you before Fido did?" Nico asked, clearly thrilled at the idea.

"You did." She left the boy beside Dante's bed and called Commander Rossi to give him the news. While she spoke, she watched Dante and Nico. He might be one of the most dangerous men she'd ever met, but he had a soft heart hidden under all those muscles. For the next while, the two of them would be spending a lot of time together. She intended to use that time to get to know Dante Strak, the man, before he turned back into Sgt. Strak, the stubborn soldier.

CHAPTER TEN

By the next day, Dante had come to realize that mandatory bed rest under Tyra's watch was like being in prison, only with better food and a far nicer view. She'd finally agreed to raise the bed so he could sit up, which meant he could watch her as she moved from station to station around the med-bay, doing countless tests to the cobalt sample his team had found while they were saving his ass. She talked to him as she worked, telling him what she was doing, what she was learning, and slowly, as the hours passed, the conversation drifted to other topics.

"I don't think I told you this yet, but the tattoo on your shoulder didn't survive. The tissue should be fully healed by tonight, but the symbols can't be regenerated the same way."

"Yeah, I figured. It's not the first time I've had to get one of my tattoos redone. Hazard of the profession."

"Can I ask what it was?" she asked.

"They were the Torski symbols for strength and

courage. Warrior is on there too, but that's more on my shoulder blade, so it's probably okay."

"Do you want to see for yourself? I should take a look and ensure everything's healing as it should, anyway."

"You're letting me out of this damned restraining field?"

She held up a finger. "Just while I check on your progress. If I'm happy with what I see, we can talk about maybe letting you up long enough to have a *brief* shower."

Right now, a shower sounded better than an all-expenses-paid vacation on a pleasure planet. "I'll take every second of freedom I can get. I'm not used to staying still this long."

"You'll be free of this bed, and me, soon enough." Tyra tapped a code into the bed's control console. The system beeped twice, but nothing else changed.

He didn't bother confirming that the field was down. Instead, he sat up and reached for Tyra, hauling her into his arms. She didn't manage to utter more than a surprised squeak before he kissed her, cutting off any protest. The moment their mouths met he knew he'd been a *fraxxing* idiot to stay away from her. He should have been getting to know her and stealing as many kisses as she'd let him. It had taken getting shot to make him realize how stupid he'd been.

Nearly dying wasn't a new experience for him. Having regrets though, that was new. Every time he'd roused during the ride back, he'd thought about Tyra. How he'd stepped back when he should have been stepping up. He'd told himself she was a distraction, but pushing her away hadn't stopped him from thinking about her.

He explored her mouth with his lips and tongue as his

hands moved over her body, learning her curves and the sweet taste of her lips as he indulged himself in their kiss. She leaned into him, one hand resting on his uninjured shoulder as she kissed him back. *Veth*, yes. For one perfect moment he forgot about everything, losing himself in the glory of having her back in his arms. That's when an ear-piercing alarm sounded, killing the moment.

"What the hell is that noise?"

"Your heart rate is too high. The bio-monitor is set to sound an alarm if there are any sudden changes to your readings."

He flung back the blankets and left the bed. "That's it. I'm sick of this place. I can't even kiss you without alarms going off. I'm fine. See? Standing on my own and everything."

"Dante Alexander Razlan Strak, get your ass back in that bed right now!"

He grinned down at her, amused and aroused by her attempt to boss him around. "Do you really think using my full name is going to make me more obedient? It never worked for my mother, and it's not going to work for you, Shortcake."

She huffed out a frustrated breath. "If you overdo it, you're going to be stuck in that bed for longer than either of us would like." Then, her expression softened, her eyes showing a hint of worry as she gently pushed against his chest. "Please get back in bed and let me see how you're doing. You took a beating last night, and the only thing keeping you on your feet right now are pain-blockers and your unbelievable stubbornness."

He caught her hand and covered it with his. "One more kiss, first?"

"You promise to get back in bed afterward?"

For another kiss, he'd do damned near anything she asked him to. "I promise."

"Okay." This time, she kissed him. She fisted the front of the hospital gown he'd been forced to wear and rose up on her toes, pulling him down to meet her. He was more than happy to oblige, closing the distance between them. He held back enough to let her be the one to initiate the kiss, but once that happened, he took over. He speared his fingers into her hair and used his good arm to haul her in tight against his body, relishing the way her soft curves fit against him.

Her kiss was a better drug than any pain-blocker, and more addictive, too. She uttered a tiny moan and parted her lips, allowing him to take the kiss deeper. Their tongues danced, every breath mingling, bodies pressed together so tight he swore he could feel her heart racing beneath her ribs.

Somewhere behind him came the unmistakable sound of a door opening, followed by a horrified groan. "Oh, *fraxx*. My eyes. I can never unsee that. For the love of gravity, Buttercup, cover your ass!"

Dante lifted his mouth a scant fraction of an inch away from Tyra's to mutter, "If you don't like it, leave. In fact, go anyway. Consider that an order, Ensign."

"I could, but then you don't get to hear the update Rossi sent me to give you. You might outrank me, but he outranks us both."

"And as I've already mentioned, when it comes to your treatment, I outrank everyone." Tyra let go of him, her cheeks darkening with embarrassment. "I believe the deal

134

was for one kiss, Muscles. You've had your kiss. It's time to hold up your end of the bargain."

"I wasn't done with you, yet," he complained. He got back into bed, though, then turned to glare at Eric, who was standing at the door grinning like an idiot. "And you have lousy *fraxxing* timing."

"Sorry, Muscles. Next time I'll knock."

"If you value your liver, that name better never come out of your mouth again. Forget it." Dante snapped.

"You'd rather be named after a weed with yellow flowers?" Tyra asked, trying to suppress her laughter.

"I'd rather be called Dante, but there's some unwritten rule in the IAF that everyone needs a *fraxxing* nickname. Just like there's some rule that says patients in a med-center have to wear stupid gown-things that don't cover a man's ass." He frowned at Tyra. "Why is that?"

"It helps keep difficult patients in bed, where they're supposed to be."

"She's got you there," Magi said. He wandered over to the bed beside Dante and leaned against it. "All kidding aside, I'm glad to see you're feeling better. You had us worried."

"You should know better than to worry about me. I'm too stubborn to die easy."

Tyra stepped between them and fixed Eric with a stern look. "You only get to stay if you don't get him too worked up over anything. Dante, are you okay with me doing the examination while he's here?"

"Yeah. I want to hear the update, and you should hear it, too."

"Alright then, sergeant. Lean forward and I'll undo the fastening so you can get out of that gown."

He almost made a joke about her wanting him naked, but something told him it wasn't the right moment. Probably the fact she'd gone back to calling him by his rank instead of his name. If she wanted him to behave while they had company, he'd do that for her. He held still while she undid the back of his gown, then shrugged it off, leaving his chest bare.

It was the first time he'd seen the damage. Even with healing accelerants and tissue regeneration, his shoulder was still a mess. Swaths of tender pink skin broke up the broad slashes of tattooed ink, the damage spanning not just his shoulder, but across his pectoral region, down his bicep, and judging by the tenderness, partway up his neck, too.

Magi whistled. "Damn man. You look worse than I did after Victor Base."

Dante ignored him and looked to Tyra. "You did a nice job of patching me up. I should have said this before, but thank you."

"I did my job. Hopefully I don't have to do it again any time soon." She carefully probed the edges of his injury with her fingers. "You're healing well, but you're not ready to go back on duty yet. The damage was deep, and it's going to take time to heal properly."

As eager as he was to get back to work, he wasn't sorry to hear he needed to stick around the med-bay. It gave him an excuse to stay in her company, and that wasn't a bad thing. "Can I have that shower you mentioned earlier?"

"Maybe." She gave him a ghost of a smile. "Can you agree to try and stay in bed if I say yes?"

"I'll try."

"In that case, once Eric's gone, you can shower." She

checked his newly repaired hand, hummed in approval, and gestured for him to dress again. "I'll finish my exam then, too. I need to take some scans to see how your ribs and lung are healing."

She left his side and went to type something into the console she'd claimed as her personal workspace.

"Okay, Magi. What do you know?"

Eric moved in close and lowered his voice. "For one thing? I know you're *fraxxing* lucky Dr. Li was here. She talked Sabre through your treatment from the moment they got you on the shuttle. To hear him tell it, you wouldn't have made it without her. I've never seen him rattled before, but after you went into surgery, he went straight to the mess and started pouring shots. It took three before his hands stopped shaking."

"She told me Sabre and Blink had me stable before I was on board. That she didn't do anything but patch me up."

Magi shook his head. "Not the way I heard it. I think your pretty doctor is being too modest."

"Thanks for telling me."

Eric nodded, then raised his voice again. "While you were lying around medical, Rossi, West, and I spent a long, sleepless night figuring out what happened to you. After you were drugged, they moved you to an unregistered craft, which is how they got you out of the district so fast. The only reason we know that is because we managed to track it for a while after it left the place the team found you, but it eventually dropped off the scanners."

"I thought the *Malora* could track damned near anything?"

"It can. Which means not only was it unregistered, it must have been fitted with modified shielding."

"That's black-market tech."

Uh huh. Just like that privacy screen your captor was using. Whoever these people are, they've got money and some very interesting toys."

"Speaking of tech, did you get anything from that *fraxxing* chip they shoved into me while I was tied up?" Tyra had already confirmed she'd removed the damned thing while she was fixing him up, which had been a relief to know.

"Not much. It was partially destroyed by the blast that charbroiled your shoulder. There's no way to pull any data off of it or any clues as to where it was manufactured. All I was able to find were trace amounts of P32 and JX9."

"Use real words, Magi, or I'll piss off the doc by overexerting myself when I kick your ass."

"They're two of the ingredients found in micro-explosives."

"That son of a starbeast put a *bomb* in my neck?" He had a sudden urge to punch something. "When we find him again, I'm going to make him regret that."

"It looks that way, yeah. I hate to say it but getting shot might have saved your ass. It destroyed the triggering mechanism before anyone could make you go boom."

Tyra cleared her throat. "I'm going to interject here and state that as your doctor, I don't recommend getting shot to prevent yourself from being exploded. How about you try to avoid both scenarios for a while? At least until you've healed?"

"I make no promises, but I will try." Despite her teasing words, Dante heard the undertone of worry in her voice.

He liked that she cared enough to worry. He just hoped that this time, he'd found a woman strong enough to accept that his line of work came with risks. Danger was part of the job, and the job was part of him.

"GOOD. I'd hate to have to turn the restraining field back on so soon." Tyra would never admit it, but she'd enjoyed having the big, tough soldier restrained and at her mercy. Not that she'd done anything unprofessional. The most intimate thing she'd done was using a cloth and a cleansing agent to wipe away the worst of the blood and other grime from his upper body while he slept. It had given her a few moments to appreciate both his hard body and the beautiful tattoos that covered it. It had also let her see the scars he bore.

"Restraining field?" Eric's brows raised. "I'm both intrigued and terrified to know more."

She only blushed a little as she shook her head, rose, and rejoined them by Dante's bedside. "Nothing like that. I just needed to keep my patient in bed instead of defying orders and trying to go back to work too soon."

"Uh huh," Eric drawled, looking annoyingly pleased. "Glad that's working out for uh…him. We need our Buttercup back at full strength."

Dante snapped his fingers in front of Eric's nose. "Hey, Magi. The update, remember? What else do I need to know?"

"Well, it's a good thing Blink thought to scan the whole crime scene with her cybernetic eye before leaving. Rossi went back this morning to do another sweep, and the whole place was gone. Torched. All we have to work with are Aria's scans, the cobalt they recovered, the DNA Cris managed to pull from your mangled body, and whatever I can dig up on our dead man."

The last bit was news to her. "What dead man?"

"According to his fingerprints and DNA, his name was Alan Darner. He was a low-level pharma dealer on Bellex 3, fully licensed, but behind in his payments to the corporation. I'm looking through data, trying to figure out what his role was. All we've got so far is that he's the one who hired the assholes who drugged you at that bar. Local security rounded them up this morning, and Blink interrogated them. They didn't know much, apart from Darner's name and the fact they've done this for him before. You were right. These guys have been making people disappear for a while now."

Dante grunted. "From what I saw, Darner was just hired muscle. He wasn't too bright, and the other guy was definitely the one calling the shots. He was the only one hiding his face, too. Darner was clearly expendable. I still don't understand how he ended up dead, though. He shot me before I could get my hands on him."

"Rossi didn't tell you?"

"He didn't tell either of us," Tyra interjected. "I would have asked to examine the body. I'm not a pathologist, but I should be able to find a cause of death."

"You were busy with Dante and then with analyzing the cobalt." Eric shrugged. "And the cause of death was pretty obvious, even to us non-medical types. After he shot Dante, he turned the weapon on himself."

"He offed himself? Why the *fraxx* would he do that?" Dante went quiet for a moment, then blew out a slow breath. "He said running wasn't an option for him. What the hell kind of people was he working for that leaving wasn't an option, but killing himself was?"

"Where's the body, now?" Tyra asked. The cause of death might be obvious, but she still wanted a chance to examine it if she could.

Eric gave her a wry smile. "Sorry, doc. Dr. Downs insisted on doing the autopsy herself. Trip observed the whole thing. It didn't take long. I mean, the guy blew his head off. There wasn't much to examine."

Irritation sharpened her next words. "What happened to the plan to keep the Bellex reps as far away from the investigation as possible?"

Dante touched her arm. "If Rossi allowed it, there was a good reason. There always is. If it came to a choice between them having access to the sample of cobalt or the body, which one would you have picked?"

He had a point. Again. "I'd rather have the cobalt. Speaking of which, I won't have a complete breakdown of its components for a few more hours. Once I do, Trip and I will start working on a way to safely neutralize its effects."

"Which is going to save a whole lot of lives." Eric agreed.

"I still don't understand why no one told me."

"Probably because Rossi didn't want to distract you. After all, you were putting together his favorite team member," Dante said.

Eric laughed. "I see your ego has already recovered. Does this mean you're ready for your debriefing with Downs and her pet lackey?"

"No, he's not. When did they find out he was even

here?" There was no way in hell she was letting Downs anywhere near Dante until he was one hundred percent.

"Bellex demanded to know why our team left District twelve without clearing it with them first. Rossi opted to tell them because it was the fastest way to cut through the bureaucratic crap. They're pissed they weren't told we had another operative on the planet, but Rossi told them to take it up with the Nova Force brass."

"You were eavesdropping again, weren't you?" Dante asked.

Eric merely shrugged. "Monitoring our Bellex guests is part of my job. If that means I happened to overhear their rather heated discussion with our commander...well, that just means I have more information to share with the team."

"Forgive Magi. He was a hacker before he decided to use his powers for good. Sometimes he forgets the rules are supposed to apply to him, now," Dante said.

"You call them rules. I like to think of them as guidelines. Very flexible guidelines."

"Given what we're up against, I'm fine with flexible. Someone killed my team, damn near killed me, and is dosing an entire population with a drug we know almost nothing about. Now they're kidnapping people and injecting them with exploding chips. They're not playing by the rules, I don't think we should, either," Tyra said.

Eric beamed at her and uttered a dreamy sigh. "You're my kind of girl. Seriously. If things don't work out with Dante, feel free to give me a call."

Dante bared his fangs and growled at Eric. "Out. Now."

Eric threw up his hands in surrender. "Right. I'm

leaving. I'm not a fan of bloodshed, especially my own. Before I go, though, Downs will be debriefing Dr. Castille this afternoon. Caldwell will be sitting in, and it will all be recorded, just like yours was, Dr. Li."

"Thanks for letting me know. Once that's done, Oran will be leaving, right?" she asked.

Eric paused before answering. "Eventually. Trin needs to finish up her investigation, first."

"She's not done yet? How long does it normally take to clear someone?"

"It depends on what we find," Eric replied.

She didn't like the way that sounded. Her review had been done in a matter of hours, and Trinity had been looking into Oran since yesterday afternoon. "I'm guessing that means she found something. I can't imagine what, but I'll wait to hear it from her."

Eric nodded. "You're both now officially up to speed on everything Rossi sent me in here to tell you, along with a few extra tidbits because I like you. Don't take any crap from this guy, doc, and if you're going to let him out of bed, please find him something to wear that covers his ass."

"I'll see what I can do. Thank you for the update," she said.

"Get gone, kid. And don't flirt with my girl again or you're going to be sucking vacuum."

Eric laughed all the way out the door.

Once they were alone again, she turned to Dante. "For the record, I haven't been a girl in more than three decades. Furthermore, I don't recall agreeing to be your anything."

Dante's lips curved up into a slow, sexy smile hot

143

enough to melt hull plating. "Wrong. You're already my doctor. The rest is a work in progress."

"You wouldn't have so much work to catch up on if you'd joined me for that drink when we first came on board."

"Instead of that drink, how about I buy you dinner? I know a place. Local. Decent food. Amazing views." He took her hand in his. "I'd like to do things right this time. If you'll let me. I have it on good authority that I'm going to be on light duty for another day or so. Doctor's orders."

"I'd like that." A thought crossed her mind right after she agreed. "But I don't have anything to wear on a date other than some borrowed training gear and some shoes that are at least a size too big."

"I'll take care of that. You should have said something."

"You were all focused on the mission, and it's not like I was going to borrow a shuttle to go on a shopping spree. These clothes are warm, comfortable, and clean. They're just not date apparel, so I thought I should warn you. Then again, you kissed me when I was wearing rags and hadn't showered in days, so I suppose you're not too worried about it."

"I kissed a very hot woman who was taking care of herself and everyone around her in adverse conditions, with no complaints. It was sexy as hell."

"You've got some odd notions of what sexy means."

He tugged her closer and wrapped her in his arms, but instead of kissing her again, he bowed his head so their foreheads were touching and they were looking into each other's eyes. "I think you're sexy, Tyra. Doesn't matter if you're dressed to kill or wearing rags."

Her stomach filled with butterflies and a delicious frisson of anticipation flowed over her. "In that case, you've got yourself a date, but not until tomorrow night. I've got work to do, and you need to rest."

"But first, I get to shower, right?"

"Right. In fact, you might as well do that now. I can run the scans once you're back in bed."

He moved his head, placing his mouth right by her ear. "Are you going to help me shower, Shortcake? I'm still recovering, you know."

She shivered as his breath caressed her ear and his words made her heart race a little faster. "Not this time. Ask me again after we've had a real date."

He nuzzled her earlobe, letting one of his fangs graze her skin for a tantalizing second. "Believe me, I will."

She believed him.

CHAPTER ELEVEN

ORGANIZING a date while confined to the med-bay proved trickier than Dante expected. Not only was he rusty on the whole wine-and-dine concept, but he needed his team's help to make it happen, since he couldn't do it himself. Aria and Kurt were back on the planet with Cris, but they'd assisted in their own way. Everyone was happy to help – for a price. The bad jokes and non-stop teasing were worth it, though, because everything was ready. He even had a few surprises arranged, and it was time for him to reveal the first one to his date.

Tyra was seated at her usual workstation, her chin propped on one hand as she stared at the screen. She'd worked tirelessly, poring over the results of her tests of the cobalt sample. She barely slept, and the only reason she'd eaten was because he'd been around to remind her to. She needed someone in her life to take care of her, and he was starting to think he was the one to do it.

"Hey, warden. Is my sentence over yet?"

She looked up with a smile. "I think so. Your last scans came back clear. Just promise me you won't overdo it for another day or so. I'd like to keep you on light duties for now. You've already had more than the recommended dosage of healing accelerant. If you get hurt again, I won't be able to give you another dose."

He rose from the bed and stretched. "You don't have a lot of faith in my ability to avoid trouble, do you?"

"In the short time I've known you, you've been shot, stabbed, captured, and beaten up. In my experience, facts trump faith."

"I had a bad week."

She laughed. "I've read your medical file, remember? The number of times you've been hurt, you should probably just hire a doctor to be on stand-by."

"You volunteering?"

Tyra's mouth opened and then closed again without her saying a word. She was silent a few seconds, then finally spoke. "Working as a military doctor isn't what I want to do with my life. I want to help those who don't have anyone else to help them. I can't do that in the IAF."

He'd learned that and a lot more about her in the time they'd been thrown together. "I know, I was kidding… mostly. I'm not going to start talking about our future before we've had our first official date. A date I can't take you on if you don't clear me to leave medical."

"Well, in that case, consider yourself cleared. You're free to leave and get yourself organized for tonight. Do I get to know the plan, yet? I mean, apart from the fact we're going to have dinner together and one of us will be severely underdressed." She tugged at her too-large shirt.

"You won't be underdressed. I called in some favors. If milady would like to return to her quarters, she should find some better selections for this evening. Also, Trinity and Blink would like me to inform you that you should have said something earlier. They both thought the other one had given you more to wear. Blink's going to see what she can find in your size while she's down on the planet. And before you say anything about paying her back, remember that she's a stubborn, slightly bionic badass and she's not going to accept your money." He held up his hands. "Her words, not mine."

"I didn't say anything because they'd already given me the clothes off their backs, literally. I'll find a way to thank them." She smiled. "And you, too."

"You don't have to thank me. You saved my life. I'm pretty sure I'm going to owe you for that for quite some time."

Her smile broadened. "You better believe it."

"I'll be by your room to pick you up in forty-five minutes." He was tempted to kiss her, but he didn't. He was going to do this right. No rushing.

"I'll be waiting." She shooed him toward the door. "I need to lock up after you go. Magi put about eight levels of security in place, and I need to activate all of them before I can leave."

Downs had been demanding access to the med-bay, and Dante, since he'd been brought back. Until now, Rossi and Tyra had kept her away, but now he was out, she'd want to question him. It would be a waste of his time, but it had to happen. That was tomorrow's problem, though. Tonight was all about Tyra.

SUSAN HAYES

BEING BACK in his own quarters was nice, but he didn't have much time to enjoy it. By the time he showered, shaved, and dressed, it was almost time to go again. He grabbed his comm and sent a message to Dax and Eric, who were acting as his wingmen.

Everything ready?

Rossi didn't bother messaging, he called instead, and when his face appeared on the screen, he looked annoyed. "I'm insulted, Strak. I run military operations for a living. Do you really think I can't handle setting up a simple dinner date?"

"Uh, no sir. I wasn't questioning your ability, I was just, uh…" he scrubbed a hand through his hair. "I feel like I'm sixteen and about to go on my first *fraxxing* date. I already screwed this up once, and I can't let anything go wrong."

Dax laughed, and somewhere in the background Dante heard Trinity giggling. "Trin, help me! Your boyfriend isn't being very helpful."

Trinity's face popped into view beside Dax's. "That's because he doesn't know what to tell you. I'm the one who asked him out, remember? All he had to do was show up and remind me why I fell in love with him the first time. He had it easy."

"I don't remember it being all that easy," Dax grumbled.

"You'll do fine, Dante. All you have to do is be yourself. She's seen you as a badass soldier and didn't run screaming. Now it's time to show her who you are when the uniform comes off."

Dax groaned. "There's a visual I didn't need. You're going to pay for that, Butterfly."

"That's not what I meant!" Trin insisted before winking at Dante. "Though, if things start going that way, remember to turn off the surveillance system. You don't want Magi getting hold of something like that."

"And this is why I asked for your help. You're detail oriented. I'll deactivate the damned thing the moment we walk into the room. Thank you, Trin."

"You're welcome. For what it's worth? I really like Tyra. I hope everything goes well tonight."

"We both do," Dax added. "Good luck."

Once the commander had disconnected, Dante set his comm aside and gave himself a final look over. His wardrobe consisted mostly of work clothes, workout gear, and casual attire, which meant his only option for tonight was his uniform. Normally he avoided reminding dates about his military connections, but he didn't have a lot of choice. Besides, Tyra already knew what he did for a living. The risks, the violence, all of it.

"Here's hoping she has a thing for guys in uniform...or out of them," he added, grinning a little as he recalled Trinity's comments. He'd like nothing better than to have his shortcake for dessert tonight, but that was her call to make, not his. He'd grown up watching his mother being abused and controlled by the men in her life. By the time he was old enough to date, he already knew he would never be like those men.

His comm chimed again. Magi was checking in.

Operation Date Dazzle is a go. Everything's in place. Good luck and try not to screw this up...again.

"Thanks for the vote of confidence, kid." Dante switched the device to emergency mode and slipped it into his pocket. He was off duty and unavailable for anything short of an imminent attack. He only had one focus tonight, and her name was Dr. Tyra Li.

He arrived outside her quarters and pressed the door chime, eager to get the night underway.

"One sec!" she called out from the other side of the door.

He stood at parade rest, waiting. He was about to ask if there was a problem when the door opened, revealing a flushed and breathless beauty. Her hair was loose and fell around her shoulders in a curtain of midnight silk, and she was wearing a simple black dress that came to mid-thigh.

"Hi. Sorry. This dress fastens in the back, and I'm having trouble with it," she explained as she looked him over. "And might I add, wow. You look amazing. I've never seen you in uniform before."

"Would you like me to do up your dress for you?" He managed to get the words out despite the fact he was having trouble focusing on anything but the vision in front of him. The dress showed off her soft curves and golden skin, and he wanted nothing more than to bury his hands in her hair, haul her in close and devour her, and dinner be damned.

"Would you? Trinity was a sweetheart to lend this to me, she even helped me shorten it a bit with tape, but neither of us thought about how I was going to get it done up once she left." Tyra turned around, moving her hair out of the way with a graceful sweep of her hand. She'd managed to get the dress partially fastened, but most of her upper back was still exposed.

"Happy to help." He stepped in close and closed the dress the rest of the way, letting his fingers drift over her skin as he did so.

"She told me you asked her to check on me and make sure I had everything I needed." She glanced over her shoulder at him. "You didn't have to do that."

He leaned down to plant a soft kiss on the nape of her neck. "I couldn't bring you flowers or take you somewhere fancy tonight, but I could make sure you had something nice to wear."

"Thank you." She turned around and offered him a shy smile. "So, do I pass muster?"

He didn't like the doubt that shadowed her eyes as she asked the question. He cupped her face in his hands and stared into her eyes. "You look incredible, but that's no surprise to me. The day we met, I thought you were the sexiest ragamuffin I'd ever laid eyes on. Tonight, looking the way you do, I'm kind of grateful we're stuck on the ship. If I took you out in public, I'd spend the whole night fighting with all the men who wanted your attention."

"And I'd be too busy fending off any women in the area to get to appreciate your efforts." She set a hand on his chest, just below the silver, five-pointed star that was the Nova Force's unique insignia. "You clean up very nicely."

He laughed, leaned forward, and gave her a slow, lingering kiss that allowed him to savor the moment, and her. "The only woman I have eyes for is you."

DANTE ESCORTED her down several corridors and down a

mag-lift to the lower levels of the ship. The only sounds were the whispered whir of distant machinery and the rhythmic beat of their footsteps as they walked. Unlike the upper levels, the floors here were bare metal, and there were far fewer doors. "We're having dinner in the bowels of the ship?" she asked as she followed him down another long hallway.

"Actually, we're having dinner at the bottom of the ship."

"So, what's down here? I mean, besides us?" she asked, curious.

"This is where the *Malora's* weaponry is housed." He turned and offered her his hand. "Come on, it's not much farther."

She laughed, the noise echoing down the corridor ahead of them. "You brought me to the weapons deck for our date? I hate to break this to you, but not many women find plasma cannons and the smell of ozone romantic."

"For the record, it's *fraxxing* sexy that you know what a plasma cannon smells like when it's fired. That being said, I did have something a little more intimate in mind for our date." He stopped in front of a reinforced door and placed his free hand on a keypad. It flashed blue, then green, and the door opened. "Dinner awaits."

She expected to walk into an armory of some kind. All hard metal surfaces and sleek weapons. Instead, she found herself standing on a small landing with stairs leading down to an impossible sight: a relatively small room whose floor and walls were completely transparent. Dante went first and she followed him in silent amazement, drinking in the view beyond the windows. Once they reached the main level, it was like standing in open space, and she felt a slight wave of vertigo as she looked down to see the planet spinning slowly beneath her feet.

Dante squeezed her hand. "It takes a little getting used to, doesn't it?"

"It does, but it's worth it. You did promise me an amazing view. You certainly delivered."

He led her to a medium sized table placed in the center of the room. It had been draped with a white tablecloth, and it wasn't until they got closer that she realized it wasn't a table at all, it was some sort of console set into the floor. Beneath the cloth red, blue, and green lights strobed and flickered softly. Most of the light came from the light cubes set in the center of the table, providing enough light for her to see two place settings and a cart of some kind covered with another white cloth.

"What is this place? I thought you said this was where the weapons were housed. It's too beautiful for that," she said, still looking around in awe. There were two large, reclining chairs facing outwards. She could see they were loaded with tech, but there wasn't enough light to tell what any of it was.

"This is the gunner's pit. The ship's AI can handle most battles on its own, but if it was necessary, we could operate all the weapons from here," he said, pulling her in close and wrapping a strong arm around her waist. "I hope you can still see the beauty in it now you know that."

She leaned into his hard body and laid her head on his chest. "I still see it. I've lived long enough to know that most things are too complex to be easily classified. There can be beauty in destruction, and sometimes the most dangerous things are the ones that are the most attractive."

"I'm glad to hear that. This is where I come when I need to figure shit out. It's special to me."

She tipped her head up to look at him without moving her head from his chest. "The view must help put everything in perspective."

"Yeah, it does." He leaned down to kiss her, then paused just before his lips met hers. "Computer, activate Dante's security program Pest Control Alpha."

"Program activated," the ship replied.

"Pest control?"

"Magi. He hates not knowing what's going on. I'd like to think he'd behave himself tonight, but this way, I don't need to worry about it."

"Your team is the best kind of crazy."

"They're the dysfunctional but loveable family I never wanted. Thing is, now I've got them I'd die to keep 'em safe."

"If I could switch places with my team, the ones that died – I would. It doesn't feel right that I lived and they didn't. If I hadn't been upstairs treating Nico at the time…"

"Then you might have died, too, and we would've never known what happened. I'd still be down there, looking for answers. Or maybe I'd have wound up getting caught again, only this time you wouldn't be there to save my life. Nico would still be stuck on the surface, and we'd have no idea what cobalt did because you weren't around to tell us what to look for. You survived, and you're doing all you can to find justice for the ones who didn't. That's all any of us can do."

"That's easier said than done. But I guess you know that already."

"I do. And I think you do, too. Let's sit down, eat, and do what I should have done days ago."

"Buy me a drink?"

"That too. But mostly I want to learn about you, Shortcake. No emergencies. No imminent threats. No one else around to interrupt us."

"I'll share my story if you share yours. But before we start, I need your assurance that if I put my drink down on this thing, I'm not going to accidentally vaporize the planet."

"It's passcode protected. The planet is quite safe."

They sat, drank wine, and talked for a while before Dante remembered to bring out the appetizers. Once he removed the cloth covering the cart, she laughed. "I'd blame Trip for stealing medical equipment, but he's down on the planet right now. So, who came up with this part of the plan?"

"Dax. According to him, it's not stealing if you're in charge of the ship."

He set down a basket of still-warm bread, some butter, and an assortment of synthesized proteins in various flavors and textures. Then he produced another basket and removed the lid, releasing a cloud of fragrant steam that was instantly familiar.

"Are those *jiaozi*? Where did you find the ingredients for dumplings out here?" She took the basket from his hands and inhaled deeply, letting the scent carry her back to her childhood, to market days where merchants would hawk their wares in sing-song voices and the scent of steamed dumplings would rise from the vendor's carts.

"We had most of the ingredients onboard, and the food dispenser managed to replicate the rest, more or less. I've never had them before, so I'm not sure they're perfect, but the one I sampled was very tasty."

She laid one of them on her plate and broke it open. "How did you know I loved these?"

"Bedrest is boring, but it gave me time to do some reading. I re-read the file I was given on you when I was tasked with finding out what happened to you and your team. I skimmed it last time, but this time I actually read your background. You were born on Earth, a citizen of Xinshi. That's where I got the idea you might like a taste of home."

"How much of my story do you know?"

He reached across the table and took her hand. "Enough to know that you didn't get into that fancy med school because your parents were rich. Axion's compensation package paid for your schooling."

"After the accident, no one came to help. It was like we didn't matter at all. It wasn't until later I discovered no one came because no one knew it had happened. Axion tried to cover it up. If it weren't for a man named Lucas Dalton, they might never have been found out. Lucas worked for Axion, and he reported what they'd done to anyone who would listen. Because of him, my father got to live the last year of his life in comfort, and I had the means to become a doctor and try my best to see that what happened to me never happened to anyone else."

He stroked his thumb over the top of her hand in slow, gentle circles as she spoke. "You chose this life because of what happened to you when you were a kid. I guess in some ways, that's what I did, too."

"Tell me."

"My mom's a hell of an entertainer, but she was never been good at reading people. Still isn't, but now she's got a good man to protect her from her bad judgement. My father didn't stick around long after I was born, and after he was gone, she always seemed to end up with someone with heavy hands and a bad temper. She got hurt a lot, and once I was old enough to know what was going on and try to stop it, I got hurt, too. So, I learned how to hurt them worse."

"And now you use those skills to protect others." Something clicked in her head. "You didn't really sign up with the IAF for job security, did you?"

"No, I didn't. In fact, I took a major pay cut, but it's what I wanted to do. To make a difference, to stand on the right side of things for once. I've done some things I'm not proud of. Being a soldier gave me a chance to make things right. That's something my…" he stopped talking long enough to take a drink of wine and then squeeze her hand. "My wife couldn't understand that, though. Which is why we're not married anymore."

"What was she like? I mean, if it's not too weird for me to ask."

"If you're worried about me making comparisons, don't be. You and Tish don't have a thing in common. She was blonde, pretty in a delicate way, and a lot like my mom, always trusting the wrong people and getting hurt. Looking back, I think that's what drew me to her. She needed someone to take care of her."

"You were her protector." Tyra nibbled at her dumpling as he talked.

"Yeah, I was. My fighting career came with risks, sure,

but I was home most nights, and we had more than enough money to buy whatever she wanted. She's the one that got me to quit moonlighting as an enforcer. That was ugly work, but it paid the bills before I got established as a fighter. I didn't like doing it, and she hated the idea of me working with dangerous people, so I stopped."

"And then you told her you wanted to join up?"

"She wasn't thrilled. In fact, she was furious. We fought about it constantly, but in the end, I knew it's what I had to do. She said she'd accept my choice, but it turned out she couldn't. She cheated on me not long after I left for basic training. When I found out, she said it was my fault. I wasn't there for her and she couldn't handle the loneliness or the constant worry that something would happen to me. The divorce came through the same day I shipped out for my first duty station."

"She shouldn't have cheated on you. If she wanted out, she should have just told you so."

"I think she was trying to, in her own way. Thing is, I'm not a very subtle guy. Something I'm sure you've noticed by now. I'm happiest when there isn't a lot of nuance going on. Makes everything nice and clear."

"Nope." She pointed her fork at him. "I'm not buying that 'I'm a simple man,' line you keep trying to sell everyone. Simple men don't get recruited to Nova Force. They don't find a way to fulfill their dreams and become pilots, either. You are plenty nuanced, and more than a little complicated, mister Strak."

His mouth dropped open in surprise. "You think I'm nuanced?"

"I do. Those muscles of yours are nice to look at, but they're not the only thing I find attractive about you."

"Any time you want to look at my muscles, I'll be happy to oblige." He flexed his free arm so that his bicep strained against the fabric of his uniform.

She knew he was teasing her, but there was an invitation there, too. One she decided to accept. He'd been haunting her thoughts and dreams since the day they met. Tonight, she wanted more, even if it was just a distraction from the darkness and chaos that had filled her life of late. She set down her fork and leaned forward. "Is that so? In that case, I think we can postpone the rest of this meal."

He gave her a slow, sensual smile that made her pulse jump as a jolt of pure lust raced through her.

"Yeah? You finally telling me it's time to misbehave?" He let go of her hand, pushed his chair back from the table, then patted his thigh. "Because if you are, then you're sitting too far away."

His voice lowered to that low, sexy rumble that left her breathless and aching to be touched. She rose from her chair walked around to his side of the table, reaching out for him with trembling fingers. "I am."

"Then, I'm a very lucky man." He caught her in his arms, lifted her easily, and deposited her onto his lap. "That's better."

"Close enough for you?"

He leaned in and brushed a heated kiss across her lips. "For now, yes."

She opened the topmost fastening of his uniform, hooking her fingers in the fabric before returning his kiss with one of her own. "Promise me one thing."

"Anything."

"The door is locked, isn't it?"

He nodded, his deep blue eyes glowing with desire. "It is. There will be no interruptions. Not this time."

"Good." She nestled herself deeper into his arms and smiled up at him, aware she was about to throw rocket fuel on an open flame. "Show me what you've got, Muscles."

CHAPTER TWELVE

SLOW AND EASY. No rushing. That was his plan. At least it was until she uttered those words. After that, all his plans went right out the airlock. He fisted her hair in his hands and kissed her hard. She moaned and tightened her grip on his shirt, popping open another fastening. He slanted his mouth over hers, devouring her every breath as he eased one hand out of her hair and let it drift up her back until he found the clasp on the dress. A light tug was all it took to undo it, leaving her back bare beneath his questing fingers.

Soft skin. Warmth. The taste of wine and spices. The silken weight of her hair between his fingers. He memorized every detail, branding her onto his senses so that no matter what happened, he would never forget this moment.

She squirmed in his lap, and he had to bite back a groan. "You keep moving like that and the only thing I'm going to be eating for dinner is you."

Her laughter filled the room. "I thought shortcake was for dessert."

He growled and kissed her again. His tongue danced with hers as they ground their bodies together. He let his hand glide down her body until he reached the bare skin of her legs. Her squirming had rucked the fabric high on her thighs and he slid his hand beneath her skirt, pushing it higher. Her legs parted in silent invitation, and he let his hand move higher, not stopping until he brushed against something that damned near stopped his heart. "You're not wearing underwear."

"I don't own any."

"You're telling me that all this time, you've been bare-assed under your pants? *Veth*, woman. If I had known that…"

"I was wearing pants, so I wasn't baring anything." She wiggled against him, pressing against his rock-hard cock until he was tempted to tear her dress off and fuck her right there on the chair.

"Well, you're going to be bare in about ten seconds. Hop up. Arms over your head. Now."

She was laughing as she left his lap and raised her arms, her green eyes bright with desire and amusement. "There was a time I found your bossy ways really *fraxxing* annoying."

He let go of her hair and caught the bottom of her dress in both hands. "And how do you feel about my bossy ways now?"

"Sexy… and still somewhat annoying. But mostly sexy."

"Only mostly sexy? I clearly need to up my game." He stood, stripping her out of her dress with a quick lift of his hands and tossed it aside without a care for where it landed. All he cared about was her. He ached to have her back in his arms, but he held back because he wanted to see her, first. All of her. Naked. Beautiful. Bathed in the light of the planet spinning beneath their feet. She was stunning. From the slender lines of her legs to the gentle rise of her breasts that peeked out from beneath the tumbled curtain of long black hair. He'd thought about this moment often enough but having her here in the flesh was so much better than any daydream he'd conjured.

She didn't wait for him to come to her. She covered the distance between them herself and started undoing the fastenings on his tunic with nimble fingers. "Standing rule. If I'm naked, you're naked."

"I like that rule." He shrugged out of his top the moment she had it undone and let it fall to the floor. Her hands rose to his chest, stroking over his skin with a hunger that made his blood roar in his ears and his cock turn to steel.

"So strong," she murmured.

He wrapped his arms around her and pulled her in tight to his body before admitting the truth he'd denied since the beginning. "Not when it comes to you."

TYRA WAS FLYING high on a heady rush of desire and happiness. At his quiet confession, she threw her arms around his neck and rose up on her toes, but his head was still too high for her to land a kiss anywhere but his chest. "If this isn't a one-night thing, I'm going to need stilts."

He cupped her ass in his big hands and lifted her into

the air, high enough she could look into his eyes. "This is not a one-night fling. I don't know what it will be or how long we'll have, but when tomorrow comes, I'm still going to want you in my life."

"Good because the next rule is this: no more disappearing acts. If you want out, all you have to do is say so. If you vanish on me again, I won't be here when you come back."

"I'm not going anywhere, shortcake." He set her down on the edge of the console they were using as a table and stepped between her thighs so that he towered over her.

Veth, she loved the way he did that, moving so close that he was all she could see, all she could feel. He was dangerous, but not to her. Her heart had known that from the first moment they'd met, and she had chosen to trust him with her life.

"Sergeant Strak, you're already in violation of our first rule." She curled two fingers into the waistband of his pants and tugged. "Why are you still dressed?"

"I got distracted." He cupped her breasts in his big hands, stroking her nipples with his thumbs as he leaned in to kiss her. It was a hard, hungry kiss. Mouths open. Tongues tangled. She let herself get lost in the moment, letting go of his pants and wrapping her arms around his waist to cling to him as her world went up in flames.

When he finally lifted his head again, she tried to follow his mouth with hers, not wanting the kisses to end. It wasn't until his hands touched her knees and he coaxed her thighs apart that she stopped trying and leaned back instead. She placed her hands on the table behind her as he parted her legs, baring all of her to his gaze.

He dropped to his knees and pressed an open-mouthed

kiss to one inner thigh, letting his fangs skim over her skin before lifting his head to stare up at her. "It's time for dessert."

She barely had time to nod before he bowed his head and pressed his face into her pussy, parting her labia with his fingers as he sought the pearl of her clit with his tongue. Her next breath came out in an explosive gasp as pleasure poured through her. If she'd been on fire before, now she was standing in the heart of a star. She let her head fall back, closing her eyes as she gave herself over to Dante's talented touch.

He was a man on a mission, using all his skill to bring her to the brink of orgasm. He sucked on her clit, using his tongue to tease and torment her until she was trembling and breathless. Only then did he slip a thick finger inside her, then another, fucking her with his hand, pushing her closer to the edge of release without letting her reach it.

"Dante, please. I need…"

He hummed in affirmation, his mouth and fingers working faster now. She became a creature of pure sensation, riding endless waves of pleasure. One of his fangs grazed a tender spot, and she cried out in pleasure, only to have him stop.

"Sorry, sweetheart."

She opened her eyes and lifted her head to look down at him. "Don't apologize. Do it again."

The look he gave her was hot enough to melt hull plating. "As my lady wishes."

He buried his face into her slick folds again, this time baring his fangs just enough she could feel them grazing her swollen flesh. She started to come, her thighs closing around his head as her release loomed. He sucked her clit into his mouth once more, closing his teeth on it with just enough pressure to send her senses spinning as she rocketed into orgasm.

She was still trying to catch her breath when he rose to his feet, gathering her into his arms for a long, torrid kiss. "You are perfection," he whispered against her lips.

"I'm not, but I'm glad you think so."

"I know so." He nipped her lower lip as he moved away from her, undoing his pants and stepping out of them with an eagerness that echoed her own.

She stayed where she was and tried to gather her scattered wits as he shucked off the last of his clothes. His legs were as heavily muscled as the rest of him, thick, hard, as if they were carved from stone. His cock was as big as the rest of him, and her breath caught in her throat.

He stepped in close again. "Relocation time."

"What? Where are we going? We're naked, remember?"

"I am acutely aware that you are naked right now, which is why we're moving. Just hold on and trust me, baby."

She reached up and took hold of his shoulders. "I can do that."

He lifted her easily, cradling her against his chest as he turned and strode across the room to one of the reclining chairs facing the windows. He sat and settled her into his lap so she faced away from him, her legs straddling his. His cock pressed against her ass, and she gave a deliberate wiggle before turning her head to glance back at him. "I don't see how this is an improvement."

"I have a plan. You'll see." He nuzzled her hair, then swept it off her neck, kissing his way down the back of her neck, not stopping until he reached her shoulder. His gentle kisses and the warm caress of his breath on her skin sent a flurry of goosebumps chasing down her back. His hands covered her breasts again, teasing her nipples with light pinches until they were hard as diamonds and every touch sent a pulse of need straight to her clit.

"This is fun, but what if I want to get my hands on you, too?"

He nipped the tender flesh at the top of her shoulder. "You will, later. You spend your life taking care of everyone else, sweetheart. Just this once, lie back and let someone take care of you."

She couldn't remember the last time that had happened. She covered one of his hands with hers and squeezed. "I'll try."

"That's all I can ask."

Dante toyed with her breasts for a few more minutes, until she was half out of her mind with need. She reached for her pussy, but he caught her wrist and pulled her hand away. "Nope. Not tonight. Tonight all of your pleasure belongs to me. Whatever you need, sweetheart, all you have to do is ask."

She caught his gaze in their reflection. He looked at her with almost predatory hunger, and it sent a dark thrill right down to her soul. "I want you inside me, Dante. I want you to fuck me until neither of us can move."

He uttered a low, primal growl that rolled through her like a rocket lifting off. "*Fraxx*, yes. That's what I want, too."

She was on her feet a half-second later, and back in his arms a moment after that, only this time, facing him, her thighs spread wide to straddle him. His cock was caught between her slick thighs, the broad head only a few inches from where she needed him to be. She rose and reached for him but froze when he shook his head.

"No touching," he reminded her.

"You're dangerously close to the line between sexy and annoying." She set her hands on his shoulders and leaned in to kiss him.

"Liar," he whispered before taking her mouth in a long, heated kiss. His tongue slid into her mouth at the same moment he moved into position, the wide head of his cock pressing against her entrance.

She didn't hesitate, lowering herself down on his shaft in one steady motion that had him groaning aloud. She didn't stop until he was buried to the hilt inside her, his thick length stretching her inner walls just enough to add a bite of pain to the pleasure coursing through her.

"So much for slow and easy," he muttered when he finally broke their kiss.

"Nothing about us has ever been easy. Why start now?"

"I'm starting to think you are the perfect woman for me." Dante reached down to flick a lever on the chair. The chair dropped back, tipping her forward and opening a gap between their bodies. His hands landed on her hips, gripping her tightly as he lifted her a few inches above him and held her there. "Hang on to me, Shortcake, and try to keep up."

Her snarky retort was cut off by a gasp as he thrust upward, filling her completely before withdrawing and doing it again and then again. He kept her suspended above him as he fucked her, her position preventing her from doing anything but enjoy the hard, rhythmic joining of their bodies. His biceps bulged with the effort it took to hold her airborne and she ran her hands over his upper arms, chest, and shoulders, loving the way his body flexed and moved beneath her fingers.

She needed him. The realization dawned as she leaned in to kiss him and found herself staring into his deep blue eyes. This went beyond attraction, beyond the passion that burned between them. This was something more, or at least, it could be. She pushed the thought away and finished the kiss instead. It was too soon to be thinking about futures and possibilities. All they had was this moment, and she wanted to make it memorable.

They chased each other across the heights of pleasure, and when he finally lowered her and let go of her hips, she rode him hard, until the friction between had them both sweat-slicked and panting.

He reached between them and pressed a calloused fingertip to her clit, rubbing it hard as his cock thickened and jerked deep inside her. "Come with me," he told her in a voice barely this side of a command.

She would never admit it was his voice that sent her over the edge, but she came within seconds, her orgasm hurtling into high orbit as he arched his back, lifting them both off the chair as he came. In the aftermath, she collapsed on top of him, heart racing and her breath coming in ragged gasps. She lay across his chest, too spent to move, listening to his heartbeat as it thundered against his ribs.

When his arms wrapped around her, she uttered a contented sigh that came straight from her soul. "S'good."

"Very good. Right now you could ask me for anything

in the universe, and I'd promise you to get you two by the time you woke up."

She laughed. "Right now, I've got almost everything I need for my life to be perfect."

"Only almost? What's missing? What can I get for you to make it perfect?"

She nuzzled his chest. "You can answer one simple question. Why do they call you Buttercup?"

He swore under his breath in a language she didn't recognize. "Promise me you won't tell Magi?"

She raised her head just enough to be able to nod in agreement. "I promise."

"I used to have a tattoo on my bicep." He reached around her to tap his right arm. "Right here. I got it for Tish. She used to wear these little yellow flowers in her hair all the time. She'd pick them off the side of the road. They weren't real buttercups, but that's what the locals called them, so I nicknamed her Buttercup. When we got married, I got those flowers tattooed on my arm. A big bunch of them, all bright *fraxxing* yellow and tied up with this stupid bow with her name on it."

"That sounds sweet." She touched his bicep, right where he'd indicated the tattoo had been. There was an ornately stylized drawing of some kind of predatory, vaguely feline animal there now.

"My fellow trainees thought it was hilarious."

"And they started calling you Buttercup." She winced. "That can't have been easy to deal with when Tish left."

"It wasn't. I...let my anger get the better of me too many times back then. It nearly cost me my career before I settled down."

"This is you settled down? I've seen you charge into a

fight against three armed men with nothing but your fists and a smile. If this is you settled, I can't imagine what you were like before."

His laughter rumbled up from his chest. "I'll tell you about my wild days another time. For now, I think we should probably enjoy our dinner."

"But then our date will be over. I'm not sure I'm ready for that to happen."

He shook his head. "Over? Not even close. There's dinner, dessert, and then I'm taking you back to my room and keeping you there until morning. I finally have you right where I want you, there's no way I'm giving that up anytime soon."

"The last time we spent the night together, you let me sleep all night and then stopped talking to me. This time will be different, right?"

"That was a younger, dumber version of me." He pointed his thumb at his chest and winked at her. "The new and improved version has plans for you tonight, and they don't involve much sleeping."

"That sounds good to me." In fact, it sounded perfect. After everything they'd been through, getting lost in each other was the best therapy she could think of, for both of them.

CHAPTER THIRTEEN

AFTER BEING STUCK in the med-bay for the last few days, the last thing Dante wanted to do was leave his soft, warm bed and his still-sleeping lover to deal with reality. Reality was a cold, miserable place full of greedy assholes and people who kept trying to kill him. The only thing that would get him out of bed and away from Tyra was a direct order, and that's exactly what he'd received a few seconds ago.

Thanks to years of conditioning he'd managed to get to his comm before the incoming alert had woken Tyra. He'd eased out of bed and left her sleeping while he read his new orders. Downs had learned he was out of medical and was demanding to see him immediately. He was to meet her in the briefing room in less than an hour to give her a full report on what had happened during his last mission. *Fraxx.* So much for enjoying a little more time with Tyra.

After a quick shower, he returned to the main room to dress to find Tyra sitting up in bed, looking like temptation in human form. "Morning, beautiful. Did I wake you?"

"You were singing in the shower. I didn't know you could sing."

"Not a lot of call for it in my line of work. I'm sorry I woke you up, though. I was going to let you sleep as long as I could before I left. After last night, I figured you could use it."

"I'm not the one recovering from a serious injury." She blushed but managed to look stern at the same time, an adorable combination that made it hard to remember he had a meeting to get to.

"Rossi's orders. Believe me, I wouldn't have left that bed for any other reason." He tapped a wall panel and pulled out a fresh uniform. "I've got a debriefing with Dr. Downs and her associate in about twenty minutes."

Tyra wrinkled her nose. "What an unpleasant way to start your day."

"Know what would make it better?" He asked as he dressed.

"Coffee?"

"Nope. I'm hoping you're going to tell me you'll still be here when I get back. I can make this the fastest meeting in the history of Nova Force if I know you're lounging around my bed, naked."

"Sorry, Muscles. Not today. I should have the results of my last batch of tests in an hour or so. I should have the results ready to be presented before noon, ship time."

He'd known what her answer would be before he asked. They both had duties to perform. He just wanted her to know where he'd rather be, and with whom. "Well, as it happens, my doctor wants me on light duty for the next twenty-four hours, which means I'm going to be around tonight if you'd like to have dinner with me."

"Dinner sounds good. This time, though, we don't let Magi make our dessert selections. I can't believe he had the food dispenser make three different kinds of shortcake!"

Dante snorted. "I can. I keep telling Rossi that kid needs more to do."

"He's been doing an amazing job of watching out for Nico. That's a full-time job. He's going to make a great father someday."

"I think so, too, but first we need to fix his taste in women. He seems to have a thing for the dangerous ones."

"His burns?" she asked.

"He told you about those?"

Tyra nodded. "He showed them to me. I got the feeling he's had more than his share of pain lately."

"He likes the dangerous ones. One gave him those scars, and the next one turned out to be an assassin." He finished dressing, tugged his uniform straight, and gave her a snappy salute. "What do you think, do I look presentable?"

"You look great. Especially since I don't think you've even had coffee yet."

"I don't drink coffee. No kick. I'll grab a quick mug of Ja'kreesh from the galley before my meeting."

Her eyes widened in horror. "You drink that supercharged rocket fuel? Do you have any idea what that stuff does to a human being's synapses?"

"I'm not human, remember? Well, not completely. I've got enough Torski in me to handle the hit." He grinned at her. "If you want to worry about someone drinking Ja'kreesh, talk to Trinity. She loves the stuff, and the lieutenant is one hundred percent human."

"You're both *fraxxing* crazy." Tyra held up a warning finger. "You may have one mug. A small one. Your body has taken enough abuse this week."

He chuckled. "Just a small one. I don't have time for anything else." He crossed the room and leaned down to plant a slow, lingering kiss on her lips. When he moved away, he groaned. "Though I'm tempted to trade the tea for more time with you."

Her eyes glowed with pleasure. "I'd like that, too, but there's not enough time. You don't want to be late for your inquisition, and I need to get back to work. Playtime is over."

"Only until tonight." He ducked down for one last kiss, winked, and headed for the door with a bounce in his step and a smile on his face. This was the best he'd felt in ages, and nothing, not even a hostile debriefing with corporate lackeys could ruin his mood.

Once the meeting started, his optimistic outlook faded fast. The two reps didn't even try to hide their agenda. They were there to try and get him to say something, anything, they could use to kick Nova Force off the planet and end the investigation.

They'd walked in together, neither one of them cracking even a hint of a smile. He rose to his feet as they entered and stood at parade rest until they were both seated across from him.

"Good morning," he said.

Instead of answering, Dr. Downs set down a recording device on the table and steepled her fingers in front of her. "State your name for the record." She spoke in Galactic Standard, but there was a trace of an accent that reminded him of Trip. She was probably from the same planet, Cassien Alpha.

"My name is Sergeant Dante Strak. Assigned to Nova Force, Team Three."

"Sergeant Strak, we're here to discuss your unauthorized intrusion onto private property, namely Bellex 3, which is owned and controlled by Bellex Corporation."

"My mission was not unauthorized. As a member of Nova Force, I go where I am ordered by my commander. The mission was fully vetted and approved by Nova Force Command."

Dr. Down's lips thinned. "So, you're admitting that you were on the planet without the permission of Bellex Corporation, the legal owner of said planet?"

Dante leaned forward and placed his hands flat on the table. "I'm saying I was ordered to go to Bellex 3 to gather intelligence about the pharma crisis and to locate a team of Boundless' medical personnel that had gone missing while investigating the medical emergency on the planet."

She sniffed and tapped the datapad she'd brought with her. "You will admit that you arrived on a civilian freighter and used a false identity to register as a freelance worker upon arrival on Bellex 3?"

"I followed orders. This was an undercover mission."

"So, you were spying," Chad Everest spoke for the first time. Unlike Downs, Everest spoke without any trace of an accent. Accents were common. The only beings he'd met without one were either cyborgs or people who wanted to erase any trace of their origins.

"I wasn't spying." He did his best to keep his

expression impassive and deliberately slowed his speech as if he were speaking to simpletons. "I told you my mission parameters already. Collect information about the crisis and attempt to locate the Boundless team. Nova Force is a law enforcement unit. We don't spy."

Downs glanced at Everest before asking her next question. "What was the name of the ship that brought you to Bellex 3?"

"Classified."

She pursed her lips and glared at him. "Is that the name of the ship or are you refusing to answer the question?"

"I'm informing you that the answer to your question is classified, which means I can't tell you."

"What about the name of the pilot?"

"Also classified." Dax had warned him they'd try to get that information.

"This will go faster if you cooperate," Everest said with a hint of a smile.

"I am cooperating. If you'd like this to go faster, I'd suggest asking questions you don't already know I can't answer."

Eventually, they changed topics and moved on the second mission, the one that resulted in his capture. This time, the questions were different. The blame game was still ongoing, but it wasn't the focus. It took a bit of time to work out what they were after, but he spotted the pattern. They didn't care about what had happened to him. The drugging. The attack. The illegal tech on the hopper that allowed him to be moved without being tracked. They asked about it all, but the only time they showed any real interest was when he talked about what happened in the room before he was rescued. They wanted descriptions of his surroundings. The sights, sounds, and smells. The man who hid his face, had there been anything about him that would allow Dante to recognize him again? On and on it went. He answered what he could and was honest about what he couldn't.

Finally, Downs sighed and looked at him with frustration. "For an investigator trained to notice the slightest details, you didn't notice much, did you?"

He didn't rise to the bait, though his patience was starting to wear thin. "I'd been attacked, beaten, and sedated at the time. A few details might have escaped my notice."

The interview dragged on. It was a pointless exercise, and by the halfway point everyone in the room knew it. That didn't stop them, though. They stuck to their assigned roles, followed the script they'd been given, and did their best to bore him to death until the very end.

"One last item, Sergeant. Please justify your decision to remove Bellex property from the planet. We're aware this was your decision."

It was the first time he'd been caught flat-footed since the interview began. "You'll have to be more specific. I don't remember removing Bellex property either time I left the planet. In fact, as we've already established, the second time I left, I wasn't even conscious."

"I'm referring to asset 749612-003," Downs stated without looking up from her datapad.

"I have no idea what you're talking about."

Everest cleared his throat and gave him an insincere smile "The boy, Sergeant. The one who calls himself Nico."

Dante rose to his feet, kicked back his chair, and

slammed his hands down on the table. "He's a little boy, not an asset!"

Downs jerked back in her chair, and for a moment he caught the barest glimmer of emotion – fear. Instead of standing up to him, she glanced at Everest.

"Is there a problem, Sergeant?" Everest asked in a voice devoid of all his usual cheer and affability.

"No." Dante straightened up but stayed on his feet. "As for Nico, I brought him to the *Malora* because he's a material witness to both the attack on the Boundless team and the later attack on our location in District Twelve. He's an unaccompanied minor, and I couldn't take the risk of him disappearing before the investigation was concluded."

"I see. Then you will be returning the asset – I mean the boy - to Bellex once the investigation is over?" Downs asked, apparently ready to take charge again.

He folded his arms across his chest and stared down at her. "That depends on the outcome of the investigation. If there are charges, Nico will have to be available to testify at the trial."

She didn't look pleased about that, and her fingers flew as she typed something into her data tablet. After a moment, Everest took over talking. "Do you think it's likely there will be charges?"

Dante managed to refrain from laughing out loud, but it was a near thing. After two hours of trying, they still held out hope that if they asked the right question, he'd give them something useful. "I'm not authorized to discuss the details of the investigation. You'll have to talk to Commander Rossi."

Downs sighed in frustration and looked up. "Since you aren't interested in being cooperative, I see no reason to continue this interview."

"I've been as cooperative as I can be."

Downs gave a limp-wristed wave of her hand. "I'm sure you think so. You may go, Sergeant. I'll be taking this up with your superiors."

He knew it was another attempt to annoy him, so he gritted his teeth, nodded once, turned on his heel, and walked away before he said something he'd regret at his court-martial.

Normally, he'd work out his frustrations in the gym, but not today. Today, there was somewhere else he wanted to be. He headed for the med-bay and the woman who could make his day better just by smiling.

TYRA LEFT Dante's quarters shortly after he did, making the short walk to her room in hopes that no one would catch her in last night's outfit, a pair of borrowed dress shoes in her hand and a serious case of bed head. She made it about three steps before Eric appeared.

"Good morning. Did you have a nice night, Dr. Li?"

"Good morning, Ensign. How long have you been skulking outside Dante's door waiting for me to appear?"

His laughter filled the corridor. "I have no idea what you're talking about. I just happened to be walking by. Just like I happened to be heading to the galley at the same moment Dante was making his way there for a mug of that unfiltered rocket fuel he drinks."

"Dante's right, you need more to do," she teased, then touched his arm. "All joking aside, thank you for your help making last night happen. And thank you for watching over Nico. How's he doing?"

"I was happy to help. Seeing the grin on Buttercup's face this morning was the only thanks I needed. As for Nico, he's great. We've got plans to hang out again tonight."

"More games?"

"Droid repair. He's fascinated by them. Plus, I figure that gives you and the big guy another date night."

"Thank you, but you're sure it's not too much trouble? You're supposed to on duty."

"And one of those duties is maintaining the ship, which includes the bots and droids. It's not a problem." Eric glanced around, then lowered his voice. "He's been telling me what it's like down there. For him. No parents. No adults at all. He vaguely remembers going to some kind of school, but he says that was a couple of winters ago. He thinks his parents died, but no one ever told him anything. One day, they just didn't come home, and he was on his own. It's not right."

"It's horribly wrong. I'm still hopeful that we'll find a way to give him a better life than what's waiting for him down there."

Eric nodded. "Yeah. Dax has me working on that. Unofficially, of course."

She beamed with gratitude, then abandoned decorum and hugged him. "Thank you, Magi. Dante has some truly amazing friends."

Eric hesitated for half a heartbeat before hugging her

back. "You're pretty amazing, yourself. Dante's a lucky man."

They said their goodbyes, and she hurried back to her room. A quick shower, a change of clothes, and she headed for the med-bay. Her brain was already buzzing with all the things she had needed to do. It was going to be a good day, she could feel it.

With Dante on restricted duty, Cris had taken his place on the ground team, which meant Tyra was managing the medical investigation on her own. Fortunately, she was used working shorthanded, and years of working with Boundless had given her a more diverse set of skills than most doctors ever needed. She checked on the progress of the various analysis programs she had running, then sat down at her desk and began working on a draft of her final report. She couldn't come to any conclusions until the last of the data came in, but she had enough preliminary information to start writing her report.

She'd been at it for about an hour when the door opened and Trinity walked in.

"Hey, Tyra. You got a moment?"

"For you? Always. Do you need me as a doctor, an investigator, or because you want to hear how last night went?"

Trinity flashed her a small smile. "I want to hear about your night a little later. Right now, though, we need to talk about Dr. Castille."

"You found something."

Trinity nodded curtly, crossed the room, and pulled up a chair. "How well do you know him?"

"Not well at all. Like I told you, he was a last-minute addition to my team. I thought he was a competent doctor and a decent human being." She sighed. "I missed something, didn't I?"

"No, you didn't. You had no way to know his family connections or his motivation for joining Boundless. Your instincts were right, though. He never intended to do more than one mission. This one."

"My instincts weren't good enough to figure out I had a liar on my team. Tell me the rest of it. Why was he on my team and what was he there to do?" How could she have missed it? She'd always prided herself on being a good judge of character, of always knowing who to trust. Had she been fooling herself?

"I haven't confronted him yet, but it looks like he was spying for his family."

"And who the *fraxx* is his family? What corporation are they aligned with? Are they the ones that pushed so hard to get us off the planet and away from Nova Force?"

"His grandmother is a Bardeaux, and yeah, it seems likely they were the ones pulling strings."

Oh no. "Bardeaux, as in Bellex Corps' biggest competitor in shipbuilding? Those slimy sons of bitches. Boundless is allowed to go anywhere because we're unaffiliated to any government or corporation. They risked destroying our reputation just so they could see what the competition was up to? We weren't even near the factories or production areas, we were focused on the people we came here to help." That's when it hit her. "*Fraxx.* You don't think he was here to steal design secrets, do you? You think this was about the cobalt."

"That's my theory." Trinity leaned forward. "None of this is your fault, Tyra. His family used their money and influence to get him a spot on your team. You took him at face value because you're a good person and you had no reason not to trust him."

"When this is over, will you inform Boundless about what you learned?" They had to know about this. There needed to be a review. Procedural changes. This couldn't happen again. It should have never happened at all.

"Of course. And I'll give you an update about what he said once I've spoken to him. I just wanted you to know what I'd discovered."

"Thank you. Do you—" She broke off, swallowed hard, and started again. "Do you think he was part of what happened down there? Is he the reason my teammates are dead? *Veth*. He's the one that told me they were dead! What if they weren't and I left them behind?" Anguish and guilt crashed over her in an icy wave.

"I think he had a hole blasted in his chest and nearly died in that attack, which makes it unlikely he had any part in it. As hard as it is to accept, I believe the rest of your team died in the first few minutes of the assault, and you only survived because of Nico. I can't tell you what Castille's role was, but my gut tells me he's not a killer."

"I'm trusting your judgment because mine's apparently pretty *fraxxing* faulty. I trusted him. I saved his damned life!"

"Of course you did. You're a good person, and that's what good people do. Don't blame yourself for that. If you hadn't saved him, everything he knows would have died with him. We need answers, and I'm going to make sure he gives us some." Trinity got to her feet. "Is there anything you can think of that I should be asking him about? Times you didn't know where he was? Locals he hung around with?"

She thought back to the first days they'd been on the planet. They'd been busy setting up equipment and letting the locals know why they were there. "Ask him about Livvy. I never made the connection until now, but he was the one who brought her into the clinic and introduced me. In fact, he was pushing for us to do community outreach before we even set foot on the planet. That's already part of what we do, but he kept bringing it up."

Trinity's eyes narrowed. "Livvy? That would be the same girl who lured Dante into that trap?"

"What? That was Livvy? No one told me."

"She left Dante a note telling him where to go, and who to speak to. It was a setup. Dante probably didn't tell you because he knew you'd be upset."

"Damn right I'm upset! Livvy's moral compass was faulty, but I never imagined she'd turn on Dante. If she were going to do that, she could have done it while we were all on the surface. It doesn't make sense."

"We think someone got to her after you were gone. They probably offered her a wad of scrip to write that note. It had to be enough to get her out of the area because no one's seen her lately. We've been asking around, and Magi's been searching for her with facial recognition. So far, nothing."

Livvy was an opportunist with minimal ethics, but she cared about her crew. She wouldn't abandon them. At least, Tyra wouldn't have thought so. Had she misjudged Livvy, too? *Veth*, had she misjudged everyone? "If you find her, what will you do?"

"Bring her here for interrogation. We're chasing ghosts right now, and it's getting *fraxxing* frustrating. If we can find her, we'll be one step closer to finding the ones behind all this."

"The final test results should be coming in soon. I'm hopeful the information will point us in the right direction."

Trinity nodded and got to her feet. "I'm glad you're here to do this for us. We all have multiple skill sets, but this level of lab work would be beyond us. If you weren't here, we'd have to send the samples elsewhere to get these results, costing us time we don't have."

Tyra stood and walked Trinity to the door. "You'll let me know what Oran has to say for himself?"

"Of course." Trin touched her shoulder. "I won't tell you not to think about what he did because I know that's not going to happen, but don't let it make you crazy. And if you need to talk? Come see me or Magi, we're currently the team's experts on trusting the wrong person."

"Only currently?"

"Everything goes in cycles, even bad judgment. I'm off to ruin Castille's day. I'll let you know how it goes."

"Thanks. If he gives you any attitude, tell him I'm filing a report with the Galactic Board of Health Professionals about his conduct. His family might be able to protect him from any legal trouble, but he won't be practicing medicine much longer."

"Nice play. I'll be able to use that. Thanks."

The moment the door slid closed, Tyra sank into the nearest chair and cursed in every language she knew. She'd been lied to, used, and betrayed. Echoes of the past stirred in her mind - memories of others who had promised to help and then left her and her father to struggle on alone. How could she forget those bitter lessons? When had she become so blind?

She forced herself back to her feet, squared her shoulders, and reminded herself of the promise she'd made herself all those years ago. *Don't trust anyone else to get the job done.* It was time she followed that advice again.

CHAPTER FOURTEEN

Two seconds after he walked into the med-bay, Dante knew something was wrong. Tyra's shoulders were slumped, and she moved as if someone had turned the gravity up.

He was at her side in seconds, and when he put his hand on her shoulder, all he could feel was tension. "What happened?"

"Trin came by." She looked up at him with a haunted expression that drove a spike into his heart. They'd been through so much together, but he'd never seen her like this.

"What did she say to you?" He briefly considered the consequences of yelling at a superior officer and decided it would be worth it.

"Easy, Muscles. She was just the messenger. Oran's the asshole."

"Details. Now. I need to know what he did so I know how hard to deck him."

"Not every problem can be solved with your fists."

"Want to bet?" he asked with a grin.

"Not really, no."

"Sorry, bad joke. Tell me what Oran's done."

"According to Trinity, he's a corporate spy. It looks like his family pulled all sorts of *fraxxing* strings to get him assigned to my team so he could report back to them about what Bellex was up to. Trinity is grilling him now. She came by to give me the heads up before she confronted him, in case I could think of any threads she could pull."

"Trinity is too nice." He tapped his fist against one thigh in frustration. "Maybe I should be there, too. What family does he work for?"

"He's related to the Bardeaux family." She finally leaned into his touch, and a little of her tension eased as she cracked a hint of a smile. "It's weirdly sweet that you want to break him for me, but I don't want you to do that. In fact, I'm pretty sure that level of activity would be a violation of your doctor's orders to take it easy. We already pushed the limits on that rule last night."

"I'm fine, Shortcake. Being with you was the best medicine in the galaxy." He lifted his hand to stroke her hair. "Seems to me like you're the one who needs some TLC right now. What can I do?"

"You could start by explaining why you didn't tell me Livvy was the one who sent you into that trap."

"With everything going on, it must have slipped my mind."

"Try again. You were sitting around my med-bay for the better part of two days bored out of your mind. You had plenty of time to tell me. I want to know why you didn't."

He gave a sheepish shrug. "I knew it would upset you. I was trying to find a good time to tell you about Livvy, but you've been working so hard, and then last night…" He scrubbed a hand over his jaw. "I wanted last night to be special, so I didn't mention it then, either."

"I wish you had. Finding out from Trinity right after she told me about Oran was a real gut punch." She leaned back in her chair and uttered a low, frustrated sigh. "I thought I could trust them, but Livvy betrayed you, and for all I know Oran is the reason my team is dead."

He dropped into a crouch beside her, his hand moving to the nape of her neck, beneath her ponytailed hair. "Cool your boosters and take it out of hyperdrive for a minute. We don't know anything for sure yet. One of the first rules of being an investigator - don't get ahead of the facts."

"I know Oran's a liar who, at the very least, risked ruining Boundless' reputation. Bellex would have never allowed any of us to set foot on the planet if they'd known his real reasons for being there. Those are the facts, Dante. Just like we know Livvy set you up."

"If you find her. Trin said there's been no sign of her since the night you got hurt.

"Which is strange. Even if she sold me out, I would have expected her to go back to her crew at least once to gather her things." It had taken him a while to see it because he'd been angry about what she'd done to him, but it was like an itch in the back of his mind. The only home she knew was the slums of District Twelve. In that world, she had a place carved out for herself, along with a family of sorts. He couldn't see her walking away from that so easily. "We will find her. We're Nova Force, remember? This is what we do best."

"This might be what you do best, but we both know I'm not really Nova Force. I'm a temporary addition to the team."

"You might be temporary, but that doesn't mean you're not a full member of this screwy crew." He massaged the back of her neck, trying to ease some of the tension there.

"I'll feel more like one of the team when I have something of value to contribute."

He rose to his feet and moved in behind her, using both hands to massage her neck and shoulders. "You don't consider saving my life to be a contribution to the team?"

"Blink and Sabre saved your life. Trip and I just patched you up after the fact."

"Don't do that, Shortcake," he leaned down to whisper in her ear.

"Do what?"

"Downplay the truth. I've talked to the others. I know what shape I was in when they found me, and who walked them through every step of my treatment. Everyone, including Trip, told me the same thing. If you hadn't been here, I'd probably be dead."

She twisted around to look up at him, a move that put her lips tantalizingly close to his. "They would have saved you."

"Maybe. But even Caldwell says he couldn't have done what you did, and he's almost as cocky as Erben." He stole a kiss before straightening again. "Thank you for saving my life."

"You saved mine twice."

He gently circled his thumbs around the twin knots on either side of her spine. "And I'll keep doing it, too. For as long as I'm in your life, I'm going to do all I can to keep you safe."

"You know, a few weeks ago I would have laughed and told you I didn't need anyone's protection. Oh, how times have changed." She pushed back against his hands in a clear invitation for him to press harder.

"The galaxy didn't change. It's always been a dangerous place. You're just looking at it from a new perspective."

"Not a new perspective, an old one. I allowed myself to forget some important life lessons. I won't do that again."

He didn't like the hard note in her voice, or the regret that weighed down every word. He didn't know what to say, though, so he continued to soothe her the only way he could. He massaged and caressed her shoulders until the muscles finally started to soften, and every time he was tempted to kiss her or let the massage turn into something more sensual, he resisted.

"That really is helping. Thank you."

"My pleasure." The words came automatically, but he was surprised to realize how much he was enjoying taking care of her. His frustration and anger at the way the debriefing had gone had dissipated, leaving him relaxed and thinking clearly again. With that clarity came the realization he needed to tell her what Downs had said about Nico. He couldn't wait for a better moment. Not again. "I know I'm about to undo all my work on your neck by mentioning this, but something came up during my meeting with Downs and Everest."

"What now?" Her tone was level, but he could feel her tension return.

"They accused me of removing corporate property

from the planet. An asset. Downs rattled off a long identification number, and I told her I had no idea what she was referring to. Everest had to clarify she was talking about Nico."

She froze. "They called him an asset?"

"Yeah. I didn't like it either, and I told them as much. I uh, may have dented the table while making that point, actually."

"I'm sorry I missed it. Did she even blink? I swear that woman is more robotic than the droids on this ship."

"She blinked, so I think she's human." Another detail struck him. "It was the first time Everest showed some backbone, too. He took over while she sat there and gaped at me."

"Chad did? Mister easy-go-lucky, I'm here to play the good guy?"

"Yeah. There's something up with him."

"My father used to call men like him snake oil salesman."

"What's snake oil? No, on second thought, don't tell me. I don't want to know. It sounds revolting…and slimy."

"I have no idea, either." She gave a small shudder and then tipped her head back to look up at him. "What else did they say about Nico?"

"I made it clear he's a material witness and under our protection until the investigation ends. They made it clear they want him back the moment he's served his purpose."

"We can't send him back there."

"I don't plan on it. They gave us some valuable intel today, though. I'll get Magi to run the recording of the interview and pull Nico's ID number. Soon, we'll know everything they do about the kid. Maybe he's got relatives who can take him in, or at least pay off his debts. We'll find a way to protect him, Tyra."

She bowed her head and sighed. "We'd better. Bellex has to be involved in all this, which means that boy will end up testifying against the people who own him."

He tried to squeeze her shoulders in comfort, but it was like caressing a marble statue. "I know. We'll think of something."

She started to say something, but one of the machines behind them chimed. He looked and saw a bank of green lights beneath the monitor.

"Finally." She ducked out from beneath his hands and bounded out of her chair, nearly colliding with him in her hurry. "Out of my way, Muscles. Those are the results we've been waiting for."

TYRA FOCUSED on the new results, shoving everything else aside for now. *Please don't be a dead end. I need a win right now.*

She tapped a screen, and streams of data flowed across it. There was too much for her to process, so she tapped a few more keys and flicked her fingers toward an empty space in the middle of the room. A projection shimmered into existence, the data reorganized into graphs and images.

"What does all this mean?" Dante asked, waving a hand through the projections.

"I need more time to put it all together, but here's the short version." She pointed to two bar graphs. "The one on the left is the chemical analysis of the cobalt sample you retrieved. The graph on the right is a breakdown of the pharma known as crimson, another designer drug that left a string of broken minds and dead bodies in its path, until Corp-Sec and the IAF had finally broken up the drug cartels creating and trafficking the drug.

THIS PARTICULAR SAMPLE was one of the first to be confiscated and analyzed before anyone knew how much of a problem it was going to be. Do you see the similarities?"

"Crimson?" he eyed the images. "Why crimson? And how can they be so alike if they cause different reactions? Crimson was a hallucinogenic, wasn't it?"

"It was. But taken in too large a dose, or too often, it could trigger a psychotic break that made the user extremely violent. They were a danger to themselves and anyone around them, and most overdoses resulted in a permanent comatose state or death."

"Which is what Markson reported was happening on Bellex 3. That was part of my original briefing. Because of that, when I first got to the planet, I was looking for the wrong *fraxxing* signs."

"Markson was right, though. They are remarkably similar." She moved to the center of the projection, organizing the images, zooming in on some, moving others, and discarding several more until she had what she needed set out around her. "These are both one hundred percent synthesized pharma, and they share too many elements to have been made separately."

Surrounded by the data, she saw confirmation of her theories and expanding on them for Dante. "In fact. If I had to guess, I'd say that this is an earlier version of the same basic formula. What if both of these drugs were created by the same group? When crimson didn't produce the desired result, they gave the formula to the cartels to sell as recreational pharma. Cobalt came later, and it did exactly what they wanted it to do – made their workforce more obedient and malleable."

"You can see all that in this mumbo jumbo?" Dante asked, then walked into the middle of the projection, lifted her into his arms, and kissed her. "You're amazing. Have I mentioned that lately?"

"I'm really not. Anyone with the right training could have done the same thing."

"Yeah, well, I think you're amazing." He frowned. "And I thought I told you to stop being so damned dismissive of your abilities."

"It's called being modest. You should try it sometime," she retorted, allowing herself a moment's enjoyment. This was real progress, and once she'd had a chance to review the finer points of the results, she was confident she'd have what the others would call actionable intel. After all the bad news this day had brought, she would happily take this win.

He grinned, flashing his fangs at her. "Nuh uh. Modesty and humility are not Nova Force traits."

"I never would have guessed."

He drew her in for another slow, toe-curling kiss before lowering her back to the ground, letting their bodies slide over each other all the way down. "You ready to let the others know what you've learned?"

"Soon. I need to go over the data first. I don't want to miss anything." She was tempted to ask him to stay, but that wasn't a good idea. She needed to do this herself, with no distractions. That thought was quickly followed by a flash of understanding. This was how Dante felt when he had tried to put some distance between them.

"I should leave you to it. Want me to let the others know you'll be putting together a briefing for later today?" Dante asked.

"Please. You'll talk to Magi, too, right?"

"He's my next stop. If I know him, he's monitoring Trinity's interview with Castille. I can see how that's going and give you an update before the briefing."

"Perfect." She looked up and blew him a kiss. "Thank you."

"My pleasure, Shortcake. Truly." He leaned down and kissed her, then left her to finish her work.

Once he was gone, she continued going through the data, compiling the highlights and key facts in a single file so she could add them to her report. Even while she worked, part of her mind focused on another problem: Nico. How could she and the others protect him? What would it take to get him away from Bellex? They thought of him as chattel, a thing to be possessed. The corporations had marked all the cyborgs with barcodes, and now they were inserting chips into human beings.

It had to stop.

TWO HOURS LATER, she stood in the briefing room and shared her findings with the team. Kurt, Aria, and Cris were still on the surface, but they were present via an encrypted comm-link Magi had declared completely secure. When she was done, everyone started talking at once, all of them enthused with what they'd just heard.

"Do we know who's making the drug?" Dax asked.

"Unfortunately, no. It would take days, maybe weeks, to run that kind of comparison, and that's if we limited it to this part of the galaxy. Even then, I'm not sure we'd find what we needed."

"Why not?" Cris asked.

Tyra called up a map of the system to help make her next point. "Because as much as I wanted this to be all Bellex's doing, I don't believe they were in it alone. They build ships. It's what they're good at. Creating mind-altering drugs requires a very different kind of knowledge, highly trained experts, and well-equipped labs." She gestured to the star map. "There's nothing like that anywhere in this system. Magi checked their employment records, too. Bellex doesn't employ anyone with that level of training. It just doesn't make sense they were doing this on their own, and if they had a secret partner…" She gestured to the map. "It's a big cosmos."

"So, you think this place was chosen as a testing ground, and Bellex agreed to it?" Dax asked.

"I do. What I don't understand is who this other party is, and why Bellex is working with them. Corporations are notoriously suspicious of each other. Who could they be in league with?"

Everyone fell silent and one by one they turned to look at Dax. When the silence stretched out, Dante rose from his seat and came to stand beside her. "She needs to know, sir."

"What do I need to know? I thought I'd been briefed on everything relevant to his investigation."

Dax nodded. "You were. But if what you're postulating is right, then this mission just overlapped with a larger problem. If we read you in, you won't be able to discuss what you learn with anyone who isn't a member of this team. Your life might depend on it."

"I understand."

Dax stared at her. "Not yet you don't, but you will soon. Erben, add a note to her file indicating that Dr. Li is being read in on the existence of the Gray Men." Everyone leaned in, and a hush fell over the room. "A few months ago, we were on another assignment, investigating the theft of DNA from a military base. The details of that investigation are classified, but we uncovered the existence of a secret group, the Gray Men. We don't know much about them, yet. They're wealthy, powerful, and some of them are members of the various corporations. They've been around a while, too. Decades, likely."

"And you think this secret faction could be the ones who created cobalt and crimson? What else have they done? Why hasn't Nova Force put a stop to them?"

"We're still putting it all together," Dax said.

"Which isn't easy when the bastards keep killing anyone we get close to," Dante grumbled. Then his head snapped up. "*Fraxx.* Do you think that's what that asshole meant when he said that running wasn't an option for him? The Gray Men aren't kind to those they think failed them."

"It's a possibility. Your report mentioned that the leader said the people he answered to don't like mess. That sounds like the Grays, too." Dax rapped his knuckles on the table. "But it's not enough to prove anything. Not yet.

So, find me proof, and until then, keep your eyes open and your asses covered."

"You said it would take days or weeks to run a comparison. Was there something in that sample with a relatively unique signature? Something I could scan for from here? The cosmos may be big, but Bellex 3 isn't," Magi said.

Tyra considered his question. "I think so. I'll send you the breakdown after the briefing and you can feed the information to the computer. Minute samples wouldn't be enough to trigger a hit, but if they're stockpiling cobalt somewhere, it could give us a location. To keep so many people dosed, they have to have a large supply of it somewhere close. If we can find a storage site, maybe that will give us a clue as to how the hell they're distributing the stuff."

Erik rubbed his hands together and cracked a gleeful smile. "I've already been borrowing Bellex's satellites to look for Livvy. Speaking of which, Bellex finally handed over her file." He looked at Dax. "Shall I?"

"Do you have anything else to report, Dr. Li?"

She shook her head and reclaimed her seat, as did Dante. "I'm all out of intel."

"Alright, Magi, you're up. Tell the others what we know."

Magi tapped the screen of his data tablet, and Tyra's display vanished, replaced by an image of a young girl with a bright smile. "This is Olivia Worth. Age, fifteen years. Parents deceased. Her file was earmarked for 'retrieval and training' once she reached sixteen years old, which happens in a couple of weeks. According to her file, she will be required to work off her parents' debts, which total more than one hundred thousand dollars once the interest is factored in."

"Interest?" Tyra was horrified. Livvy wasn't a good person by any stretch of the imagination, but no one deserved what Bellex was doing here.

"Her parents died eight years ago. These bastards have been charging her interest on her parents' debt until she's old enough to start working it off."

Tyra stared at him. "Why is this allowed to happen?"

"It isn't. Indentured service is allowed, but charging interest on the debts is not." Dax stated. "Bellex screwed up when they gave us that file. It proves they're breaking the law. Erben, send a copy of that to HQ and tag the relevant passages. I don't want us getting sidetracked from our mission, but this needs to be looked into."

"Yes, sir." He tapped the screen once. "And…done."

"Show off," Dante muttered under his breath.

"Am not. I'm just efficient…and better than you," Eric replied.

"Children…" Dax's voice rumbled in warning, and it was all Tyra could do not to laugh. Even in the midst of dark news, the team still found a way to hold onto a little light.

Dante didn't say another word, he merely glowered at Eric as he methodically cracked the knuckles of his right hand.

She leaned in and set her hand on Dante's back. "Behave. You're still on light duty. No kicking ass until I give you the green light."

He looked down at her with affection. "Yes, ma'am."

"Holy *fraxx*. She's done the impossible," Kurt said.

"They have to be pranking us. Magi, are you messing with the feed?" Aria demanded.

"Nope. That was live and recorded for posterity." Magi could barely speak between gales of laughter.

Dante folded his arms across his chest and straightened, somehow making himself look even more massive than usual. "Laugh while you can. When I'm back on duty, I am going to kick all your asses."

"And he'll have my permission to do it," Dax added. "Or do you think I've forgotten about the crap you put me through when Trin and I were figuring things out?"

The snickering and laughter stopped instantly.

"Do you have anything else to add, Erben?" Dax asked.

"One more thing. Thanks to Dante, we now have more information on Nico. I uh…acquired his file a little while ago, and no, you do not want to ask me how I did it, Commander."

"Right. What did you learn?"

"Not much." Eric waved his hand and the image of Livvy – Olivia – shimmered and vanished, to be replaced with a picture of younger and far happier looking Nico. "Meet Nicolas Martinez. Age eleven. Like Livvy, he's an orphan with no listed next of kin. His debt load is also accruing interest, and by the time he comes of age, he'll owe Bellex at least thirty-five years of labor to pay it back."

"They can't have him back." The words left her lips before she could stop herself.

"We're working on that," Dax said. "None of us want him setting foot on that planet again."

"Especially now we suspect the Grays are involved. They don't leave loose ends." Trinity said.

Dante wrapped an arm around her and hugged her to

his side. "I'm not going to let anything happen to him, Shortcake. You have my word."

She believed him. She didn't know what the future held for her and Dante, or even for herself once this was over, but when it came to this, she was certain. Dante would protect Nico to his last breath, and so would she.

CHAPTER FIFTEEN

DANTE SAT in silence as Trinity took over the last part of the briefing, updating everyone on everything Oran had confessed to.

"The second I told him I knew who his family was and why he was on Bellex, he started talking. Honestly, I think he was relieved the truth was finally out," Trinity said.

"What did he tell you? Did he know we were going to be attacked?" Tyra asked.

"He said he had no idea, and I believe him. I had Magi monitor the entire interview, complete with bio-scans I've already reviewed. There's no indication he lied about anything."

Tyra exhaled softly and sat a little farther back in her chair. She'd been wound too tightly since learning of Castille's lies. Maybe this would help her unwind, at least a little. They were all pushing themselves. Well, everyone but him. He was still stuck on light duty, and it chafed him to be sitting idle while others had to take up the slack.

"So, what did he confess to?" Aria prompted.

"Mostly mundane issues. Lying about his reasons for applying to Boundless. He confirmed that his family bribed several people, including the doctor whose place he took on your team, Tyra." Trinity gave her a sympathetic look.

"Wonderful. I guess I'll be making another report to the Galactic Board of Health Professionals," Tyra said.

He dropped his hand to her thigh and squeezed it gently. She flashed him a tiny smile of gratitude, then turned her attention back to Trinity.

"One thing that caught my attention was his admission he was there to get a sample of cobalt. That's how Livvy came into the picture. She was his contact on the planet. He didn't know how it had been arranged, but he was given her name and told she'd be bringing him a sample. Only by the time she was hired, the supply was already drying up and she couldn't get it for him."

"Did he know what it was? What it did?" Kurt asked.

"He had a fair idea, yeah," Trinity confirmed. "Apparently, Bardeaux discovered it was being tested on Bellex 3, and they wanted to get their hands on it. He was the perfect spy, because he's never worked for Bardeaux Starliners or any of their affiliates, and isn't part of their social circle, either. He didn't want to do it, but they blackmailed him. Something about a cheating scandal at his college that his family paid to cover up."

"Being rich certainly has advantages. No insult intended, Caldwell." Dante had grown up resenting people who had everything offered to them without having to work for it. It wasn't until he's joined the IAF he'd met a different kind of rich kid—the ones who chose to refuse to toe the family's line and walked away from them, and the money it offered. Cris, whose full name was actually Crispin Charles Caldwell the fifteenth, had left a powerful family, and eventually so had his little sister. Having met the family at Alyson's wedding not long ago, Dante could see why neither sibling had stuck around. Their parents were the most judgemental and unhappy people he'd ever met.

Cris scoffed. "No offense taken. There are times I miss some of those advantages."

Dax rapped his knuckles on the table. "Stay on task, guys. Bardeaux knew about cobalt. What it was, and where it was being tested. What does that tell us?"

"That at least one of them is connected to the group that developed it," Aria stated.

"And they decided to use that information to their own ends. Want to bet we have a dead Bardeaux executive show up in the next few weeks?" Dante added. They didn't have much hard intel on the Gray Men, but they didn't tolerate anyone stepping out of line with their agenda.

"No bet," Eric said with a shake of his head.

"I'll let the Colonel know. If anyone from that company dies, for any reason, she'll need to open an investigation."

"If things get any busier, the brass are going to need to commission another Nova Force team," Dante said.

"I think that's already being arranged. With us stationed on the Drift now, there's room for another team at HQ." Dax ran a hand through his dark hair, and for a moment his expression darkened. "These are rough times, and it's not going to get better any time soon. If we don't do our jobs, it might never get better. The corporations are at each other's throats. There are rumblings another corporate war is coming. And now we've got more problems that link back to the Gray Men." He got to his feet. "We're the last line of defense. I don't know about the rest of you, but I don't plan on standing by and letting them tear the galaxy apart again."

Dante rose with the rest of them. "No, sir!"

"Not on our watch."

"Not happening, sir."

Even Tyra stood, her voice softer than the others but filled with the same determination. "Never."

Dante looked down at her, taking in her fierce expression, the hard line of her jaw, the set of her shoulders. She was beautiful. Glorious, and in his eyes, utterly perfect. His stomach dropped, his heart raced, and his entire world shifted, re-centering itself around Tyra.

Fraxxing hell. He was in love. The thought sent his heart slamming against his ribs so hard he expected the others to hear it and comment. He wanted to lift her up, kiss her senseless, and tell her how he felt. He also wanted to wrap her in his arms and never let go, because if he did, he wouldn't be able to protect her. He looked over at his commander, standing with the woman he loved at his side. How the hell did the two of them do this?

He reached down and rested his hand on the curve of Tyra's back. He'd ask Dax how he managed it once he'd gotten a few minutes alone with Tyra. There was something he needed to say, first.

AFTER THE BRIEFING, Tyra lingered for a moment to talk to

Eric. "Would you please send me over a copy of Nico's file?"

"Anything for you, gorgeous." He winked and dropped into a low, dramatic bow.

"Quit flirting with my woman!" Dante bellowed, his heavy footfalls making the floor shudder as he stomped toward them.

"Gotta go! The file will be on your computer shortly." Eric took off at a brisk jog, keeping the table between himself and Dante as he headed for the door.

"You can stop growling now, he's gone. Besides, he only flirts with me to get a rise out of you." She turned to smile up at Dante as he reached her side. "And who said I was yours?"

"I said so." He hauled her up against his hard body and kissed her hotly, his lips branding hers.

She didn't argue with him. Wouldn't have tried even if she had the breath to speak. She hadn't belonged anywhere, or to anyone, since her father's death. She went where she was needed, to whatever place she could do the most good. But being needed wasn't the same as being desired, and for once, she wanted more. She wanted a small portion of happiness for herself, too.

It was a long time before he finally raised his head and loosened his hold on her enough for her to be able to lean back to look up at him. "You are mine, aren't you, Tyra?"

She lay her hand over his heart and nodded. "For this moment, right here and now, I'm yours. I don't know what the future holds, though, or how—"

He cut her off with another kiss that lasted even longer than the first one. "We'll figure it out. Just like we're going to figure out how to protect Nico. All I needed to know is that you're with me, Shortcake."

Joy filled her, like tiny, shimmering bubbles of pure light. "I am. Are you with me?"

"To the end of the universe and back."

She grabbed hold of his uniform with both hands and pulled herself onto her toes. Even then, she couldn't reach high enough to kiss him, but he cupped her ass in his hands and lifted her until she closed the gap between them. Even as she kissed him, she knew there were a hundred reasons it could never work out, but for now, she wouldn't let it stop her from stealing a few moments of happiness. For now, she belonged. To the team, to this mission, and to Dante.

He started walking without letting go of her or even breaking their kiss. When they got to the door, she expected him to put her down, but he didn't even slow his pace.

"Where do you think you're going?" she asked.

"My quarters."

"Why?"

He uttered a low, dramatic groan. "I think I need to go back to bed, Dr. Li. Immediately, and possibly for the rest of the day. As my physician, you really should come with me and make sure I'm not having a relapse."

She pointed in the opposite direction from the one he was headed and struggled not to laugh. "If you're having a relapse we should be going to the med-bay, not your room."

"My bed's bigger. Also, the door locks."

"I usually charge extra for house calls."

He stopped long enough to kiss her again. "I'll pay in orgasms. What's this gonna cost me?"

Her entire body lit up like a torch at his rough words. Her clit throbbed, her nipples tightened, and her next breath came out as a soft moan. "At least two."

"You're undercharging. How about three?"

A flood of raw need hit her system like a drug, driving everything else from her mind. "Yes, please."

Dante broke into a jog and navigated the rest of the distance without stopping once, even pacing during the short ride in the mag-lift. He keyed in the code to his door and hustled them both inside, then spun around to press her up against the door for a hard, demanding kiss the moment it closed.

She was already working on the fastenings of his uniform, eager to get him out of his clothes and into bed. She wasn't in her right mind, and for once, she didn't care. Reality and duty would call them back soon enough. Until then, there was just the two of them and the shining start of something wonderful.

"Need you naked. Now." He grabbed her shirt in his fists and tugged.

"Borrowed clothes. Don't tear them," she reminded him.

He uttered a frustrated grunt. "Then take them off quickly."

"This would go faster if you put me down." She pulled the shirt over her head, gasping when he palmed one of her breasts in his hand the second it was bare.

She was still trying to get the shirt off when the distinctive chirp of a comm filled the room.

"*Fraxx*. I need to take this. It's the commander. I'll go voice only."

Her head was still swaddled in her shirt as he set her down and stepped away. The moment she had her bearings, she pulled her shirt back down.

"Strak here. What is it, sir?"

"I forgot to tell you before the briefing ended, West and I would like you to sit in on our next meeting with the Bellex reps. Think the doctor will clear you for that?"

"Let me ask her. Shortcake, am I allowed to sit and look threatening during a boring meeting with some cranky corporate types, or would you rather I stay in my quarters with you?" The cocky son of a starbeast actually grinned as he outed her.

She made an obscene gesture with both hands before answering in the steadiest voice she could muster. "Since you're clearly over your sudden relapse, I see no reason why you can't attend the meeting."

"Dr. Li? Sorry for disturbing your uh, medical consultation with the sergeant. Dante, if you're fit for duty, we'll meet you in briefing room two in fifteen minutes."

"I can make that work. See you then, sir."

He flicked off the device, dropped it onto the nearest flat surface, then raked his gaze over her. "We've got thirteen minutes. Why are you still dressed?"

"I can't believe you did that! Now he knows where I am and what we were going to do."

He undid the last few fastenings on his uniform and shrugged out of it, then dropped it on the floor. "Not were. Am. I remember promising you three orgasms. If you don't get naked, we're only going to have time for two."

"But you told your commander—!"

He stood directly in front of her, bare-chested, feet planted, his thumbs caught in the waistband of his pants. "I did. I'm tempted to stand in the middle of this ship and yell the news to the stars, too. You said you're mine, Tyra Li. I'm not keeping that a secret. It's not like they didn't know about us already. I was just making it official."

She opened her mouth, closed it, and opened it again. He never claimed to be a subtle man. She shouldn't have expected him to be any different about this. She pulled her shirt over her head again and tossed it on the floor with his. "Next time, could you try to be a little lower key? It's bad enough Magi was grinning like a lunatic when he spotted me sneaking out of your room this morning. Now, I'm going to blush the next time I see Dax."

He wrapped her in his arms and nuzzled her hair. "He's happy for us. No need to be embarrassed about that. I cheered him on when he and Trinity found their way back to each other. He's just returning the favor." He picked her up and carried her over to the bed. "Enough talk. Get naked."

That was one order she was happy to comply with. Bellex, the mission, and all her questions would still be there later. This moment was about the two of them, and nothing else.

She stripped out of her clothes as quickly as she could, but Dante was faster. Her pants were tangled up with her shoes when he moved in behind her and gently pushed her forward onto the bed.

She landed on her hands and knees and immediately glanced back to look at him. "Was that necessary? We're not in that much of a hurry."

"Yes, we are." He dropped to his knees beside the bed,

so his mouth was tantalizingly close to her already wet pussy. "I made a promise, and I intend to keep it."

He pressed an open-mouthed kiss to one ass cheek as he moved his hand between her thighs. She widened her stance, and he gave a low hum of approval, then slid a finger past her slick outer lips to stroke over her clit. A few deft touches of his fingers and she was pushing back against his hand, craving more of his touch.

"And a moment ago you were complaining I was in a rush. Now which one of us is in a hurry?"

"Just trying to help you keep your promise."

He laughed and pressed one long, thick finger into her channel. "You ready for orgasm number one?"

Before she could answer, he added another finger, fucking her with one hand while reaching around to toy with her clit with the other. He was relentless, teasing and pleasing her with a hard, fast tempo that left her gasping on the bed, arms braced to stop herself from falling forward.

"You like that? Are you ready to come for me yet, Shortcake?"

She uttered a soft moan, too far gone to even form words anymore.

"I love the sounds you make when I'm making you feel good. Sexiest sound in the whole *fraxxing* galaxy." He slowed the pace a little and changed the angle of his fingers, curving them upward so his fingertips brushed over her g-spot with every stroke.

Her legs were shaking and she moaned again as an orgasm began to bloom deep inside her. Dante's fingers stroked and fucked her without mercy, and soon the onslaught of sensations was more than she could take. She was lifted high on a wave of pleasure that crested, then crashed over her, sending her tumbling into release.

"That's one," he murmured as he eased his hand out from between her thighs. "You've got thirty seconds to get ready for round two."

CHAPTER SIXTEEN

FOR THE SECOND time that day, Tyra found herself slipping out of Dante's room. At least this time there was no one lurking in the corridor, and she made it to her quarters without seeing anyone.

He'd kept his promise and given her three mind-blowing orgasms before he kissed her goodbye and left for his meeting, still doing up his uniform as he hurried out the door.

She freshened up quickly and then sat down to review the file Eric had sent over. Nico's entire life was summarized in two heartbreakingly brief pages, so it didn't take her long to find what she was looking for. When she spotted it, she sighed in relief. Nico's chip had been inserted when he was an infant. It allowed him to be geo-tracked and could be scanned for identity purposes, but there was nothing in his file to indicate it would be dangerous to remove it. At least, not for Nico.

If she did this, she'd be tampering with corporate property. She could be brought up on charges, lose her reputation, end her career, or most likely, experience all three outcomes. The risks were high, which is why she wasn't going to share her plan with anyone else. If Bellex came after her for this, Dante and the rest of the team would be absolved, and Nova Force's reputation wouldn't be tarnished. If the others knew her intentions, they'd want to help, and they'd done enough for her and Nico already.

"Computer, where is Nico Martinez currently located?"

The Malora's AI answered immediately. "That being is currently in the mess."

Of course he was. With everyone busy, he was probably enjoying an impromptu feast. The crew quarters, the med-bay, and the galley and attached mess, were all off-limits to the Bellex visitors, protecting Nico and the research she'd been doing from prying eyes. Eric had the ship's AI watching their guests to ensure they didn't enter an area they weren't supposed to. So far, they hadn't attempted it, though she'd heard from the others the pair complained non-stop about the restrictions. They also made repeated complaints about the food, their lodgings, and the fact they'd only been granted the use of a single service droid each.

She headed to the mess and found Nico enjoying an ice cream sundae slathered in whipped cream and awash in a sea of caramel. He was dwarfed by the metal furnishings that filled the room, all of it built to accommodate full grown adults. His feet dangled nearly a foot off the floor, and his shoulders barely reached the tabletop.

"Hi, Dr. Li." He waved at her with a sauce-splattered spoon, most of his face hidden behind his dessert.

"Hi, Nico. Hungry again?"

"No." He answered honestly. "But I don't know how long I get to stay here, so I'm eating all the stuff I can while there's still time."

She wanted to hug him and promise him he'd always be safe. That there was no need to eat until he burst because he might never get another chance. "The team isn't done their investigation yet, so I think you've got a few more days at least."

He put down the spoon. "Yeah? That's good, 'cause I don't think I can eat the rest of this."

"How about we put it in the freezer for later? I thought you might like to come to the med-bay with me."

"You gonna run more tests?" He asked, looking doubtful. She'd done a full workup of him the first day they'd come on board, and he'd quickly grown bored with all the scans.

"Just one. I want to show you something, and then ask you a question."

"Something wrong with me?" he asked. It amazed her how quickly his vocabulary had changed. He spoke more clearly now, and while his words were still accented by the patois of this world, it wasn't as pronounced as it had been.

"Nothing's wrong. Come on, let me show you what I'm talking about." She held out her hand, and her heart swelled as he hopped off the bench and took hold of her without hesitation. "Okay. But first, we should put the ice cream away."

THE LAST TIME she had scanned him, she'd shown him the

results as a holographic display, explaining what all the readings meant and even showing him a digital model of his heart beating in real time. This time, she didn't run the display at all, and she kept her data tablet turned away from him while the imager did its work. She didn't know how he'd react when she told him about the chip, and she didn't want him figuring it out before she could explain. When the scan was done, she prepped the display to show a model of his head and shoulders but didn't activate it,.

"You ready to see yourself?" She asked.

"Yeah. Can I see my heart beating again? That was cool."

"Not this time." She moved the imager out of the way and moved in right beside him, placing her hand on his thin shoulder. "Before I show you this, I need to ask you something. Did anyone ever tell you what this mark on your neck means?" She reached up to gently brush her finger over the small, triangular tattoo on his neck.

"It means I'm a Bellex 'ployee."

"The word is employee. And yes, that's what it represents."

The boy nodded. "When I get older, they'll come get me and train me to work in one of the factories. I seen some of the others who got taken. They say they get to eat food tabs and sleep in real beds and even get clean clothes to wear."

"Is that what you want to do when you get older? Work in a factory?"

Nico shrugged. "That's the only choice I got."

"Maybe not. But if you wanted to do something else, I'd need to take that mark off your neck."

His eyes widened. "Then I wouldn't belong to Bellex

anymore?"

"Something like that." She turned on the display. "This is you. Do you see that object in your neck? Right about where your mark is?" She pointed to the tiny, circular object the computer had shaded a brilliant yellow.

"What's that?" He leaned forward, his eyes locked on the image as his fingers probed the area under his tattoo. "I don't feel nothing there."

"It's a microchip. It's too deep and too small for you to feel with your fingers, but it's there."

"What does it do? Am I a cyborg? Does it give me powers like them?"

"I'm afraid not. What it does is carry your information. Your name. Your birthdate. And it tells Bellex where you are."

"It knows my name?"

"It has that information, yes. Your name is Nicolas Martinez. It has other information about you, too. Like the names of your parents. Would you like me to give you a copy of your information, Nico?"

He nodded, looking slightly dazed. "I'd like that. And maybe a picture of my parents. I don't remember what they looked like. Do you think that chip thing has that?"

"If it doesn't, I think I know where we can get one." She'd ask Eric to search Bellex's files. If a picture of Nico's parents existed, he'd find it.

He looked at the model again. "It's awful tiny to have so much important stuff on it."

"It is. If you wanted to leave Bellex 3, it would have to be removed. I'd like to do that for you right now, but only if you want me to."

He frowned. "Will it hurt?"

"Not even a little bit. I'll have to put you to sleep though. You'd need to stay very still, and I know you don't like that."

"I get all itchy if I has to keep still too long," he agreed.

"Right. So, you'll go to sleep right here, and I'll take the chip out. Once that's done, I'll use a tissue regenerator to fix the little hole in your neck. You remember how those work? I fixed your arm with it the day you saved Dr. Castille and me from those bad men."

"I remember. That was fun to watch." He touched the mark on his neck again. "When I wake up, no more mark?"

"No more mark. No more chip. But only if you agree. This is your choice, Nico."

He straightened up, and his expression turned solemn. At that moment, she could see a hint of what he'd look like as a grown man. She wanted that man to have a life beyond that of an indentured slave.

"Take it out. I don't like them knowing where I am all the time. Maybe if they can't find me, I won't have to work for them."

"That's my hope, too." She wrapped her arms around his thin shoulders and gave him a hug. To her surprise, he hugged her back and didn't let go for a long time. Her life had never brought her to a place where she'd considered having children. She was at peace with that but holding Nico, she briefly wondered what that life might have been like. Fulfilling, sure, but in a different way than the path she'd chosen.

After everything that had happened this mission, she wasn't sure it was a path she wanted to stay on. Her team – her friends – were dead. Two people she trusted had betrayed her. Boundless had been compromised. It would be better for them if she stepped away, especially after what she was about to do

She stayed with Nico until he let go of her, enjoying the moment of closeness. When it was over, she prepped for the procedure, keeping up a running chatter the whole time. When she was ready, she had Nico lie down and close his eyes. She held his hand as she pressed the injector to his upper arm and administered the anesthetic. He was asleep in seconds.

"Computer, activate sterility field and initiate surgical protocols for med-bay." With the model projected above the sleeping child to help guide her, she picked up a laser scalpel, made a small incision and began the process of removing the chip from Nico's neck.

It didn't take her long to locate the chip. Removing it took significantly longer because she didn't know what sensors the tiny device might have, and she didn't want to inadvertently alert Bellex to the fact Nico's chip had been removed.

The extraction was done slowly and carefully, using a set of field-generating forceps that created a tiny bubble around the chip, allowing her to ease it out of his body. Once it was out, she had the ship's AI place a temporary shield around the object until she could get it sealed into a signal-blocking container.

Only then did she breathe a sigh of relief and return to Nico. It wouldn't take long to close the small incision and inject him with a small dose of healing accelerant. When he woke up again, he'd be one step closer to freedom.

Dante arrived for the briefing with a minute to spare, though he'd jogged the length of the ship to do it. He paused in the corridor, brushed a bit of dust off the front of his uniform, and managed to slow his breathing before activating the door and entering the room.

Dax and Trinity were already seated, but there was no sign of Downs or Everest, yet.

"Sorry about before," Dax said as he gestured for Dante to take a seat. "I didn't realize you were with the doctor. We've got a few minutes before the others get here. I needed some time to get you up to speed on the plan."

"Not a problem. I'm still figuring out how to make this thing with Tyra work. I mean, Nova Force is my family, but Tyra…"

Trinity beamed. "Is an amazing woman who deserves your time and attention, too. Believe me, we understand."

Dax gave her an affectionate smile. "Yes, we do. It's not easy to juggle it all sometimes, but it can be done."

"Usually with minimal bloodshed," Trin added.

"Well, if it comes to that, at least Tyra knows how to put me back together again. *Fraxx* knows she's had to do it enough times already."

They laughed and changed the topic to the upcoming meeting. Dax laid out his approach and objectives in succinct terms, checking the time more than once to make sure he got the pertinent information to Dante before the meeting began.

The scheduled start time came and went with no sign of the Bellex representatives. "They're playing games with us," Trinity muttered in frustration.

"Annoying, but not surprising. I'm not sure how the corporations actually get anything done with all the petty politics they indulge in." Dax leaned back in his chair with a disgruntled sigh. "Computer, please confirm the location of Dr. Downs and Mr. Everest."

"Both beings are currently in the private mess assigned to visitors, Commander Rossi."

"Of course they are. Probably making last minute plans about how to handle this meeting," Trinity said.

"Computer, please notify me when Dr. Downs and Mr. Everest are 10 meters away from my location."

"Yes, Commander Rossi," the ship's AI replied.

The three of them spent the next while chatting quietly, discussing the mission, their theories, and concerns. Most of those concerns were about Nico. None of them wanted him to wind up back in Bellex's hands. If this went the way they all suspected it would and Nico wound up testifying against the corporation that owned him, he'd need more than just his freedom from Bellex. He'd need a place, and people, willing and able to protect him.

Eventually, Downs and Everest made an appearance. Neither of them even acknowledged their tardy arrival, never mind apologizing for making everyone wait. Downs looked even dourer than she had during his meeting with her only that morning, though Everest seemed as affable as ever. He selected the seat directly across from Dante, and as he sat, Dante was struck by a sense of familiarity.

He'd had Eric pull Everest's company file earlier that day. His parents had been mid-level Bellex employees, both deceased. Everest had scored well on his qualifying exams and been selected for executive training. He was moving up the ranks with impressive speed, but so far, none of his assignments had taken him outside the shipyards of this system, and Dante had never been to the Bellex system before this mission.

Downs shifted her chair, putting a little extra distance between herself and Everest. She set down a data pad and looked squarely at Dante, her lips drawn into a tight, disapproving line. "Why is the sergeant here? I've already spoken to him today. In fact, I wanted to relay to you how uncooperative he was."

Dante folded his arms across his chest and stared at Downs while he waited for Dax to speak. This was the commander's show. Dante was here for one reason—to look intimidating.

Dax lifted an eyebrow. "I reviewed the footage of the interview, and I stand by Sergeant Strak's responses. You were informed from the beginning there were some elements of this investigation you would not have access to. By asking about matters you already knew were off limits, it might be construed that you have violated the agreement that allows you to be here at all."

"It does not! We were led to believe that you and your team would be cooperating fully with us. Instead, we've been stonewalled, kept in the dark about the status of the investigation, and denied access to the med-bay, which we know is where you're conducting tests on the sample of cobalt you obtained. I was sent here because I'm the best equipped to run those experiments, and you won't even let me into that part of the ship."

"Bellex might consider you the best equipped, but my superiors elected to have Dr. Li manage that part of the investigation. She is more than qualified, as well as being an unbiased outsider."

Downs snorted. "Unbiased? Really? It's come to my

attention that at least one member of her team was a corporate spy."

"How did you learn about that?" Trinity demanded.

"You're not the only one investigating what happened to Dr. Li and her team. The local Corp-Sec team uncovered the truth and let me know, since it seemed Nova Force didn't feel like sharing that piece of information."

"That's one of the reasons I called this meeting, actually. You'll find it listed on the agenda you were sent." Dax leaned forward and pushed a data tablet across the table toward Downs. "The other reason we're here is to discuss Dr. Li's findings." He tapped the tablet before withdrawing his hand. "I'd like here your explanation as to how Bellex 3, a planet solely owned and controlled by Bellex Corp, became the testing ground for a mind-altering drug with alarming similarities to a recreational pharma known as crimson."

"A testing ground? Crimson? Is this the narrative Nova Force has spun to try to put Bellex out of business?" Downs snatched up the tablet and started reading, her brow furrowing deeper with each line she perused.

Dax responded while she was still reading. "Nova Force doesn't try to put corporations out of business. We investigate crimes and suspicious incidents. If we find evidence of wrongdoing, we proceed accordingly. Our mandate is to ensure the corporations obey the laws as set out in the Unified Galactic Agreement. We don't spin narratives, we enforce the law."

She set the tablet down on the table hard enough it clattered. "I don't see it that way. I refuse to accept these findings until I see the supporting documentation. Then I want to replicate these myself to verify them."

"The data was provided to you as a courtesy. Whether you accept it or not, our findings have already been sent to Nova Force Headquarters. Furthermore, now that we have sufficient cause, I'm formally requesting that you allow us to take blood samples from a randomly selected group of Bellex workers so we can screen it for cobalt."

"This is unacceptable. You've been moving so slowly on this investigation I wasn't sure you were accomplishing anything at all, and now, suddenly, you're fast-tracking the process and giving us no time to process what's happened or respond."

"We've been moving as fast as we can. Investigations, done properly, take time to piece together."

Everest cleared his throat, then spoke in a gratingly cheerful tone. "Dr. Downs, We're all on the same side, here. I'm as frustrated as you are, but I think you can agree that everyone has been working hard to get this investigation done the right way."

Her reaction was surprisingly understated given how agitated she'd been only a few seconds before. "Oh. Well, yes. Of course we're on the same side, but this could have been done much quicker if I'd been allowed to do the job I came here to do."

Everest replied before Dax could, trying once again to diffuse the situation. "Speed is not always a virtue, Dr. Downs. Rushing leads to mistakes, and mistakes are messy."

The others kept talking, but Dante wasn't listening anymore. He was staring at Everest and replaying the last words he'd said. Words he had heard before. The voices droned as he raised his hand, using it to block out

Everest's face while leaving the rest of his body visible. *Son of a* fraxxing *bitch.*

He was on his feet the next second, lunging across the table to grab Everest by the shirt and hauled him off his feet. "You! I knew you were familiar! You bastard, you jammed an explosive chip into my neck. Did you think I'd forget you after that?"

The room erupted into chaos. Downs screamed and scuttled backward, Trinity dove into the fray, and Dax barked out an order that overrode Dante's fury. "Put Mr. Everest down and explain yourself, Sergeant!"

Dante wanted to tear Everest's head off, but he knew better than to disobey his commander. He let go of the smaller man, dropping him onto the table with a satisfying thunk before turning to face Dax, coming to attention, and snapping off a crisp salute. "Apologies for the disruption, sir. I've been trying to figure out where I know this man from since I first saw him. It didn't hit me until just now. I recognized the phrase he used, sir. Word for word. It's the same thing my abductor said while I was held prisoner on the planet."

Everest had struggled back to his feet while Dante explained, then backed as far away from him as the room allowed. "I was on this ship during that event. It couldn't have been me. Your entire crew is my alibi!"

"I can't explain it, sir. But I know he was there. Though, I got the impression the man I met on the surface was older…but it's the same man. The voice. The hair. The build. I'm certain it's him."

"You'd better be. You're putting your career on the line here, Strak. And so am I." Dax turned to Everest. "Chad Everest, you are hereby taken into Nova Force custody."

"For what? I've done nothing. Nothing! I was here with you during the entire event on Bellex 3. This is insane." He turned to his cohort, and Dante caught an edge of command to his next words. "Debba, tell them this isn't acceptable."

Dax raised a brow, which told Dante he'd caught the shift in tone, too.

Downs didn't react as if she'd been given an order, however. Instead, she stepped away from Everest and shrugged. "As you pointed out earlier, we are all on the same side, Chad. We both know you were on the *Malora* the whole time, so the sooner we cooperate with this farcical demand, the sooner you'll be exonerated."

"Are you sure that's the best course of action?" Everest asked in a lowly, silky smooth tone that set Dante's teeth on edge.

The doctor's gaze dropped to Everest's hands. His finger was resting lightly atop a slender band of polished silver. Another fragment of Dante's memories clicked into place. He'd seen that band before, too. "Put your hands on the tabletop right now, Mr. Everest."

Everest didn't look happy, but he complied with the order and grudgingly set his hands on the table. The moment he did, Trinity stepped in behind him and looked at Dante. "What did you see?"

"That band on his left wrist. I don't know what it is, exactly, but I think it's some kind of weapon." He glanced over to Downs. "You know what that is, don't you?"

She did her best, but her micro-expressions revealed the truth before she uttered a word. "I don't know what you're talking about."

Trinity removed the object from Everest's wrist with

care and handed it to Dax, who examined it briefly and then turned his attention to his two guests. "Dr. Downs, I assume you will want to notify your superiors what has happened here. You may do that now, if you wish, while Lieutenant West and I have a word with Mr. Everest, here."

"I uh. Of course. They will not be pleased about this. Not at all. Your treatment of Mr. Everest and I will be reported."

"I'm sure it will." Dax didn't look concerned by the news. They'd heard it all before. Every time one of the corporations got caught breaking the law, they went on the attack.

"Sir, I'd like permission to be part of the questioning of Mr. Everest," Dante said.

"Permission denied. You're to give this to Ensign Erben for safekeeping." He handed over the metal band. "Then I need a supplemental report from you detailing your actions today and why you felt they were necessary."

"Yes, sir."

"Dismissed, Sergeant."

Dante nodded and turned to Downs. "After you, ma'am."

He kept his eye on her as they left. She didn't look at Everest even once, and as they left the room, he saw her shoulders sag. He didn't know what the *fraxx* was going on with these two, but it was clear things were not as they appeared. One day, they'd have a nice, simple, straightforward investigation where the motive was obvious and no one lied. Today was not that day.

CHAPTER SEVENTEEN

T YRA STOOD at Nico's bedside and watched the boy sleep. He was resting quietly after the procedure, and by the time he woke up, the minute incision she'd made wouldn't show at all. She'd left the tattoo for now.

She checked his vitals one last time, then left him to take another look at the microchip she'd removed. It looked so harmless now. It was smaller than the one Dante had been injected with, which she assumed was because it was only made to carry information, not explosives.

Later, she'd give it to Eric to look at. Of course, she'd have to tell the others what she'd done, first, starting with Dante. Once he'd finished scolding her for keeping her plan a secret, he'd help her find the right way to inform the commander.

When the med-bay door opened, she assumed it was Dante. She set the chip down and turned to greet him, only to stare in confusion. There was no one there.

"Well, that's odd," she muttered to herself and turned away.

"Not odd. Just good tech." A woman's voice came out of thin air somewhere to her left.

Tyra spun in that direction in time to see the air dance in distorted waves to reveal Dr. Downs with a blaster in her hand and a cold smile on her face. "Hello, Dr. Li."

Tyra kept her shock at bay long enough to position herself between Downs and Nico. "I don't know how you got in here, but you can't have him. Nico deserves so much better than anything Bellex could ever give him."

Downs actually looked surprised. "You think I'm here for the boy?"

"You're not? What else could you want? I'm damned sure you can get your hands on a sample of cobalt anytime you like."

"You're right." Downs' calm confession hit Tyra like a runaway comet.

"I'm... what?"

"Right. About all of it. Bellex, the cobalt, the hellish and probably very short life that boy will have if he goes back to the company." She waved a hand at herself. "They own me, too. At least, they did. You're going to help me change that."

"Like hell I am."

Downs lowered the blaster slightly. "I don't have time for this, so I'll make it simple. You managed to get the chip out of the kid's neck, and now you're going to remove mine. That's all I want."

"How did you know about that? And how the *fraxx* did you get in here?" Tyra's mind was racing as she tried to make sense of everything.

Downs growled in frustration. "There's no time. Right now, your teammates are distracted, and so is Everest. This is my chance. My only chance. Whatever tools you used to get that thing out of the boy, grab them and come with me."

"No."

"If you don't, I'll kill him." She stepped to the side and pointed the blaster at the bed where Nico slept. "You can try to stop me, but it will take the others a while to get here, and I'm a decent shot. The odds are not in your favor."

Tyra knew that if she went with the other woman, the chances of her living to see another day were close to zero, but she wouldn't risk Nico's life to save her own. Dante would understand. If the worst happened, he'd take care of the boy. In fact, he'd be the perfect protector and mentor. The thought gave her pause. If she lived, she'd have to give that more consideration.

She nodded. "I'll go with you, but only if you leave him alone. And he stays here. If you want a hostage, you'll have to make do with me."

Downs lowered the blaster. "Like I said, he's of no interest to me. Get moving. We don't have long."

Tyra went to the sterilizer, pulled the instruments out she'd need, and placed them in her med-kit. While she was doing that, she managed to pull her comm out of her pocket and tuck it into the kit without Downs noticing. "You still didn't tell me how you got in here, or how you think we're going to walk out of here together."

Downs patted a small device attached to her belt. "It's called a personal shield generator. I don't understand the technobabble, but basically, it bends light around the wearer, making me more or less invisible. Very handy little gadget. We're not going to walk out of here—you are. At least, that's what the ship's sensors will think."

"You're not hiding at the moment, though."

"No need. This ship's AI was very helpful. It explained that it was monitoring the corridors of the off-limit areas, not the rooms themselves."

There hadn't been time to activate the distress beacon on her communicator in the second she had to smuggle it into the kit, but eventually, Downs would let her guard down. All Tyra had to do was be ready to move when that moment came. She closed her med-kit and set the strap over her shoulder. "I'm ready. Where are we going?"

"Not yet. Where's your comm?" Downs demanded.

"On my desk, along with the chip I took out of Nico," she lied.

"I'm surprised you didn't call for help the second I showed up."

"I was distracted by the crazy lady pointing a weapon at me and an innocent child."

"I'm not crazy, I'm desperate. This chip in my neck contains an explosive. Fun fact, they designed these things to heat up to over one hundred degrees before they go boom, which means if I screw up, I don't just die, I die screaming. I've seen it happen, and I'm not going out that way." Downs gestured to the door. "Move it. And remember, you're walking alone. Nice and casual. No trying to attract attention, no sudden moves."

"Got it. Since I can't see you to follow you, you're going to need to tell me where we're going."

"Deck two. Shuttle bay four. I need to put as much distance between me and this *fraxxing* place as I can before they figure out what's going on. I don't know what the range is on the detonators, but it can't be that far, or they wouldn't have sent Chad on this mission."

"Chad? What detonators? You still haven't told me how you knew I removed Nico's chip, either."

"You are full of *fraxxing* questions, aren't you?" Downs touched a switch on the shield generator, and a second later she had vanished from sight, with only a faint shimmer marking her location. "I'll make you a deal. Do what I tell you when I tell you, and I'll answer all your questions once you've got this chip out of me. After that, I'll tell you every Bellex secret I know."

Tyra walked into the corridor and set out for the shuttle bay, hoping with every step that she'd cross paths with someone so she could signal them for help. She held onto that hope until she stepped on board the Bellex ship and the door sealed behind her with an ominous thud.

"Strap yourself in. It's going to be fast launch. Once I'm sure we're in the clear, you're going to take this thing out of my neck and give me my life back."

Tyra took her seat without saying a word. She hugged the med-kit to her chest and tried to work out a plan. If she activated the beacon now, the team would stop Downs, but Downs would have more than enough time to kill her before they got inside. Once she removed the chip, Downs would kill her anyway. That is, if she managed to remove it without setting off the explosives and killing them both. She needed to time this carefully if she wanted to get out of this alive.

The only thing she was certain of was that the moment she hit the beacon, Dante would come for her. No matter what happened next, she wasn't alone anymore.

Dante left the briefing room and headed to Eric's domain, a cubby-sized room aft of the cockpit. Inside the heavily-shielded room resided the electronic brain of the ship, along with an ever-expanding collection of partially repaired systems, tools, and spare parts that Eric affectionally referred to as his hoard.

He considered stopping by the med-bay to update Tyra on his way but decided against it. Dax would want a full report on what Everest's odd fashion accessory was and how it worked, and he'd want it soon. Dante had let his temper get the better of him back there, and that meant he needed to stay on target for the next while or he'd be on the receiving end of a verbal ass-kicking from his commander.

Eric was in his usual spot, reclined in a chair, feet propped up on the desk. His eyes were closed, and his slack expression clued Dante into the fact Eric was jacked directly into the *Malora's* system even before he spotted the telltale cord trailing from his arm jack.

He smacked Eric's boot. "Wakey-wakey, Magi. Commander's got a job for you."

Eric's eyes snapped open, and he held out a hand expectantly. "And hello to you too, Buttercup. Whatcha got for me?"

"A new toy for you to play with. I think it's some kind of weapon, so try not to blow us up while you're figuring out what it does."

Eric sat up and took the band from Dante eagerly. "Oh, shiny. Where'd this come from? Details, big guy. I'm going to need details."

"You weren't listening in?"

"Not this time. I've been running surface scans trying to find a match to the chemical signatures your Daisy gave me earlier."

"My Daisy? Please tell me that's not the nickname you've chosen for Tyra."

"You like it? It was that or Tiger Lily, but she seems more like a Daisy to me."

"What is it with you and the nicknames? You need a hobby. Get out more. Maybe try talking to people in the real world instead of that tribe of digital delinquents you call friends."

"The last time I tried that, it didn't go well for me, remember?" Eric's words were colored with hurt and regret. "I should probably stick to the digital world for a while. The real world is a little *too* real for me these days."

"You couldn't have known. You were only just getting to know her."

"I should have known something was up. That's our whole *fraxxing* job, and I didn't see it. Maybe if I had, she'd still be here. Maybe they'd all still be here."

"Yeah, and if wishes and buts were candy and nuts, no one would ever go hungry."

Eric's lips quirked into a momentary grin. "That's your sage advice? Really?"

"My mother wasn't big on wisdom."

Eric scoffed. "Or empathy, apparently."

"Not so much, no. Now, if we're done discussing the many ways the women in our pasts have let us down, can we get back to your new assignment?"

"Tell me about this shiny gizmo and what I missed while I was hooked in and tuned out."

Dante leaned against the wall, the only spot he fit in the cramped space, and recounted the highlights of the meeting with Downs and Everest. He included his recollections of his brief captivity. Eric interjected with occasional questions that helped jar loose a few more snippets of memory, and by the time he was done, he was even more certain Everest and the man he'd met on the surface were closely related.

"You got access to the DNA we pulled off me after I was taken?" he asked out of the blue.

"Yeah. Most of it belonged to the guys who gave you that beatdown."

"Any of it unmatched?"

Magi held up a finger and closed his eyes for a few seconds, scanning through the digital records through his data port instead of doing it manually. When his eyes opened again, he was grinning. "How'd you guess?"

"Playing a hunch. I'll ask Rossi to get a DNA sample from Everest and run it against our mystery match. They have to be connected somehow."

"It's worth a shot. I trust your hunches more than most people's facts."

"Thanks. I'm going to leave you to it. I need to talk to Rossi, and then I want to let Tyra know what happened."

"Say hi to Daisy for me," Eric gave him a jaunty wave before picking up the wristband.

"She's going to hate—" He was cut off by a strident alert erupting from his communicator, as well as Eric's.

"That's the emergency alert!" Eric exclaimed, dropping the band and activating a holographic display that filled the air around him with streams of data.

"Is it the ground team or Dax? Where do I need to be?"

Dante itched to be moving, but he needed a destination before he took off running, and Eric already had the information flowing directly into his mind.

"Neither. It's Tyra. Son of a starbeast, when did that happen?"

"When did what happen? Damn it, Magi, what's happened to Tyra?" He tried to lock down his emotions and think clearly. He grabbed his own comm and checked it. There was no mistake. The emergency beacon was from Tyra's device, and it was…

"When did she leave the *fraxxing* ship?"

"Hang on, big guy, I'm trying to figure that out."

"Do it *fraxxing* faster and tell me when you know something. I'm headed to the cockpit."

Eric merely nodded and kept working as Dante headed for the cockpit, dropping into his chair with enough force it groaned in protest. He ignored it and got to work, activating the standard drive engines while ignoring the computer's attempts to make him follow the required checklists and procedures. After a few seconds of fighting with it, he slammed his fist down on the edge of the console and snarled. "Computer, pilot override code gamma-seven-delta-three-zero-strike-zero. Authorization Strak, Dante. Confirm."

The computer chattered in what he swore was the electronic version of alarm and then replied. "Override code accepted and confirmed. Pilot has full manual control."

"Finally." He watched the displays show the engines wind up to full power. Not that it mattered. He couldn't go anywhere until he had a destination. Tyra was out there, and he needed to get to her. Now.

"Magi! Get me some *fraxxing* coordinates," he roared, not bothering with the communicator, or even turning around in his chair.

"Are we going somewhere?" Dax's voice cut through the red fog of anger and worry that clouded Dante's mind.

"Tyra's distress beacon went off. She's not on the ship, sir!"

"I know. Which is why I'm here. You're about to head after her in my ship, leaving our ground team unsupported on the planet." Dax clapped a hand on Dante's shoulder. "Take a breath, Strak. You're no good to her if you're not thinking clearly."

He sucked in a lungful of air, exhaled sharply, and turned to look up at Dax. "Now can I go after her, sir?"

"Now *we* can go after her. Permission to leave orbit granted...once we have her location." He raised his voice to a shout. "Magi, we need coordinates."

"Got 'em! Should be coming up on your screen right now."

Dante locked the coordinates into the nav-computer. She was headed out of the system on a damned fast ship. Luckily, the *Malora* was faster. He hit the maneuvering thrusters, turning the ship end over end and pointing her away from the planet, then opened the throttle. "I'm coming for you, sweetheart. And when I find you, I'm never letting you out of my sight again."

CHAPTER EIGHTEEN

TYRA COULDN'T EVEN LOOK at her comm to confirm her emergency beacon had activated. She'd done exactly what Eric had instructed, pressing the power button three times in rapid succession and then holding it down for a three-second count. After that, she'd dropped it to the bottom of her med-kit and continued pulling out the instruments she'd need for a surgical procedure she had no intention of performing.

The ship she was on was the epitome of luxury. The area she could see had soft lighting, deep taupe carpets that muffled the sound of the engines, and tasteful furnishings that made the most of the limited space. There was even a small dining area with a polished wooden table and matching chairs.

"How'd we get away from the *Malora* without them noticing?" She asked.

Downs was still piloting, but she twisted around in her seat to answer. "The ship's AI thinks we're still sitting in the shuttle bay. I'm relaying our transponders' signal through another nifty gadget my employers provided me. Getting the bay doors open was a little trickier, but nothing this ship's AI couldn't handle. It's a lot smarter than the *Malora*."

"Where do you want to do the procedure? I'll need to sterilize the area, and it should be somewhere you can lie flat. It would be best if you were sedated, too, but I don't imagine you're going to agree to that."

"Sedation? Not going to happen. If I take a nap, I'm going to wake up in restraints…if I wake up at all."

Tyra finished sorting through her med-kit. She'd been looking for anything she could use was a laser scalpel. It wasn't long enough to do serious injury, but it was better than nothing. "You still haven't explained why you think I can remove your chip without setting off the explosive, or how you knew I'd taken Nico's chip out."

"Nico's chip has similar anti-tampering technology to mine. The difference is that his was only designed to emit an alert if it was messed with. Mine has, well, let's just call them far more aggressive settings."

"If I didn't set it off, how did you know about Nico's?" She was missing something, and if she ended up doing the surgery, she needed every bit of information she could get.

"You didn't set off the primary alert. You set off the backup, which is triggered when the chip is exposed to normal atmosphere for more than two minutes."

"And yours has the same settings?"

"As far as I can tell, yes. Which means once you get it out, your next move will be to toss it out the nearest airlock. Right over there." She pointed to a hatchway midway down the room.

"It would have been safer to do this back on the *Malora*.

I'm not sure either one of us is going to survive this. What if we went back and—"

"No. Everest isn't the only one who can detonate my chip. There are others, and I need to put as much distance between us as I can. These things have to have a finite range, and I've got a head start. I'm not giving that up."

She pointed to the dining area. "We'll use the table. Don't worry about sterilizing it. The incision isn't going to be big enough to be a concern." Downs fixed her with a fierce stare. "Right?"

"Of course not."

She took everything she'd need and set it up by the table. Downs was still at the controls, which worried Tyra. By now, Dante and the rest of the team should be coming after her, and she didn't want Downs spotting their approach.

"Ready when you are."

"I suppose this is far enough. The computer can take it from here." Downs tapped in some commands then rose from her chair and stepped out of the cockpit.

"I'm going to administer the pain blocker myself, and I'll be making the incision. Nothing personal, but there's no way I'm letting you near my throat with a scalpel."

"You're going to operate on yourself? How?"

"You're going to help, but I'll hold the blade." There was an odd gleam in Down's eyes now, a tiny spark of madness that warned Tyra the other woman was at her breaking point.

"Whatever you want." Tyra gestured to the laser

scalpel she'd laid out with the other instruments. "It's right there."

The second one was already tucked up her sleeve. She didn't know when her opportunity would come, but it had to be soon.

"Then let's get this done." She walked past Tyra, set down the blaster, and grabbed the bottle of old-fashioned antiseptic Tyra kept in the kit for emergencies. For a moment, Downs was vulnerable. This was her chance.

She dropped the scalpel into her hand, activated the blade, and drove it into the other woman's neck as she tried to push past Downs to reach the weapon. She fumbled the grab, only managing to knock the blaster off the table out of her reach.

Downs screeched and turned on Tyra, tossing the antiseptic solution at her. The solution stung her eyes, making it almost impossible to see.

Downs was on her a split second later, lashing out with wild, uncontrolled strikes that sent Tyra scrambling backward. She still had the scalpel in her hand, and she slashed the air in front of her in wild sweeps, trying to hold the other woman at bay while desperately rubbing her eyes with her sleeve, trying to recover her vision.

They fought like that for what felt like forever but was likely only a minute or two.

"Proximity alert. Proximity alert. There is another ship approaching rapidly. Maintain course?" The ship's AI interrupted the fight.

"That's the *Malora*," Tyra announced triumphantly.

"No! You've killed me. Do you understand? I'm a dead woman!!"

Downs came at her again, and this time Tyra managed

to slice open her cheek with the blade. It cauterized as it cut, but that didn't lessen the pain.

"I'm not the one who chose to work for monsters. You brought this on yourself."

Downs stopped fighting. She dropped to her knees, her injured face cradled in her hands. "That may be true, but I still don't want to die."

Tyra looked down at the broken woman and made an offer that surprised them both. "I can take it out. Right here. Right now. I just need to let the others know I'm alright, first, and then I'll do it."

"Why would you do that?"

"Because I still remember the oath I took when I became a doctor."

Downs lifted her head a little and parted her fingers so she could look up at Tyra. "Contact them. Do what you need to. Just please, don't let me die. I'll tell you everything I know, just like I promised."

"Prove it to me. Tell me something valuable, right now."

Downs sniffled. "You couldn't find the cobalt because we added it directly to the water supply at the factories. Only the workers were supposed to get it, but someone got greedy. Stupid. They sold it as recreational pharma. Some of the factory workers tried it and overdosed because they already had it in their system and didn't know it. That's when the trouble started, and by the time we got the mess cleaned up, word had gotten out. The people I work for don't tolerate mistakes like that, and they terminated anyone they thought might have been involved."

"And my team? Why were we targeted?"

"Bellex should have never let you on the *fraxxing* planet. When they caved to outside pressure, it caused all sorts of problems. By the time they told us you'd arrived, it was too late. Your team had seen too much to be allowed to leave, and we couldn't move on to the next stage until you were out of the way. I'm sorry about your team, but I had my orders." She touched the side of her neck. "It was them or me."

"You killed some of the best people I knew. They were my friends."

"I know. And for what it's worth, I really am sorry."

"Darner had a chip in his neck, too. You removed it during the autopsy, right? That's why he killed himself."

Downs nodded. "Yes. There, I'm cooperating. Do you think that's enough to get Nova Force to agree to protect me?"

For Tyra, it wasn't nearly enough to make up for what she'd done, but it was a start.

"If you continue to cooperate, I believe they'll protect you." Tyra kept the scalpel in her hand and gave Downs a wide berth on her way to her med-kit. She retrieved her communicator and sent a ping to the entire team to let them know she was ready to communicate. It was only a few seconds before Dante's face appeared on the screen. "Tyra? Tell me you're okay. Where's Downs? What happened to your face?"

"I'm okay. Dr. Downs and I had a fight. I'm not badly hurt, but she is. She's ready to surrender and give you all the information she has in exchange for Nova Force's protection. If you agree, she'll come quietly."

Dax joined the conversation, his face appearing as an

inset image in the corner of the screen. "Tell Dr. Downs she has herself a deal."

"I will. I just need to remove a chip from her neck before you all come aboard. There's a small chance it might explode, so you should probably stay away until I'm done."

Dante stared at her through the monitor. "What the hell am I going to do with you, Shortcake? You can't keep trying to save the people who want to kill you."

At her feet, Downs wailed in pain and clawed at the side of her neck, leaving bloody tracks carved into her skin. "No. No. Please, no. Not this." She looked up at Tyra with wild eyes full of terror and pain. "It's burning me. Inside."

"Tyra? What the hell is happening?" Dante demanded.

Tyra ignored him and stared at the woman kneeling broken and bleeding, on the floor. "The chip?"

She gave a frantic nod, her breathing ragged now. "You have to get away from me."

"Maybe there's still time to get it out."

Downs shook her head, and her last word came out as an agonized shriek. "Run!"

"I'm sorry." Guilt at abandoning Downs to a horrible death tore through her as she turned and ran toward the airlock, the doctor's screams accompanying her every step of the way.

She made it to the door and slapped at the controls until it opened, then hurled herself inside. She forced herself to stop and think before touching anything on the inner panel. If she hit the wrong key, she could wind up dying in the vacuum of space instead of being blown up. She closed the door and moved away from it, pressing her back against the outer wall of the ship. It was quiet inside, but the agonized screams of a dying woman still reverberated inside her head.

"Tyra! Damn it, talk to me! What's going on?"

She finally remembered she hadn't told Dante what was happening. She lifted the communicator and tried to muster a reassuring smile. "I'm okay. But... keep the *Malora* clear. Someone activated the chip in Debba's neck. She's going to die, and I can't stop it. She told me to run..."

"Where are you right now?"

"The airlock."

Dante's expression softened the slightest bit. "Okay. Airlock is good. Solid. It should survive—" An explosion tore through the ship, sending her to her knees as the floor jerked and bucked beneath her. The screen of her communicator flickered and then died. The artificial gravity ceased, the lights went out, and she was left floating in total darkness, listening to the random pings and groans of the wounded ship outside the airlock door.

She curled into a ball and drifted, eventually remembering to try the communicator again. It turned on, but no one answered her messages. She was alone again.

DANTE HAD BEEN in more crisis situations than he could count in his life, but none of them hit him as hard as this one. Dax had ordered him to retrieve Tyra before he could even ask for permission to go, and he'd made the trek to the shuttle bay at a full sprint

Whoever had triggered Dr. Downs device had gone for

a double event and taken out Everest as well. The simultaneous explosions had rocked the *Malora* and temporarily taken down some of her systems – including communication. He had no way to talk to Tyra. No way to know if she had survived the blast that had blown a hole in the smaller ship's hull.

It was the first time he'd left his team during a crisis. The Malora was damaged, her systems crippled. He was needed on board, but Tyra needed him more.

Magi updated him on the condition of both vessels as he ran, and once he fired up the smaller of the Malora's two shuttles, he could see the readouts for himself. He cried out in relief as a single life sign appeared inside the Bellex ship. Tyra was still alive. "Hang on. I'm coming, sweetheart."

As he maneuvered the shuttle toward the drifting wreck of the Bellex ship, he could see the damage for himself. The explosion that had killed Downs had punched a relatively small hole in the hull, and the shattered contents of the ship were now floating around the wreckage. The explosive decompression had forced everything through the hole, making it wider and tearing the larger items apart in the process.

There would have been a similar hole in the hull of the *Malora*, but her hull-plating was military grade and contained the blast. The only permanent damage had been to Everest himself. Their prisoner was dead, his body reduced to a bloody jigsaw puzzle with most of the pieces gone.

The explosions had happened at the exact same moment, a clear announcement that someone, somewhere, had deemed it time to tidy up their loose ends. Dante suspected the decision had been triggered by Tyra's action. He'd been too focused on her to notice anything else, but Magi had noted that when Tyra had opened a channel to them, she'd done it without activating the encryption keys. They could never be certain, and he'd never tell her, but that small lapse likely gave their enemy enough information to know their assets had been compromised.

He docked the two ships via their airlocks, grateful again that Tyra had the good sense to pick one of the most reinforced parts of the ship to hide in, as well as the one with the easiest access for rescue. He stepped into the airlock and began the process of sealing, then opening, the various doors on his side. If Tyra was hurt or unconscious, he'd have to override the other ship's airlock from the outside, costing him precious time. There was breathable atmosphere in her part of the ship, but the room was small, and there was no life support. He had to get her out of there before she ran out of oxygen or froze to death.

The outer door on his ship finally opened, exposing the hatch of the Bellex vessel. He reached for the release handle, but someone was already moving it from inside. *Tyra.*

The second the door opened, she cried his name, launched herself into his arms, and then tumbled as she crossed over into the artificial gravity of his shuttle. He caught her before she reached the ground, cradling her close to his chest.

He couldn't stop smiling as he looked down at her bruised and bloodied face, part of his mind taking inventory of her injuries. Someday, someone would pay for this. The deaths. The suffering. The hurt. But for now, he was grateful to have her back in his arms, alive and well. "Hey, Shortcake. You okay?"

"I am now."

He bowed his head and kissed the cold skin of her forehead. "Don't you ever scare me like that again. I thought I might have lost you back there."

"The thought crossed my mind, too." She reached up and slipped a freezing cold hand behind his neck, pulling him in closer. "That's when I realized something kind of important, and I promised myself I'd tell you as soon as I saw you again, so here it goes. I love you, Dante. I know the timing sucks, and it's probably too soon, but well, I do."

"About time you figured it out. I've known how I feel about you for a couple of hours at least."

"Yeah? And how do you feel?"

"You're going to make me say it?"

She laughed, nodding, and the last worry and fear fell away from his soul. "You bet I am."

He lifted her higher in his arms, his mouth a fraction of an inch from hers, now. "I love you, Tyra Li. To the end of the universe and back again."

He didn't know which of them moved first, but once their lips met, he poured his heart into that kiss, crushing her to him. She was his, now, and no matter what it took, he'd find a way to keep her with him, always.

CHAPTER NINETEEN

DANTE KEPT her in his lap for the short flight back to the *Malora*. They talked the whole way, updating each other with the highlights of what they'd experienced with since they'd parted only a few hours ago. It was hard to take it all in. Everest's involvement. Dante's suspicions that he was related somehow to the stranger who'd planned to experiment on him. And now, Everest and Downs were both dead, killed by some terrible, secret organization she hadn't even known existed until recently.

Dante listened intently to everything she shared too. He even took an audio recording of her recital of events, though he stopped the recording when she told him about taking the chip out of Nico's neck.

"*Veth*, woman. You should have told me what you were planning."

"If I had, you would have been complicit in my crime. I didn't want my decision affecting anyone else on the team."

He gave her a look of rueful frustration. "And how did that work out for you?"

"Not great," she admitted.

"And what did we learn?"

She stuck her tongue out at him. "That you're not nearly so sexy when you're lecturing me."

"Apart from that."

"Next time, no going it alone." She leaned in and kissed his cheek to take the sting out of her next words. "But that goes for you, too. You don't have to prove your worth to anyone, Dante. Your team, your commander, and me, we all know what kind of man you are, and how important you are to us."

"I'll do my best, but charging into danger is kind of my forte."

"I remember. If you hadn't, I wouldn't be here now. I don't need you to stop being who you are. I just don't want you doing it alone. If you bring your team with you, I know they'll bring you safely home to me."

"I can do that. I like the idea of coming home to you."

"I like it, too."

As he set the shuttle down on the floor of the shuttle bay, she settled deeper into his lap and asked the question that had been foremost in her mind since she'd found herself adrift in a dead ship. "What happens now?"

Dante chuckled. "It feels like something monumental should come next, doesn't it? I feel that way too, but the truth is, nothing much is going to change. Not yet. We still need to wrap up our investigation, which means the only one of us going anywhere is Dr. Castille. He's got a lot to answer for."

"Yes, he does. But at least I know now that he wasn't

the reason my team was killed. That was Downs, and she got her orders from the Gray Men." Just saying their name made her feel uneasy. They were still out there, and she was on their radar, now. Even if she wanted to go back to her old life, it wouldn't be the same. It was time for something new.

Dante tightened his arms around her in a comforting hug. "We'll find them eventually. And when we do, we'll end them. That's why Nova Force exists. It's what we do."

She believed him. But between today and the day they found the last member of the Grays, she knew the only time she'd truly feel safe was when she was with him.

When they landed, Dante insisted on taking her to the med-bay to get checked out, despite the fact the only one around to do the check was herself.

Once they were there, he folded his arms across his chest and glowered at her. "You're not doing it yourself. You'll slap on a bandage and tell me you're fine. Get the diagnostic system to look you over. If it says you're good, then I'm letting you out of here, but not before."

"This is your revenge for me using that restraining field to keep you in bed while you healed, isn't it?" she asked.

"Maybe. But it's still happening," Dante stated.

"And I'm backing his call," Dax added. The commander had met them in the shuttle bay with the latest news. They'd found Nico in the med-bay and moved him safely back to his quarters, where he was still asleep. Castille was secure in his holding cell, and the rest of the team were on their way back to the *Malora*. Eric was still working on getting some of the systems back online, but he'd restored communication, and help was on the way.

One advantage to being in the middle of a system-sized shipyard—getting the *Malora* repaired would not be an issue.

"Alright. Alright. I'll run the damned program, but I'm telling you, I'm fine."

"Sweetheart, have you looked in a mirror, lately? You know I think you're gorgeous, but a black eye is not the sexiest look for you."

"I've got a black eye? Why didn't you tell me? I thought it was just swollen from the antiseptic she threw in my face."

"This is going to be an interesting report to read, isn't it?" Dax asked Dante.

"You have no idea, sir. My Shortcake kicked some serious ass."

"Which is not something you should be proud of. I'm a doctor. I'm supposed to heal people, not hurt them."

"Special circumstances, remember?" Dante reminded her.

"You're going to need to keep reminding me of that for a while." She hit the scan button and held as still as she could manage. Now that she was paying attention, she could feel the aches and pains that she hadn't let herself register before. Dante was right, again. She was a bit of a medical mess.

The system finished and beeped at her, and the diagnosis flashed up on a screen, along with its recommended course of treatment. There was nothing seriously wrong. Just abrasions, bruises, and a slightly lowered body temperature from her time in the airlock.

"See? Even the computer thinks I'm fine. More or less.

All I need is a mild pain-blocker, some healing accelerant, and rest."

"You take care of the first two, I'll see to the last one." Dante looked over at Dax. "Permission to escort the doctor to her quarters and ensure she gets to bed? After that, I'll help Magi with repairs."

"Trin is already helping Magi, and the others will be here soon. You're assigned to debrief the doctor and see to it she gets the rest she needs. You're still supposed to be on light duty, anyway, Buttercup."

Tyra went over to the dispensary and selected the medications she needed. "I'm never going to get used to that nickname for you."

"Wait until you hear yours," Dax said, laughing now.

"I have a nickname? Who gave me that?"

"Magi, of course. Apparently, your new name is Dr. Daisy."

She considered that while injecting herself with the prescribed medications. "It could be worse. I was prepared for any nicknames to be dessert-related."

They all laughed at that, then Dax took his leave.

"You're really okay?" Dante asked as he wrapped her in his arms in a tender hug.

"I am. Honestly, I probably look worse than I feel right now. The pain-blocker is already helping, though, and in a few hours the swelling and bruising will be mostly gone. I'm going to be fine."

"How long will it take for you to forgive yourself for not being able to help Downs?"

"That recovery won't be as quick. I know she wasn't a good person, but the way she died..." She would be hearing those screams in her nightmares for a very long time.

He gave her a gentle squeeze. "I know. Stuff like this leaves a scar. Just don't let it cut too deep, okay? I'm not exactly the galaxy's most gifted communicator, but if you need to talk about it, I'm here."

She let her head rest against his chest and nodded. "Thanks."

"You ready to head out?"

"I think so."

"Good. Because despite your insistence that you're fine, I'm not going to believe that until I've seen for myself." He released his hold to take her hand and led her to the door.

"This is all a ruse to get me naked again, isn't it?" she teased.

"Maybe. But it's also true. When we got your distress signal and I realized you weren't on the ship, I lost my mind. Then there was the explosion, and I lost my mind again not knowing if you were okay." His hand tightened around hers. "I promised to take care of you, and I failed."

"You didn't fail. I'm still here, aren't I? I went with her to protect Nico, but it was an easy choice, because I knew you'd come after me." He'd been there for her since the day they'd met, and in her heart, she knew he always would be.

As badly as Dante wanted to get Tyra safely ensconced in his quarters, there was one more stop they needed to make on the way. The moment they turned left instead of right, Tyra's footsteps quickened.

"We're going to see Nico?" she asked.

"Yeah. He's going to hear about your off-ship adventure eventually. This way he won't be worried. Plus, I know you'll want to make sure he's healing up after the procedure you did."

"You're right on both counts." She was smiling now, and it looked good on her.

It took Nico less than two seconds to open the door, and the moment he saw Tyra the boy's eyes widened and he flew into her arms. "You gots hurt! How?"

"I'm okay, Nico. It's just a few bumps and bruises."

The boy clung to her. "You was gone when I woke up."

Tyra stroked Nico's hair, beaming down at him with obvious affection. "I know. Some bad things happened, and I had to go for awhile. I'm back now, though. How's your neck?"

Nico gave her a calculating look. "If I tell you it hurts a little, can I have the rest of my ice cream?"

Her answering laughter was the most beautiful sound in the world. "You can have your ice cream even if it doesn't hurt at all."

"Okay. It doesn't really hurt, but I'm starving! I haven't eaten in hours."

"Go get your ice cream, you little con artist. I need to take Doc Li to get some rest."

Nico nodded, gave Tyra one last hug, stepped back, and gave Dante a startlingly adult look. "You take good care of her."

Dante raised a hand and gave him a crisp salute. "Yes, sir. That's exactly what I plan on doing."

Nico's face erupted into a broad grin and he stood ramrod straight. "Carry on then, Sergeant." Then he ran off giggling.

"He's quite amazing, isn't he?" Tyra asked as they watched him vanish down the corridor.

"Yeah, he is."

"If he's going to be a witness, he's going to need someone to take care of him for the next few months. Like a guardian."

Dante nodded. "Yeah, he is. The Commander and I were talking about that earlier today."

She leaned into his side. "I think it should be you."

"You do? Why? I don't know a damned thing about kids."

"He idolizes you already, and there is no one in the galaxy I trust to take better care of that little boy than you. Bellex isn't going to want him to testify, and we both know they're more than capable of silencing him forever if they thought it would help their case. I can't protect him from them, but you can."

He scooped her into his arms and carried her the rest of the way back to his quarters.

The moment they were sealed inside, he set her down and leaned back against the door.

"Clothes off."

"You know the rule, big guy. If I'm naked, you're naked."

"Right." He shed his uniform with a speed borne of years of practice, and came to help her finish undressing. Despite her assurances, she was moving slowly, and as she bared her body to him, he saw why. Her ribs and stomach were bruised in several spots, and even though they were already responding to treatment, he knew firsthand they'd still be tender.

He circled her, taking inventory of the damage. "First thing we're doing is taking a long, hot shower together. Then I'm going to kiss every one of these booboos better. Then, I'm keeping you in bed for the rest of the day. The droids can bring us something to eat later. Sound like a plan?"

"Sounds like the best plan I've ever heard."

He stole another kiss, planting a hand on the soft curve of her ass. She ground herself against his already hard cock, tempting him to forgo the shower in favour of going straight to bed, but he didn't give in. She'd been through hell, and nothing fixed that feeling faster than the bliss of a long, hot shower.

He led her to the sanitation room, and for once didn't lament the lack of space. It meant they were wrapped around each other from the moment they stepped inside the shower cubby.

"Not too hot?" he asked as the water flowed over them.

"Perfect."

"Tell me if I hit any sore spots, okay?" He slipped an arm around her waist while his free hand reached up to cup one breast in his hand. She reacted with a soft sigh and closed her eyes, letting her head fall back so the water hit her upturned face and streamed through her hair. He bent his head and kissed her, enjoying the sweet taste of her lips as he released her breast to slide a hand carefully down her stomach. When he reached her pussy, he parted it with his fingers, exposing her clit to his touch.

She rocked herself against his fingers, moaning again as he worked the delicate bundle of nerves between his thumb and forefinger. He kissed his way from her mouth to her jaw, and down the side of her throat. When he reached the point where her neck met her shoulder, he paused to press an open-mouthed kiss to the spot, and grazed her skin with his fangs. She shivered and proof of her arousal coated his fingers.

It was one of a thousand reasons she was perfect for him. She wasn't afraid of who or what he was. She not only accepted his differences, she embraced them. Fangs and all.

He continued to pleasure her with his fingers as he started a slow inspection of her body, pressing a feather-light kiss to every injury he found, starting at the crown of her hair and working his way lower, until he was kneeling at her feet.

Tyra reached down to rest a hand on the top of his head. "I like you on your knees. It's the only time I get to be taller than you."

He withdrew his hand from between her legs and moved in close to her body. "Any time you want me on my knees, you just say the word." He tapped her right leg and she lifted it, letting him drape it over his shoulder and she leaned back against the wall.

"So beautiful," he murmured as he drank in the sight of her body rising above him. Neither of them was young anymore, but that made her more attractive to him. She was a woman in the prime of her life, and she was his.

Her fingers tightened on his scalp, drawing him in closer. "Need you."

He didn't answer her aloud. Instead, he buried his face between her thighs and lapped at her pussy, letting the scent and the flavor of her desire fill his senses. He parted her folds with his fingers so his tongue could find its way deeper, seeking out her clit again.

"*Veth*, that feels good. Make me come, Dante. Please?"

He'd been hard and aching from the moment he'd seen her naked, but once she uttered the word please, his cock turned to steel and his control frayed.

She must have sensed how her words affected him because she lowered her voice to a husky whisper and spoke again. "I don't care how but make me come soon. I need to forget everything. Everything but you. Fingers, tongue, cock. All of them. Any of them. Just do it."

He lost his mind. He rose to his feet and brought Tyra with him, taking care to slide her body down his so she didn't hit her head on the showerhead above them. She wrapped her limbs around him and laughed, the joyful sound filling the tiny space. Her legs gripped his waist and she ground herself against his cock, rubbing her pussy against it until they were both shaking with need.

"Ready?" he asked as he took hold of her hips, guiding their bodies together at the perfect angle.

"So ready."

He lowered her onto his cock in one slow, steady move that didn't stop until he was buried to the hilt inside her. She buried her face in the crook of his neck and moaned, her fingernails digging into his skin. He lifted her slightly as he rocked his hips back, then drove into her with a hard thrust that made her gasp. Her pussy walls pulsed around his dick, and he let himself go, fucking her with hard, steady thrusts.

She raised her head and kissed him as he claimed her, her heels dug into the small of his back. He varied the angle of his thrusts until he found the one that made her quiver and moan into his mouth. He leaned forward, pressing her against the wall as he increased the pace, filling the room with the sounds of sex.

Her inner walls gripped him tight, milking his length as she reached orgasm. Flushed with pleasure, she lifted her head and stared into his eyes as she rode out her release. Her passion didn't ebb with her orgasm, though, she continued to ride him, urging him to join her in bliss.

"I love you," she whispered. "Now come for me."

He grinned. "It's so damned sexy when you try and tell me what to do." He let himself get lost in her body, the pleasure of her touch, the sheer wonder of knowing she loved him. Within seconds, he was teetering on the edge, and when she kissed him again, he came hard enough he saw stars.

They stayed that way for a long time, wrapped in each other's arms, surrounded by water and steam. When he finally set her down on her feet again, he took his time and washed her from head to toe before finally shutting off the water, bundling her into a towel, and carrying her to his bed.

"How do you feel?" he asked as he curled up behind her, spooning her against his big body.

"Better."

"Good. Then get some rest. As my doctor has pointed out to me repeatedly lately, it's the fastest way to heal."

He held her as she drifted off, counting his blessings that despite everything, everyone he cared about still alive and well. At some point, he fell asleep too, because the next thing he knew they were both being woken up by the annoyingly persistent chirp of his comm.

"Strak here," he answered it in audio only mode without bothering to check who was calling.

"Audio only? You're naked again, aren't you?" Eric's voice was rife with humor.

"Aren't you supposed to be busy repairing my ship?" Dante shot back.

"I've already got that fixed, sort of. She's jury-rigged but holding. Your baby is fine."

"Glad to hear it. Please tell me you didn't wake Tyra for a status report."

"Hey, Daisy. Glad you're back with us. Trust me, you're both going to be happy to hear what I have to tell you. I got the results of the DNA cross-match you asked me to run on Everest and your mystery man from the surface. Turns out you're smarter than you look, big guy."

"They're related?" Dante asked.

"Weirder than that. They're identical."

"How can they be twins?" Dante asked. "The guy on the surface seemed older to me.

"Not twins. The samples show different age markers."

Tyra sat up and joined the conversation, looking horrified. "Clones? The Grays are making clones?"

"So it would appear. There's no line these bastards won't cross," Eric said angrily.

"Does Rossi know about this?" he asked.

"Not yet. I thought you and the doc would want to know first. Rossi is next on my list, though."

"Thanks for telling us, Magi," Tyra said.

"Anything for you, Daisy. You know that."

Dante growled. "I told you to quit flirting."

Tyra just laughed and patted his arm. "He knows I'm taken. Don't you, Magi?"

"I do. But making your boyfriend all growly is my new hobby."

Dante closed the link and set the communicator aside again.

"Did you just hang up on him?"

"Yep. He's got work to do, and you're supposed to be resting, remember?"

She snuggled into his side. "I think we should both get some rest. Tomorrow you can go back to protecting the galaxy."

"Tomorrow, *we'll* go back to work. You're part of this team now, and no matter what you decide to do next, you always will be."

"Not sure what comes next for me, but I'm sure that whatever it is, it somehow includes you and a certain little boy with a love of hamburgers."

He wasn't sure what the future held for any of them, but he was going to do his best to make sure that they faced it together.

EPILOGUE

DANTE PACED the corridors of Astek station's main docking ring as he waited for Tyra's transport ship to finalize their arrival and debark. She'd been gone for almost two months, and he was anxious to have her back in his arms again.

It had taken two more weeks to finish the investigation of Bellex Corporation, and more than that to process the evidence and submit all the reports. Bellex stock was already plummeting, and rumors of backstabbing, hostile takeover bids, and even bankruptcy filings were everywhere. Bellex might not have created cobalt, but they'd willingly exposed their workers to the drug, violating a host of laws in the process. Because of their actions, the policy of allowing corporations to transfer debts to family members, especially minors, was coming under scrutiny, too. The wheels of justice moved slowly, but Dante was certain that in the end, Bellex would answer for everything they'd done.

One day, he and the rest of Nova Force would make the

Gray Men answer for their actions, too. Downs and Everest weren't the only ones to die in an explosion that day back in Bellex system. When they finally found the warehouse full of cobalt, they'd found two more bodies nearby, both of them suffering the same catastrophic bomb damage as the others. Evidence in the warehouse led to the discovery of two black site labs on the planet, too. One was a production space for the cobalt, the other was something far, far worse – a research site where cobalt was tested on unwilling subjects. It had to be where Dante's abductor had intended to bring him, a hellish place full of suffering and death.

The moment it was safe to do so, Boundless had sent more teams to Bellex to help with the rehabilitation of the addicted workers. They'd asked Tyra to lead the mission, but she'd declined and later resigned from the organization despite their pleas for her to reconsider.

Dante was selfish enough to be thankful she hadn't listened to them. He wanted her with him, not caring for people on a distant world where he couldn't protect her.

Bellex, in an attempt to curry favor, had done more than simply repair the *Malora* for them. They'd upgraded her engines, enhanced her weaponry, and added enough bells and whistles to her computer system that Eric hadn't stopped grinning the whole trip back to Astek Station. While they were gone, their new headquarters was finally completed, including quarters for the entire team. The Drift wasn't just another stopping point for them anymore. Now, it was home. At least, it would be, once Tyra got here.

Finally, the arrival light turned green, and passengers started leaving from the ship. He didn't have to wait long.

Tyra was one of the first to arrive, and the moment she spotted him, she hurried through the throng as fast as she could.

"Hi," She dropped her bags and threw herself into his arms with gratifying eagerness. "Miss me?"

"Every second you were gone." He gathered her close and kissed her, letting the taste of her lips and the warmth of her body fill him until he felt whole again.

"Where's Nico?" She asked when he finally set her down again.

"In school. He doesn't know you're back yet. If he did, he would have never gone to classes today. I thought it could be a surprise. I should warn you though, you might be the one who's surprised. He's growing so fast I had to buy him new pants again this week."

They'd used Nico's status as a witness against Bellex to bring him back to the Drift. Officially, he was under Nova Force protection. Unofficially, Dante had taken Tyra's suggestion and stepped in as Nico's guardian. He'd never imagined himself as any kind of father but taking care of the boy wasn't much different from taking care of the rest of the team. Nico just moved faster and defied orders more often. His fondness for Nico was growing into something that felt a lot more permanent than just being his assigned protector, and he'd already made some inquiries about what the next steps might be.

He kissed Tyra again. She was here, and he wanted to believe that meant she was ready to talk to him about the future. Hers, his, and theirs.

"We're causing a bit of a scene. Maybe we should continue this back at your place?"

"They're just jealous." He set her down and scooped

up her bags, tossing them both over one shoulder before taking her hand in his and guiding her through the crowd. "It's a bit of a walk."

She only got a few steps before she stopped and tapped his shoulder, right over the new addition to his uniform. "What's this?"

"You are dating a Master Sergeant, now." He grinned. "New rank, same job, better pay."

She squealed and hugged him again. "You didn't tell me! When did this happen?"

"A couple of days ago. I didn't even know it was in the works. Dax recommended me and headquarters approved it. I figured I'd be a sergeant for the rest of my career."

"You earned it." She bounced on her toes. "I'm so proud of you. We'll have to do something to celebrate." She looked around the crowded promenade of Astek Station. "This is a recreational station, right? There's got to be a good restaurant around here, somewhere."

"There's several hundred, actually. But some of the best food on the Drift is at the Nova Club. We're invited to dinner there tomorrow night. I've got some friends who can't wait to meet you."

"Is one of them the doctor you told me about? Trip's sister?"

"One of them is Dr. Alyson Jefferies, yes. She runs a med-clinic here on the station. You'll like her. She's the one who found a way to reverse what the corporations did to the female cyborgs so they can have children again. She's also got an open-door policy, treating anyone, of any race, whether they have the scrip to pay or not."

"Sounds like my kind of doctor. I don't suppose she's hiring? I looked into what it costs to live out here. For a bunch of ancient stations on the edge of nowhere, this place is expensive!"

"As a matter of fact, she is. I've told her about you already, and she's interested. I mean, if that's what you want to do. I didn't make her any promises." He didn't want Tyra thinking he was committing her to anything. She was considering changing her life so they could be together. How that happened needed to be her choice, not his.

"That's fantastic! You've been busy setting things up, haven't you? Nico's going to school. I might have a job. Bellex is up on charges. You have any other good news for me? I could use some. Visiting all those families was the right thing to do, but it was harder than I imagined it would be."

"You did an amazing thing, going to see everyone." While he and the rest of Team Three had been finalizing their reports and making sure that the case against Bellex was as tight as they could make it, Tyra had taken on the task of visiting the family of every fallen member of her team. She couldn't tell them everything, but she shared what she could, offering her condolences and support to the grieving families.

"I did what I needed to. For them, and for me." She leaned into him. "I've never cried so much or hugged so many strangers."

"If you need to talk about it, you know I'm here for you."

She smiled up at him. "I'll take you up on that eventually. Right now, I just want to enjoy being with you."

He lifted her hand to kiss her fingers. "I do have a little

more good news for you, actually. Livvy is starting to recover."

"Really? That's wonderful! When you told me they'd found her locked up at that horrific research site you all uncovered, I had such hope, but then you said she was in bad shape and when you never said anything more I thought..."

"She was in rough shape when they found her. She was malnourished to start with, and the dosage of cobalt they hit her with must have been enough to trigger an overdose. She was unconscious and barely breathing when they found her, but she's a fighter. Most of the others were too far gone to make it, but the Boundless teams have made real progress with treatment options, and Livvy is a tough kid. I got word this morning. It looks like she's going to pull through."

"I hate to ask, but..." She looked around and lowered her voice to a whisper. "Any sign of our Gray friends, or more clones?"

"None. Mr. Money pulled a vanishing act. We still don't know how he got off the surface, but he must have had help to disappear so fast and so completely. Someone scrubbed the records, too. Everest's entire file was wiped, and the copy Magi lifted for us is totally falsified. His parents, his name, his place of birth—none of it was real. We know what he looks like, though, and facial recognition software has been programmed to look for his face everywhere. It's the biggest manhunt we've ever undertaken, but if someone's got clones running around..."

She nodded. "That's a major violation of galactic law.

No one's supposed to be using that technology on sentient species. Not since the cyborgs were freed."

"The Grays don't seem too concerned about the law, ethics, or anything that gets in the way of their agenda. We just need to figure out what the hell that agenda is, and how to stop it."

"You will." She winked at him. "I've been told that's what Nova Force was created for." They walked in silence for a bit, as she looked around them with interest. The promenade was a lively place any time of day or night. Food vendors hawked their wares alongside pharma dealers and entertainers, while brightly lit signs advertised a wide variety of shops, pleasure dens, bars, and restaurants. Astek was where the asteroid mining crews, cargo pilots, and more than a few criminals came to spend their money and enjoy their downtime. Anything imaginable was for sale, if the buyer had the scrip and inclination. "So, this is home for you, now?"

"This is home." He guided her to a bank of mag-lifts. They were headed to one of the upper levels, where things were a little quieter. He led her out into a well-lit corridor that was only ten feet across instead of the vast stretch of space that was the promenade. Astek had made some improvements to this part of the station—the air here was fresher than on the lower levels, the machinery all worked perfectly, and even the walls had been touched up with a fresh coat of pale gray paint.

"It's quieter here," she noted.

"Astek leased this entire area to Nova Force. Which means we're the only ones in this part of the station. The whole place is ours." It was a rare luxury in a place where every square centimeter had value and privacy was something only the rich could hope to have.

They rounded the last corner and stepped into a courtyard. Ahead of them were the main doors to the newly created Nova Force headquarters, and to the left was another, smaller set of doors that led to what they'd taken to calling the barracks. In actual fact, they were far nicer than any barracks ever designed, with private suites for all personnel, as well as common areas for socializing, fitness and training, and a dining hall with well-stocked food dispensers.

"Do you want the grand tour now, or would you rather head straight to my quarters so you can relax?"

"Your quarters. You and Nico can show me the rest later. He's due home soon, isn't he?"

"Two more hours. He's staying after class right now for some extra help. He's got a lot of catching up to do. He's doing great, though. And he likes it, for the most part."

"It's a lot to get used to." She gestured around them. "No sky, no weather. A whole host of rules and expectations, and no need to steal or fight to keep what's his."

Dante chuckled. The kid was still getting used to the 'no fights' part of the agenda. He'd been involved in more than one fracas, but most of them were either because he was standing up for himself, or for someone else. Dante couldn't fault him for that. In fact, he was proud of him. They had their good days and bad ones, but overall, Nico was making progress.

They reached the door to his quarters. He pressed his hand to the scanner, and the door slid open. "Welcome home."

Tyra stepped past him and looked around. "This is nice."

He had to agree. The furnishings were simple but comfortable, all designed to take up minimal space while still serving their purpose. Monitors on the walls displayed images that made them appear to be windows looking out over a garden, and the lights were designed to mimic sunlight, warm and cheerful without being overly bright.

He followed her inside, setting her bags down near the door. "Do you like it?"

"I do. But you really need to decorate a little. This is your home, now. But it doesn't feel very homey. Not yet."

He stepped in behind her and wrapped an arm around her waist so he could pull her up against him. "I was waiting for you."

She laughed. "I have no idea how to decorate a home. I haven't had one in years. I'm a nomad, like you."

He bowed his head and kissed the crown of her hair. "I know. That's not what I meant, though. I thought we could pick some things out together. I don't want this to be just my home, Shortcake. I was hoping you'd stay with me and make it *our* home."

She canted her head back to look up at him. "I could stay here? I thought this was military barracks."

"It is. But soldiers have families, and families live together." He stared down at her, his heart pounding now. "I'd like you, me, and Nico to be a family."

Her mouth was open, but no words came out. Then she nodded slightly and spun in his arms, so she was facing him. "We're going to be the weirdest family on the station."

"Wait. You jumped ahead a bit there. Is that a yes?"

She beamed. "Yes, it's a yes. I'm not sure what I'm even agreeing to, but I came here because I wanted to try and make a life with you. We didn't talk about the future while I was gone, and I wasn't sure what to expect. I just…I wanted to be with you."

He stroked her cheek, dazzled and humbled by the fact that this incredible woman wanted to be part of his life. "I wanted you to be free to make your own choices. We'd have figured out a way to make this work, even if you were still with Boundless." He grinned at her. "But I have to admit, this is much easier."

"It would have been even easier if you had talked about what you were planning."

"I wanted to ask you in person. That way if you said no, I'd have a chance to change your mind." He waggled his brows. "I planned on being very persuasive, and if that didn't work, I was going to sic Nico on you. I was pretty sure you couldn't say no to him."

"He's definitely the charmer in this family."

He pulled her in close and kissed her hard. "I like the way you said that. This family. *Our* family."

"I like it, too. It's going to take some time to get used to, though. Just like everything else." She gestured around them. "I have a new home. A little boy who needs a lot of loving, and maybe even a new job."

"Yeah, you do. You also have me to help with all that. I won't be able to come home to you every night, but I will be here every minute I can be. We'll figure this out together."

"Yes, we will." She rose up on her toes and managed to latch onto his shoulders, pulling him down for another long, heated kiss that had his pulse pounding as his tongue speared into her open mouth.

"I love you," he whispered against her lips.

"I love you, too. I didn't need you to offer me a home, though, Dante. The second I stepped off that ship and into your arms, I was already there."

The End

BONUS SCENE – ERIC

UNLIKE THE REST of his team, Eric wasn't enjoying his new quarters. They were spacious and more than comfortable, but he hadn't slept a night on Astek station. He'd met a woman here, on the Drift, and she'd died here while he was away on a mission. He didn't believe in ghosts, but for him, the station was haunted, which was why he spent his nights sleeping on the *Malora* instead.

They hadn't known each other that well. In fact, he wondered if he'd known her at all. The laughing, sensual woman he'd spent a few passionate nights with seemed to have nothing in common with the person she'd turned out to be. That thought consumed him as much as the memories of their brief time together. Had she played him for a fool? Was any of it real?

She'd left him a message. An encrypted file marked with his name. He'd hoped it held answers, but all it contained was an audio file with a brief message. He'd committed her words to memory, but they didn't bring him peace.

"I'm sorry, Eric. What we had was never meant to be. I was dead before we ever met. If I meant anything at all to you, save her. You're the only one who can."

He knew that the *her* she referred to was her batch sister. Another cyborg by the name of Nyx. That information had been left in another file, one given to the IAF to investigate.

He'd left them to do their jobs and buried himself in work, so he didn't have to face the facts - he'd been an idiot who fell for a killer just because she seemed to be able to look past the implants and scars that marked him.

Since they'd arrived back at the station, he'd developed a routine. Every night, once the barracks got quiet, he'd take his gym bag and head to the ship. If anyone spotted him, he'd claim he was going to work out. In the morning, he'd head to the gym before arriving home again to grab a coffee, a shower, and start his day. If the others knew what he was doing they'd worry about him, and he didn't want that. There wasn't anything wrong, really. He just needed some time to figure shit out.

When he got to the ship, he set his hand down on the palm scanner and spoke the passphrase keyed to his voice. It wasn't the standard one he used during normal hours, though. It was a code he'd programmed in himself. One that let him come and go from the ship without it showing on the log. It wasn't regulation, and his commander would kick his ass if he ever found out about it, but it was small rebellions like this that made life interesting.

He walked onto the ship with a smile on his face, and promptly froze when he found

Lieutenant Commander Kurt Meyer was waiting for

him inside in a fresh uniform and with a dour look on his face. "We need to talk, Erben."

Fraxx. "Evening, sir."

"It's not evening anymore. It's damned near the middle of the night. Care to explain why you're not in your quarters?"

"I couldn't sleep," Eric tried the usual excuse, but something told him Kurt wasn't going to buy it.

Kurt shook his head. "And now I owe Rossi dinner. He bet me you'd say something like that. I figured you were smart enough to come clean right away."

Eric wasn't sure what stung more: the fact his commander had expected him to lie, or the look of disappointment on the lieutenant's face. "You know I've been sleeping here, then." It wasn't a question.

"Come with me. If we're going to have a heart to heart, we might as well do it in comfort."

Eric fell in behind Kurt. "How much trouble am I in, sir?"

The lieutenant kept walking. "That depends on two things: why you keep sneaking onboard the ship every night, and if you lie to me again."

"It wasn't a total lie, sir."

That made Kurt turn to look at him. "Hold that thought until we're somewhere with chairs. I have a feeling we should both be sitting down for this."

"Yes, sir."

Kurt led them to one of the newer briefing rooms and sat down on one side of the table, then gestured for Eric to take a seat across from him. Eric's ass barely hit the chair before Kurt leaned in. "Explain yourself."

"I can't sleep on the station, sir. I've tried."

"So you've been coming here to sleep? That's it? No extra curricular activities?"

"Just sleep." He knew there wasn't any point in lying to his XO. He shouldn't have even tried. The man was a walking lie detector, trained to read micro-expressions and body language.

Kurt relaxed a little, the hard lines of his mouth softening. "Alright then. Why can't you sleep?"

"It's the station, sir. Every time we come back here, I remember…" he trailed off and raised his hands in a frustrated gesture.

Kurt nodded. "I thought that might be it. Being on the *Malora* makes it easier?"

"It does."

"How long do you plan on doing this?"

"I don't know, sir. How long are you and the commander willing to let me?"

"If you need some time, you've got it. But from now on, you'll use your normal access code. You and I are going to disable the other one before I leave tonight. Do that again and there will be hell to pay. Clear?"

"Yes, sir."

Kurt relaxed and leaned back in his chair. "Now that the official ass-chewing is over, I want to talk to you as a friend. You can't keep running from your demons forever. It doesn't work. Believe me, I've tried. Eventually, you have to face them."

Everyone on the team knew Kurt had lost someone he cared about. He didn't talk about it at all, and the only one who knew the details was Rossi. Despite his unending curiosity, Eric hadn't gone looking for the story. "I keep thinking if I put it off, it might hurt less when I find out the truth."

"It won't help. In fact, it just prolongs the suffering. If I could go back, I'd tell myself to stop running. I can't do that, but I can give you the advice. It's going to suck either way, so why prolong your suffering?"

"Anyone tell you that you're lousy at giving pep talks?"

"It's been mentioned." Kurt shrugged. "If you wanted hugs and sympathy, you would have let Trin or Trip know what was going on. You didn't, so…"

"You're right, I didn't want sympathy." He grinned and opened his arms to his XO. "You sure I don't get a hug, though?"

Kurt snorted and got to his feet. "Not *fraxxing* likely." He did circle the table to stand at Eric's side and placed a hand on his shoulder. "Figure your shit out, Magi. If you need help doing that, you know where to find me."

"I will." Eric slapped his friend's hand. "Thanks."

After Eric removed his extra access code from the system, Kurt left the ship. Eric considered going with him, but he wasn't ready, yet.

He went to his work area, settled into his chair, and jacked into the system. If he was going to do this, he would do it in the one place he truly felt at home - cyberspace. He soared through the realm, revelling in the flows of data, the sense of connection, the limitless freedom of cyberspace.

He went to the digital fortress he'd created for himself and retrieved the files he needed. A copy of all the information she'd left for the IAF. Phaedra, a friend and fellow cyber-jockey, had given it to him. He hadn't looked at any of it until now. Kurt was right. It was time he faced his demons, and that meant finding Nyx.

OPERATION FURY

Nova Force – Book Three
Releasing Winter 2019

She's fighting for her survival. He's fighting for her soul.

Nyx was created to be the perfect killer, with death and violence encoded in her DNA. After years of tests, torments, and trials designed to push her to her breaking point, she's survived by focusing on one thing—revenge.

Nova Force investigator Eric Erben lost someone he cared about. Now he's on a mission to fulfill her last request—free her sister from the shadowy group holding her captive. Rescuing Nyx from her captors is the easy part. Saving her from herself will be a battle only love can win.

ABOUT THE AUTHOR

Susan lives out on the Canadian west coast surrounded by open water, dear family, and good friends. She's jumped out of perfectly good airplanes on purpose and accidentally swum with sharks on the Great Barrier Reef.

If the world ends, she plans to survive as the spunky, comedic sidekick to the heroes of the new world, because she's too damned short and out of shape to make it on her own for long.

You can find out more about Susan and her books here:
www.susanhayes.ca

35868018R00176

Printed in Poland
by Amazon Fulfillment
Poland Sp. z o.o., Wrocław